BOOKS BY **FRANK ROSS**

SLEEPING DOGS   (1978)
DEAD RUNNER   (1977)

SLEEPING DOGS

SLEEPING DOGS

Frank Ross

ATHENEUM   1978   NEW YORK

Library of Congress Cataloging in Publication Data

Ross, Frank.
    Sleeping dogs.
    I. Title.
PZ4.R82255SL   1978   [PR6068.0796]   823'.9'14
ISBN 0-689-10850-8   77-88911

Composition by Dix Typesetting Co., Inc., Syracuse, New York
Printed and bound by Halliday Lithograph Corporation,
Hanover and Plympton, Massachusetts
Designed by Kathleen Carey
First American Edition

TO ALASTAIR MACLEAN AND LEN DEIGHTON

For applause when it counted

PART ONE **NIGHTMARE**

1. NOVEMBER 1958

Mr. Randolph paused at the door and ran a practiced eye over the décor. The club was dressed overall for Thanksgiving Day and even the bar had not escaped Chuck Rabin's zealous hand.

He'd done well. A little overgenerous, perhaps, on the exotica of dried corn and squash gourds; the table centerpieces in the dining room were tasteful, but a purist might find it just a shade gauche to have the theme repeated in the bar alcoves.

Still, it was Chuck's first year and he was coming along fine. The papier-mâché turkey, which he had molded and painted himself, was his big success and the paper streamers, in their fall colors of russet, gold, and yellow, lent the room a rare warmth. They were all set.

The bar was full, all thirty-two of them were there, and Mr. Randolph paused long enough at the door to make his presence felt before he strolled over to the nearest unoccupied swivel-top stool. Not one head turned, not one conversation hesitated as he did so, but he knew instinctively that every one of them had noted his arrival and judged his mood. He was proud of them.

Pete was swapping gossip with Deke Somerfield at the far end, but he scurried down the bar as Mr. Randolph settled himself and, without consulting him, measured two thirds of Bacardi into his shaker, added the juice of a fresh lime, a sixth of Grenadine, and slicked into his Latin-American cha-cha rhythm. As he strained and poured, he offered up the usual evening banalities. There was a subtle precision about Pete's bartop gab; sounds without shape, words devoid of meaning. Verbal wallpaper.

Perfect.

At the far end of the bar Tom Lister turned from his school of four highball drinkers and yelled loudly, "Hey, Pete, you down there for the rest of the night?"

His huge pink face, droop-jowled and perpetually damp with perspiration, wore an angular grin that revealed only the teeth at the left of his mouth. It drew the sting from his words but his eyes never quite reached Mr. Randolph's. Tom was mainline Madison Avenue and baiting his hooks for a vice-presidency. He was also fishing with quiet desperation for a positive reaction from Madge Schwer, whose auburn pageboy was just visible above the shoulders of the men towering over her. Tom's loud-mouthed challenge was strictly for her benefit.

Mr. Randolph smiled at Pete and angled his head in Lister's direction. The bartender winked and moved away.

Dick Harrington's Alabama drawl rose above the hubbub to Randolph's left.

"What do I have to say to you, Paul? Stay in blue chips, you want it safe and cozy. Depends what you want out of life; survival or the silk purse. Now me, I'm on a scientifically designed program to double the client's portfolio value at four-year intervals. You won't make that at the conservative end of the market is all I'm saying."

Paul Connor, cool as a Saks Fifth Avenue window dummy in a white silk shirt and an Ivy League gray three-piece suit, examined the glittering toes of his handsewn black moccasins and waited for Harrington to run out of steam. Paul was one of life's listeners, the perfect foil for his Wall Street friend.

Mr. Randolph swung on his barstool and, almost at whisper pitch, inquired, "How'd the market close today, Dick?"

Harrington wheeled instantly, his eagerness intense. "Up 0.37 to 566.24, Mr. Randolph," he said quickly. "It's been one helluva seesaw day down there. The turnover, I guess, was around four million three hundred thousand shares."

"Very excitable," purred Randolph.

4

"It'll settle tomorrow, take my word for it. If you're thinking of buying, do it first thing tomorrow morning. If you're selling, hold on." The youngster was poised to expand the thesis, but Randolph swung the barstool halfway around, and presented his back to the anxious young face. There was a pause, brief but measurable, before Harrington returned to his conversation with Connor. This time, his pitch was fractionally less confident.

Mr. Randolph sipped his daiquiri. Harrington was sharp, intelligent, and he had the ability—a giant's capacity for memorizing minutia, even that very special hunger that set apart the truly brilliant from the merely excellent. But he still lacked presence. He wasn't into it yet—not really *in*. He was poised on tiptoe over it like a potential suicide over a ravine, not doubting his capacity to jump but questioning the reason. He would need at least another year before he had the confidence to jump on the word of command.

There was a roar of laughter from the crowd over by the long window, and Mr. Randolph allowed his attention to settle on the figure standing on the perimeter. Glass in hand, mint julep untouched; two long artistic fingers lightly, characteristically, touching the bottom lip; body relaxed, face gently creased to mirror the laughter of the others but not sharing it; eyes opaque. Randolph knew that behind the eyes the brain was functioning with a cool detachment. The personality was a skin; natural, but manmade.

It was a great temptation, he thought. He had planned to make the announcement tomorrow at the Thanksgiving Day luncheon, or better still, at the dance on Saturday night when he would have stopped the music, gathered them around him— the men formal in white tuxedos and black ties, the women in strapless gowns of tulle with wide satin cummerbunds. It would have been more . . . proper.

However. . . .

He had an overpowering urge to indulge himself, shock them if necessary. If possible. He slid from the barstool and meandered through the drinkers to the window and stood with his back to it. Again, there was no break in the conversation around the bar but he sensed a stiffening, a new watchfulness. The tall figure he had studied a moment ago turned to him, nodded, and turned away. The other three who were grouped around Teddy Schwarz ignored him.

Schwarz, a mercurial little Jew with a vaudeville comic's build and style, smothered his punch line in midsentence and looked over his shoulder at Randolph.

"Sorry," he said impulsively. Poor Teddy.

Randolph took in their faces with one silent sweep of the room. Without turning his head, he placed one hand on the shoulder of the tall figure, the other on the slim arm of the one to his right, thereby embracing the group of four. Teddy Schwarz recognized his exclusion from it and retreated a half-dozen paces.

Mr. Randolph smiled at his audience and the talk stopped instantly. He nodded left and right, encompassing the four for the benefit of the rest. "I have an announcement, ladies and gentlemen," he said.

Teddy Schwarz quailed. Tom Lister stiffened.

"Our colleagues here," said Mr. Randolph, "will be leaving us this weekend. They will be fully operational as of Sunday morning. They'll be at the dance Saturday night, of course, so make the most of their company while you can. That's all."

He turned away toward the window and the drinkers crowded forward to shake hands with the lucky four. Mr. Randolph smiled inwardly. It was most satisfying.

Outside, beyond the double glazing, snow fell heavily in the square below, filling in the shoveled path to Lenin's tomb. There was another fuel shortage this winter and only a handful of lights pinpricked the night from the offices overlooking the Kremlin wall. In the distance, two lonely cars sloughed through the slush. In the street below, an old man pushed a handcart into the teeth of a howling northeaster, his clothes flapping about him.

6

Moscow, reflected Mr. Randolph comfortably, was a lion in winter.

2. JUNE 1978

Sam Hanlon punched the water with one final stroke and let the wavelets of the falling tide carry him the last few yards to the edge of the surf.

He grounded in the sand and sprawled in the suck and drag of the sea, arms outstretched, feet wide, lungs heaving. Five years ago—he could remember the day exactly—he'd stopped timing his morning swim, although he still buckled on the old diver's watch out of sheer habit before he left the house. There had to be a moral in that somewhere.

Anyway, who needed a watch to prove that age played hell with a man's performance?

He saw the funny side of that and grinned to himself. Performance. He wedged his chin in the streaming sand and looked up the beach to the town.

A slender plume of smoke rose in the quiet air from the fish cannery just out of sight behind Mackie's Point, and there was a token ripple of movement in the narrow streets above Old Harbor. At six-fifteen, only the incoming fishermen and a handful of longshoremen blessed Teague's Landing with an impression of wakefulness.

He made a cushion of his arms and squinted into the new sun at the canopy of elegant houses nestled on the forested slopes of the Ridge. No movement there. Not a rustle. The Ridge was commuterland, a pine-covered subtopia where escapees from Boston's inner city mortgaged their careers and laid their hang-ups out to dry.

His own house was inescapable. White. Apple green roof tiles, apple green shutters, apple green venetian blinds—still

7

drawn. The fishermen used it to mark their course as they wheeled southwest on their way home from George's Bank. Hanlon's Mark.

He snugged his hands close to his body, palms flat, and reared into the ritual thirty press-ups. He made it thirty-one to prove he still had something in reserve, sprang to his feet, and ran up the beach through the littered remains of last night's clambakes, knees high, pumping his heart. He stopped at the rail by the Bait Shop, climbed into his tracksuit, tucked the towel around his neck and into the zipped top.

As he moved across the boardwalk he was stopped by the flash of his own reflection in the darkened window. He looked back over his shoulder to the beach, then left and right, and, when he was sure he was alone, he stopped and appraised himself. The tracksuit credited him, absurdly, with more youth than he would ever dare credit himself. It sloped nicely over the middle bulge; stretched tight across the shoulders, over muscled thighs and calves. There was an undeniable dynamism in the way he stood, in the set of his shoulders. Unconsciously, he raised himself up on his bare toes and dropped into a fighter's crouch.

Only inches above his head, a gull squawked its ridicule and feathered to a landing on the Bait Shop roof to watch the performance.

Performance.

Hanlon straightened sheepishly and loped off along the boardwalk to the road.

He was panting hard when he reached the house, but he trotted on through the orchard to the frame shed that Joe Sayer had built to house his exercise paraphernalia and did three minutes with the Bullworker—the minimum he permitted himself. It was the only regime that worked over his left shoulder till the wasted tissue throbbed with life.

He went back to the house, showered, threw on a terry-cloth robe, and perked some coffee.

8

Carrie's eyes were closed and he tiptoed cautiously into the bedroom as if he really believed she was asleep. He set the coffee on the bedside table without a sound and leaned over her. They had never talked it over, this morning pretense, and he had long ago accepted it as a ritual too important to her for debate. From the first morning after their first night together—a twin-bedded motel room near Aspen with orchestrated bedsprings—Carrie had feigned sleep for the pleasure of his awakening.

Performance.

He spanned her with his arms and lowered his mouth into the auburn silkiness of her hair until he found the perfect shell of her lobe. He touched it with the tip of his tongue. Carrie moaned softly, a childlike release of pleasure. She twitched her nose. He did it again and her face came round to reach instinctively for his. Her arms followed, encircling him in the warm, dry, musk-laden embrace of her private dream.

To be tongue-deep in Carrie was an infinite wonder. Familiarity breeding adulterous sensation. Thunder in the head, panic in the arteries, brimstone in the loins.

"Oh, my God! Sorry!"

Bobby, in sweat shirt and jeans, burst through the door and out of it again with the speed of a starting buck.

Carrie choked on instant laughter and Hanlon's passion collapsed into hysteria. They shook together till the spasm passed, then he sat up and ruffled her hair.

"Your son lacks breeding, mama."

"Not on my side of the blanket, he doesn't," she said, mock prim. "I gave him all I had, gene-wise. That boy is a palanquin of virtue. I can't speak for your side of the blanket, of course."

"We could experiment further."

"Sure we could. Carrie Hanlon, human incubator. I married you for love, brother. Not reproduction."

"Gee, thanks. I'll pass that on to my shrink."

"Please do."

They sipped coffee until Bobby knocked a loud, long warning at the door and came in with the mail and *The New York Times*.

He was a big boy for twelve: loose-limbed, collected, handsome. His brown doe eyes, soft like his mother's, might have dominated the face with a limpid sensitivity had he not also inherited his father's dimpled snapjaw. Childe Harold out of Rocky Marciano.

"Sorry about the freak-out," he said.

No embarrassment. That was the best part of their life together. No secrets. Privacy-in-the-round.

"Our freak-out, baby. Not yours," said Carrie. "Gimme a kiss." Bobby obliged.

"Why the early start? You going somewhere?"

The boy shrugged.

"Nowhere much."

"As usual, you mean."

"Kind of. I guess so."

Carrie raised beseeching eyes and hands to heaven in theatrical disbelief. "At school he's intelligent. He communicates. He articulates. At home he's a dummy. Somebody tell me where I failed!"

Bobby rode the tease good-naturedly. "Dan's coming over. He wanted to take off early so I said okay. You know Dan."

Sam grabbed his son, rolled him expertly across the bed, and flicked the boy's carefully brushed helmet of long blond hair over his face. If Daniel Carradine planned to hold up a bank, Bobby would keep it to himself and go along if only to avert disaster. Bobby had been propping up young Daniel since they were three-year-olds. When Dan discovered beetles, Bobby had trapped and imprisoned them for his petrified inspection. And tadpoles. And frogs. When Dan tried to match the speed of his brain to the lumbering mechanics of his unmuscled body, Bobby was there to catch him on the fall.

He had to be.

Young Carradine spent seven eighths of his day in the back of his head. Not dreaming, because dreaming was a scandalous waste of cerebral electricity. Daniel was a thinker, a creator, an energy source. Without Bobby he was a closed circuit. With Bobby to provide the dynamics, Carrie often said, Daniel would one day move the world.

Sam pushed his son over the far side of the bed. The boy rolled like a paratrooper and landed on his feet.

Sam said, "Just keep him in one piece. And you'd better tell his mother where you're going. Okay?"

Carrie stuck out her tongue at him, but this time took care not to let Bobby see the gesture. The boy chewed the inside of his cheek. "Dan wouldn't go if he hadn't checked it out with her first," he said defensively.

The pejorative *her*.

"Well, check anyway. And be back here at noon sharp. The picnic doesn't start without you. Now beat it."

When the door closed, Carrie said, "You'll give him a complex. Why can't we let the two of them work things out themselves? If Margo had her way, Danny'd live in a cage with a notice pinned on the bars: Human contact with this biological specimen is strictly forbidden."

Sam reached for his coffee. "Keep your Dr. Spock to yourself, mama," he growled. He opened the paper and pretended to read, but, as always, his wife's irritation troubled him.

For a psychotherapist, Margo had made one hell of a mess of her son, and Carrie had been the first to see it and attach the blame.

As a doctor, and a damn good one at that, Frank Carradine should have done something about it. Had he observed the same vexed condition in any one of the three or four hundred families on his list of patients in Teague's Landing, he would have acted swiftly and punctiliously.

But Frank wasn't that kind of father and he couldn't be that kind of husband. He'd acquired a wife and sired a son as any

11

other professional would equip himself with the essential tools of his trade. They formed part of the screen around him—along with his home, his social work, his archery, his shyness, and his air of permanent melancholy.

In Teague's Landing, Frank Carradine meekly endured a reputation as a wife-dominated weakling who had failed his son. He endured it—and polished it and projected it.

In the beginning this knowledge had poisoned every second Hanlon spent in Frank's company. In those first weeks of his arrival in the town in April 1963, he had played the surveillance of Frank Carradine strictly according to the book. Remotely.

The passage of fifteen years had changed that because Hanlon had changed beyond his own recognition. He had gone into business as instructed. He had made friends as instructed. He had married Carrie Holmes, not on instructions; however, it had not been difficult to persuade his case officer, and Langley's official blessing had followed quickly. It was curious, too, the way he had come to like Carradine. Slowly at first; hesitantly, like a phobic clutching at the object of his revulsion. Then their sons had been born within months of one another, and the coincidence turned mild friendship into an easy interdependence.

Each year, Hanlon reminded himself that the bond existed to be broken. Scrape away the years of familiarity and there was still only one reason for their friendship.

One day he would be ordered to kill Frank Carradine.

3.

From: Dmitri Orlov, Director, First Directorate, KGB
To: Marshal Vasili Bunin, First Deputy Chairman of the Council of Ministers of the USSR

MOST SECRET.

Following our recent informal discussion, I feel it worthy that I inform you of news just received from within the office of the Chairman of the KGB, Stefan Andreyev. A draft statement has been prepared for the Praesidium and the Council of Ministers, outlining the agreement of the Soviet Union to participate in tripartite talks to be held at the United Nations in New York.

These talks will involve the personal presence of the Premier, the President of the United States of America, and the Prime Minister of the People's Republic of China.

The subject: détente.

The outcome is irrevocable. There is nothing that can now be done politically to prevent such a meeting. I need not amplify my feelings on this matter, except to stress my dismay—which will be shared by many.

From: Marshal Vasili Bunin, First Deputy Chairman of the Council of Ministers of the USSR
To: Dmitri Orlov, Director, First Directorate, KGB

SECRET.

Your note has disturbed me greatly. I shall, of course, be at the meeting of the Praesidium when the matter is raised, but by then it will be a *fait accompli*. Are we to sit back, like children, Comrade?

From: Dmitri Orlov, Director, First Directorate, KGB
To: Marshal Vasili Bunin, First Deputy Chairman of the Council of Ministers of the USSR

I am more than delighted at the speed of your reply. It has come to my attention that a Russian cell, seeded in the United States of America in 1958, is capable of immediate activation. I shall examine the consequences of so doing.

I am informed that all four members of the cell are highly

13

trained and, despite their inordinately protracted period of dormancy, are fully equipped to carry out any assignment. The group, code named KINGFISH, was seeded when the present head of the KGB, Stefan Andreyev, was head of the First Directorate in charge of foreign surveillance and assignments. The group's activities could, technically, be judged his personal concern. I feel sure I do not need to enlarge on the advantage of such a situation.

4.

Jonathan Haskill had escaped from the British compound at White Plains in June 1783 where, history had it, he was under sentence of death for declaiming against the imperialist tyranny of George III. He had acquired a battle sword and a brace of pistols and, in the heat of the day, broken his bonds and escaped, shooting and skewering a platoon of English soldiers in the process.

He traveled on foot for fifteen miles, running with the speed and staying power of an Indian brave, until he came upon a redcoat patrol in the woods above Pound Ridge. With unbounded courage he overcame three soldiers, leaped into the saddle of the best mount, and rode to his destiny—the founding of Teague's Landing.

Why he changed his name to Jonathan Teague seemed irrelevant to early historians who preferred this saga of patriotism to a considered analysis of the facts. It was as late as 1927 before a town archivist hit on the truth of Jonathan Haskill, and he was wise enough to keep it to himself. On his death, his writings revealed that Haskill had been awaiting the death sentence for rape, that he had escaped by strangling a whore and making off in her clothes.

For two years, Haskill lived in a cave above what was now Old Harbor. The arrival of three settler families on the Ridge had led him astray yet again. He attempted rape on all three of the wives, was attacked, and ferociously butchered the three husbands.

Haskill/Teague lived to establish his patriarchy, a small fishing port and a community of swarthy, inbred, inhospitable sons of the sea who survived by adapting themselves to smuggling and occasional piracy.

None of this dissuaded the people of Teague's Landing from celebrating Founder's Day on June 12, the day of Jonathan's heroic escape from White Plains.

The town picnic had lost some of its innocent appeal in the fifties and sixties, but it was revived in the early seventies. The general view was that Vietnam had done the trick. The town had lost seven of its sons in three years; people had turned willingly to the dead past for gentler, simpler images of community life. Perhaps they thought they'd found them in the Founder's Day ritual. Hanlon could have pointed out that Jack Shawn had resurrected the picnic. A predictable gesture by a cartoon-cutout American who'd gotten his values knotted in a time warp.

The Ridge terminated in a pillar of sandstone called Jonathan's Rock, and on its landward side, ringed on three sides by pine woods, lay the clearing. Jack Shawn, in his third year as mayor, had filled it with sideshows for the kids, a couple of merry-go-rounds, a shooting gallery, and a crude covered platform for dancing.

Hanlon stretched his long legs on the warm grass and closed his eyes. At the table behind him, Carrie poured iced tea and unpacked sandwiches, cookies, and Coke. The Carradines had gone for a stroll, Marvin and Grace Fish were dozing on lounge chairs a few feet away, and Doug Cater and his wife, Joan, lay side by side on a plaid blanket reading magazines.

The high school band brought "Can't Buy Me Love" to an

abrupt end and slipped, almost in unison, into "Friendly Persuasion."

A bee zizzed suicidally above Hanlon's nose; he snatched at it but missed. He opened his eyes into the glare of the sun and rolled onto his stomach to avoid it.

Joan Cater eyed him obsessively. "You just can't relax, Sam, can you?"

Her husband raised his head, caught Sam's eye, and fixed a comic expression on his fleshy features. Doug was well practiced in defending the world against his wife's advances.

"Maybe he can if he's left to do it in peace," he said.

"No, I mean it," Joan persisted.

"He knows you mean it, goddamnit. You never stop telling him." True—she never did. For a dike, Joan Cater had an unusually compulsive appetite for observing Hanlon as a physical specimen.

"Hey. Wait a minute you two," Carrie interrupted. "Today is closed season on Hanlon. Leave him alone, Joan. You can mother him tomorrow." She emphasized the word "mother."

"That's a date then, Sam," Joan snapped spitefully. "Tomorrow. That's if you can make it between the morning swim and the eight o'clock start at the office and the morning tour of the Center and the business lunch and the stint at the cannery and a couple of hours at the Town House and the run down to the port. Any woman who wants to make it with you. . . ."

"Shoots me full of holes first," cut in Carrie. There was an overbright smile on her face. Hanlon rolled back into the sun.

Joan and Doug Cater had no children. According to Frank Carradine that was Doug's fault—medically—but Hanlon knew better. Frank had a vested interest in maintaining Doug Cater's image as a decent, uncomplicated citizen and his domestic arrangements as unfortunate, but in trying to protect him against public knowledge he was guilty of overplaying his hand.

But then, all four of them constantly overplayed their hands. After fifteen years, it would have been a miracle if they hadn't. Taken as a whole, their teamwork was little short of masterly.

16

Their lapses had been minor ones, probably a result of the sheer unrelieved concentration involved in living to order. Not for the first time, Hanlon wondered how it would be if the situation were reversed. Could he have kept it up under surveillance himself?

Maybe. He'd kept the worst of it from Carrie, from Bobby. His innocence was intact. At least, it seemed so. And as far as Frank, Doug, Marv, and Jack were concerned, he had one incontestable advantage over them. They were visible. He was not.

"Oh boy, could I handle a shot of something adult." Helen Shawn dropped onto a chair beside Carrie, kicked off her shoes, and elevated her feet to the handle of a picnic basket. She shook out her long blonde hair, stretched her body luxuriously. Hanlon ogled her openly.

Doug Cater pushed himself up on one elbow, dug into a pocket of his jacket, and produced a neat silver hip flask. He carried it everywhere—the cross to which he had once been nailed. He carried liquor to prove he had no further use for it.

He said, "Here. Take a belt of this."

Helen sniffed it suspiciously.

"What is it?"

"Brandy, baby. In case of summer chills."

"I always knew you were one of the good guys, Doug. What a man!" She tipped the flask and gulped. A flash of golden liquid fell onto her brown throat. "Damn!"

Joan said icily, "It'll make your head ache in this heat."

"Right. But it might numb the senses, too, and that's all I care about right now. If I have to defoliate one more five-year-old up to here in ice cream, I think I'll scream."

Joan Cater dumped a paper plate full of sandwiches in her lap. When she felt for Helen Shawn had to be camouflaged constantly. "The pride and the passion of community leadership, dear," she cooed spitefully. "Next time Jack comes up for election, remind him of Founder's Day. That'll bring him down to earth."

Carrie prodded Hanlon with her foot and he took a plastic

mug of tea from her. Through the trees he could see Bobby and Dan. They were lobbing a baseball back and forth with that studied monotony of rhythm that twelve-year-olds can keep up for hours on end. He envied them.

"Where's Margo and Frank?" Carrie, a plate of sandwiches in each hand was looking for landing space. Marvin Fish inched upward on his lounger, saw the Carradines approaching through the trees, and brayed loudly, "So who cares?"

"I heard that!" Frank Carradine shouted across the clearing and broke into a jog-trot, leaving his wife behind. Hanlon turned to watch her. Margo was tall and spare, breastless, curveless and erect. Her face was long, handsome, and taut, accentuated by her rolled, plaited hair. She wore a checked shirt, flared pants, brogues, and, ludicrously, a pair of light kid gloves. Margo always wore gloves. Hanlon would dearly have loved to hear her professional reading of that piece of symbolism.

Carradine dropped to the grass beside Hanlon and bit deep into a sandwich. He ignored Margo who reached for a chair and dusted it with a paper napkin before she sat down. They all felt the tension, definable as ether.

With a clatter, Bobby and Daniel blundered through the trees into the clearing and plunged into the grass at Carrie's feet. The high school band exhausted their selection of Sousa marches and made a ragged entry into The Deadwood Stage. Carrie stuck cans of Coke into the boys' automatically outstretched hands.

Hanlon felt Carrie's eyes on his neck. He turned to her and she made a face and nodded her head furiously at Frank Carradine. Hanlon grimaced. She mouthed the word "coward."

"Frank?" she said slowly. Hanlon turned away.

"Uh-huh." His cheeks bulged as he ate.

"Bobby's going up to camp in Maine again this summer. He was wondering if you'd let Danny. . . ."

"No!" Margo's voice was pitched low but the emphasis she contrived to put into that one word was daunting.

"Margo, we just thought that . . ."

18

"I mean *NO*, Carrie."

"But Bobby has an absolutely fantastic time there. You wouldn't believe. . . ."

Margo turned to face Carrie. Her unpainted face developed tight lines at the mouth and the corners of her eyes. Margo Carradine was never embarrassed to display hostility.

"I wouldn't believe that any responsible mother would *presume* to tell another what's best for her child. Least of all you, Carrie. Danny and I will judge what he needs."

The revelation escaped everyone but Hanlon and Carradine in the silence that followed.

Carrie was ashen-faced but she kept her temper. "I didn't mean to suggest for a second, Margo, that you don't know what's best. I just . . ."

Margo turned away. "I don't think there's any point continuing this, dear," she said coolly. "Let's talk about something else, shall we?"

Frank Carradine opened his mouth and closed it again without a sound. He winked at Hanlon but the gesture was pathetically devoid of humor and he lowered his gaze quickly.

"Hey, Frank, you want to stretch your legs?" Hanlon rolled to his feet, resolutely averting his face from the women.

"We've just walked a whole half-hour," Margo retorted acidly. "Frank doesn't have your college-boy constitution, remember." There was a subtle crinkling of skin around her mouth—the living lie of a smile.

Her husband got up, his mouth set hard. He said, "Sure I could use a walk Sam." Courage in the face of the enemy. "And these two young hoodlums, as well." Above and beyond the call of duty. Danny looked doubtfully at his mother, but Bobby was already on his feet and dragging at his arm.

"*Frank!*"

Carradine turned his back on his wife's word of command and strolled off across the clearing. Marvin Fish poured canned beer into his delighted smile, and Doug Cater glued his eyes to his magazine. The high school band declared war on "The

19

Halls of Montezuma." Hanlon snapped a hand on the boys' shoulders and shoved them after Carradine.

The kids were rolling boulders down the fall from Jonathan's Rock to the sea. Hanlon and Carradine lit cigarettes and watched them. Carradine's show of strength seemed to have drained him. He hadn't spoken a word during the ten-minute climb through the woods.

Hanlon felt sorry for him. He said, "I didn't want that to happen, Frank. Carrie should've kept her mouth shut."

Carradine shook his head. "Not her fault. I mean, what the hell's so unthinkable about a kid wanting to be with his friend?" He sucked hard on the cigarette and blew smoke over the winking sunspecks of the Atlantic below.

Hanlon said, "Maybe Margo's right. Summer camp's fine for Bobby; he's that kind of a nut. Danny . . ."

"Needs help." The passion made his voice shake, but the professional in him asserted itself quickly. Thin grin. "All right, Sam, say it if you want. If a kid needs help, he expects it from his father or his doctor. I struck out on both counts a long time ago. Right? I've got no one to thank for this but myself. That's what they all say behind my back, isn't it? They have the right."

Carradine had gone this far in conversations before. Intimate disclosures, admissions of guilt. The highwire performer extending the limits of his compact with self-destruction.

"*Your* son. *Your* marriage. *Your* business," Hanlon replied.

They watched Daniel struggle in vain with a firmly rooted boulder a hundred feet below them. Bobby, always at hand, rushed over to lend his muscle. Together they wrenched it free and sent it rolling. Halfway down it struck an outcropping and launched it self on a long arc outward into space. It hit the sea with a blip of spume. The boys danced and waved and hollered up the hill. Hanlon raised an arm in salute, but Carradine stared sightlessly out to sea.

"You think I let Margo get away with too much, huh?"

Hanlon shrugged. "I never said that. Not even behind your back."

Carradine touched his arm: affection mixed with forgiveness. "Sure. It's a joke, you know that. The way Margo railroads me and you defend me. Big joke. I heard two of my own patients talking in surgery the other day. They thought you'd live my marriage for me if you could. 'What Margo needs is a good lay—know what I mean?' They had you elected."

Hanlon felt real anger. "Don't even *think* it."

"I'm at the age when I think of nothing else, Sam. Look at me. When I came up to the Landing in '63, I thought I was coming to the Promised Land." He probed the long coarse grass with the toe of his moccasin. "I thought I could change everything. Start from scratch. Margo was part of it. There was still hope, then. We were trying for another child and, boy, were we uptight about it. We'd already lost one in '59. Miscarriage."

He slipped a pack of cigarettes from his shirt pocket and lit one. "The way it came out, I did everything and changed nothing. I'm fifty-three years old and I've thrown it all away. Margo and Dan, too. I lay awake at night sometimes thinking: What would Sam do about Dan? How would he handle it?" He sniffed derisively.

"So you see, they're not so far wrong. If I could live things your way, I would. I guess Margo might even get to like that."

"You can make a great start by not feeling so damned sorry for yourself," Hanlon snapped brutally.

Carradine took a shred of tobacco from his tongue with the tip of his forefinger and studied it for a long time.

"You're right. Too right. If I had what you have, Sam, I'd do it tomorrow. Today. Now. Fact is, I *am* sorry for myself. I mean, clinically. It's a condition I can't explain to you. You wouldn't understand the causes. You couldn't interpret the symptoms. You've a nice, sound, coordinated, aggressive Ameri-

21

can male. More than a little materialistic. Sure of yourself because what little you know of yourself you like."

"Thanks for the citation."

"Don't be cynical, Sam. It *is* a citation." He dragged that deep sigh through his nose again. "Let's just say I'm buying futures in the friendship market." He chuckled, suddenly relaxed. "I might need you—posthumously, that is. You never know; this condition of mine could turn out to be terminal."

5.

Alec Lamb shifted his bulk in the chair and glanced at his watch. The gift-wrapped secretary produced a technical smile to acknowledge his impatience but did nothing about it.

Lamb hated Langley. He approached it as an unfrocked priest would approach the confessional, with a sense of guilt wrapped in genuine doubt. The day-to-day mechanics of his life were at best monotonous, at worst sordid. Langley sublimated them, gave them a sense of religious purpose. Lamb had only to walk by the wall motif in the lobby with its Delphic legend, "Ye shall know the truth and the truth shall make you free," to feel soiled.

The secretary's desk communicator gave out a soft tone and she flicked a switch. The Assistant Director's voice said, "Come."

He was at his desk, reclining in the great chair, flanked by a deftly draped Old Glory and a huge phony-antique globe of the world. Three young men, two of them spectacled, sat stiffly on couches around the walls, and George Strauss perched his shapeless, tweedy mass on one end of a low coffee table.

"Sit down, Alec. You know everyone, of course." The Assistant Director pointed to a chair and Strauss raised his head in greeting. Lamb had never met the others and the AD knew it.

"The subject of this meeting is not for circulation beyond this office," the AD said smoothly. "No one takes notes. What we discuss here is strictly between you, me, and the VATs."

The CIA did nōt use Voice-Activated Tape Recordings on the executive floor at Langley. It was the AD's little joke. Nobody laughed.

"Okay, George. Tell him."

George Strauss flicked through the file of papers on his lap.

"Alec, we've come up with a bad one. As of now, I guess you could say we don't know how bad, and there're some people who think it's a put-on. Okay. First, we're assuming it's exactly what it appears to be."

He combed his riot of gray-white curls with long, thick fingers. "The background first. Communications picked up a transmission channel in 1963. It was Russian, staged through Helsinki. We marked it low-profile because they used the public cable service and the code predated the Soviet switch to computers. Fine. The messages were informational and usually financial. Told us nothing we didn't already know."

Lamb said, "Unless it was a code-within-a-computer-code."

Strauss shook his head. "We thought of that. The Brains Department said no way."

"How were they passing them?"

Strauss consulted a yellow sheet. "The old interception technique. They filed their cables to a nonexistent industrial address in the East Fifties."

"How was that making it easy for them?"

"Simple. Western Union received, tried to deliver, failed, and routed the cable to their Trace Section."

"Where," broke in the AD, "it was picked up by the interceptor. A clerk specializing in Finnish. Neat."

"Sounds like a lousy operation to me," Lamb said. "It's uncertain, amateurish. One mistake and it's dead."

"Quite," said Strauss dryly. "Except it worked. Anyway, it was an infrequent service."

Lamb stared at the toes of his burnished black shoes.

"Where do I come into this?"

"You came in about twenty-eight hours ago. We think. This transmission channel has been closed since September 12, 1964. No termination message at that time. They just stopped using it. We assumed the channel was deactivated. At six sharp yesterday morning, a cable was filed from the same old Helsinki source. Same code. Same pickup. One difference. We think it's a kill order. The code suggests that much, but that's where it also works against us. We don't know the target."

"But if the code's that easy to break . . ."

"It isn't," broke in the AD. "They're using random word coordinates for the important part. The target is coded as 'shall.' It doesn't take a genius to work that out. They're using book references. A certain word on a certain line of a certain page of a book preselected by the code operator. That word is given a fixed identity—a person, a time, a place, a method—anything you want. The system is antediluvian, but it's watertight."

"And where does that leave me?"

George Strauss watched Lamb carefully. "The cables previously pushed through this channel concern a sleeper colony—Kingfish."

"Teague's Landing," Lamb said quickly.

"The cable we picked up yesterday is also aimed at Kingfish."

The AD leaned across his desk. "I don't want you to read too much into this, Alec. Just take it as it comes and leave the imponderables to me. As far as you're concerned, this could be a kill order directed to a group under your sphere of influence. Don't go looking for fancy undertones, understand me? You play it for real."

"Do I get reinforcements?"

"Not for the moment," the AD broke in. "What I want you to do now is get alongside your fieldman, Hanlon. I want you up there fast. I want to know why this cell can get a trigger message without his knowing about it. I want you to go through every report he's submitted since 1963 for any evidence he's recorded of a change in the character or intention of the Kingfish cell. George'll give you a list of the Helsinki messages. Match 'em against Hanlon's reports."

"Wait a minute." Lamb sat bolt upright. "Are you telling me we let this message through?"

George Strauss looked at the floor. The Assistant Director cleared his throat. "Communications logged the cable at 0600 yesterday. The clerk had it in his hands at 0535. He arrived at his desk a little after five. He had to know it was coming. We're assuming he passed the message on before we picked him up."

Lamb got to his feet and reached for his briefcase.

"Well, I can get a rundown on that, I guess. Twenty-five minutes. In that time he could only phone or send a telegram. If it went to any of the four in Teague's Landing, Hanlon will know about it."

The AD held a hand across the desk. Lamb shook it awkwardly.

"I hope for your sake he does, Alec," he drawled.

They gave him time to close the door, cross the outer office, open and shut the second door, and walk at least fifty paces along the corridor to the elevators. They sat in silence, avoiding each other's eyes. George Strauss broke the pattern.

"I don't like it," he said.

The Assistant Director yawned. He had been roused from a troubled sleep at 0615. "What don't you like, George?"

"When you stop trusting your own men on the ground, you throw the motor into reverse. You think Hanlon's been sleeping on the job? All right. I'll buy that. It's a possibility. But Alec Lamb! You haven't got a finer officer on the team. He gave us the lead on Kingfish in the first place. Take him out of the

25

sequence and we end up trying to contain Kingfish by remote control."

"Your personal loyalty's showing, George," the AD said slowly. "No one's taking out Alec Lamb. I just want to be sure about him, that's all."

"I'm sure about him—all the way," Strauss persisted doggedly. He had protuberant eyes underhung with deep redrimmed bags. He looked at that moment as aggressive as a King Charles spaniel.

"With respect, sir, it's not a matter of personal confidence." The gold-framed spectacles of the young man nearest the AD's chair flashed as he turned to face Strauss. The tone was deferential but with a hint of mild impatience. He raised his head, questioningly, at the AD who nodded at him.

"We've had to make lightning judgments, sir. We need to double-check them," said the flashing spectacles efficiently.

Strauss directed a hard glare at the AD. "No judgments have been made, as far as I know."

The AD waggled a finger. "Correction, George. No judgments *since you arrived*. We had to work fast." He turned to the young man again. "Go ahead, Jeff."

The young man got snagged up on Strauss's stare. He turned for comfort to his bespectacled colleague.

"We see it this way. Kingfish was made operational to the best of our knowledge in November 1958 and seeded in Teague's Landing in March 1963. Hanlon was *in situ* from April 1963. It's got to be said: there's been nothing out of Hanlon since then to suggest that Kingfish is fulfilling its role as a clandestine unit. We know about Hanlon. Berlin Allied Intelligence Staff, 1951 to 1953. Army Intelligence Staff for Soviet Military Surveillance, 1953 to 1955. Berlin Station covert activities, 1955 to 1959. Arrested Prague in July 1959.

"Bad mistake. He was acting independently and outside Station influence. The persuaders got to him. He's never been the same—physically, anyway. Muscles of the left shoulder were

badly torn. Exchanged for a KGB captain, Ernst Bemmel-
mann, in May 1960. He was ripe for retirement. I see from the
records, sir," he blinked nervously at Strauss, "that you recom-
mended him for surveillance on Kingfish."

He raced on before Strauss could reply.

"The file has it all. Hanlon was old-style muscle. That's what
he was trained for and that was his experience. Cold War
muscle. Fine. Nothing wrong with that. He was right for his
time. Competent, committed. What we have to ask ourselves is:
Can we trust him? I'll qualify that. Can we trust him as an
agent, and can we trust him as an individual? I'd say the answer
to the first part is a halfway Yes. The second part, one hundred
percent No."

George Strauss breathed heavily, his eyes on the floor. "And
you come to these instinctual conclusions on the basis of your
long practical experience of working in the field, huh?"

The young man's face twitched and colored. The AD swung
his chair around thirty degrees.

"Cut it out, George. So you're high on loyalty. Great. Show
me some good old country suspicion, too, and we'll get somewhere. What Jeff was getting around to was this: Hanlon's
suspect and in my book that makes his case officer suspect.
Efficiency-wise. We don't have time to prove them one way or
another, so for a couple of days we let the two of 'em gnaw
away at each other's doubts. Meanwhile, I want a support operation mounted on Kingfish."

"To exclude the two men who know Kingfish best?"

"If that's the way you want to read it, yes."

"Am I allowed to ask who gets to run the new cover?"

The AD beamed, a generous display of confidence. "You do,
of course, George. You're Lamb's Controller. But . . ." He
steepled his fingers. "This time we start all over again. I want
to know if Kingfish really is functional, but I also want to know
how many more have been added to the cell, if any. Maybe
we're doing Hanlon an injustice. He started with four named

27

sleepers. He's stayed with them. There may be more now. The center may not be operating from Teague's Landing. Find them."

Strauss finger-combed his wild gray hair.

"I'll need to talk to the Western Union clerk."

The AD came forward in his chair.

"Forget the clerk, George. I'll take care of that end. I don't want you or anyone else fraternizing with the FBI. If they thought the Agency was running its own surveillance effort here at home, they'd take it all the way to the White House and that'd drag in the Domestic Operations Division." He relaxed into the chair. "We just can't handle a demarcation dispute at this point in time, George. Let's keep it simple."

Strauss examined the carpet again. The Assistant Director had been appointed a little over a year earlier. He was a former Navy logistics planner and an Annapolis product like the Director who had brought him in. There was too much White House identity in this package to make a policy fight worthwhile.

"I'll get a team together, then," Strauss said.

The AD switched on his anxious-to-please expression again. "Sure, George. Sure. I've been thinking about that. I want you to meet someone. He's downstairs. He could be just the man you're looking for."

6.

Hanlon was at the station to pick up Alec Lamb and they drove into town in silence. The bronze Mercedes 350 SL sports car was open to the sun and the wind, and Hanlon had quadrophonic tapes playing loudly. Lamb allowed himself total immersion in the mighty choral stanzas of Carl Orff's *Carmina Burana* and postponed thoughts of the crunch to come.

The station was lodged in a natural fault between the Ridge and the long spiky hill that obscured Old Harbor and the smokestack of the cannery. The road dropped through the pine woods to Main Street and then into the square. In the far right-hand angle of the square stood the Hanlon Center, a two-story conglomerate of shops and utilities built in an extended H-shape. On the crossbar of the H, the Center climbed to six stories. Hanlon's personal office suite was the glass-walled penthouse.

Lamb accepted a Chivas Regal in a stubby Rosenthal glass and settled himself in a wide, low Italian leather chair on the raised platform in the center of the room. Hanlon took the chair behind the desk.

Alec Lamb was the ultimate professional; there was no room in his makeup for narrow emotional responses. He exhibited envy as rarely as he experienced joy. On the other hand, he found it difficult to avoid comparisons between his own modest rented apartment in Westchester and Hanlon's Sybaritic surroundings in Teague's Landing. Lamb had never set foot inside the house on the Ridge, of course, but he'd talked to people who had. And this. . . .

When they shipped Hanlon in, Langley had ordered him to develop a solid business background. In due course, they provided the capital for Hanlon's ventures through one of their own banks and, in 1968, he'd gone public through the Agency's brokerage house on Wall Street. Hanlon had displayed an unforeseen talent for corporate law and company manipulation. It was an irrelevancy in terms of his role in Teague's Landing but Langley was delighted. The CIA was then at the midpoint of its drive to develop investments in industry and commerce, and Hanlon undoubtedly earned himself favorite-son status with the Directorate of Management and Services.

The CIA now had a higher corporate yield than General Motors, and Hanlon had a life style that relegated his case officer's to Third World berry-picking standards.

"I didn't expect you this early in the month," Hanlon probed gently.

"Yeah. I needed a breath of fresh air."

"You want a run-through since you're here?"

"Why? You got anything new?"

"No."

Lamb sipped his whisky. A green light winked on Hanlon's desk set and he pressed a square key.

"Mr. Schapp's secretary is on the line. Will you confirm lunch for today, one-fifteen?" his secretary inquired.

"Tell him something's come up, Jean. I'll get back to him later." He flicked the key.

"Thanks," said Lamb.

"You want to eat?"

"Yeah. How about here?"

Hanlon eyed him curiously, then called through an order of ham on rye, sardines, a French wine whose name Lamb didn't catch, and a dessert of cheesecake and coffee.

"How're the dogs?" Lamb made it sound as superfluous as a comment on the weather.

"No change," Hanlon said slowly. "If you really want to know, we can do a run-through like I said."

"Yeeeeeaaah." Lamb brought it out with an effort. He got up and strolled over to the big telescope facing southwest over the Ridge. It was floor-mounted on a single steel shaft. An electric motor in cylindrical white casing sat on the crossmembers below the instrument, and, above the eyepiece, on a slender stalk of stainless steel, was a beautifully compact Japanese movie camera. Lamb bent to squint through the eyepiece.

Helen Shawn lay on the springboard over her pool, her brown athletic body glistening with suntan oil, naked breasts stretched tight, nipples erect. Her folded arms cushioned fluffy yellow hair tied with a blue bandanna. Lower down, he could see, she was a true blonde, but he couldn't make out the essential bodywork. She had her ankles crossed.

He looked over his shoulder at Hanlon.

"You sure you're happy in your work?"

Hanlon grinned. "Helen Shawn?"

"As if you didn't know."

"See one, you've seen 'em all."

Lamb returned to the eyepiece. "Are you filming this kinda thing?"

"No. Jack gets home around six-thirty at night and he leaves at eight-thirty in the morning. The cameras just make sure he comes and goes. If anyone's with him, the bugs in his car and on the outside of the house, front and back, trigger the electric motor on the telescope and the camera."

"Very scientific," said Lamb. He was still enjoying the view.

"But not exactly new. You know what it's all about, Alec. Why're we playing games?"

Lamb straightened up and swilled Scotch into the back of his throat. There were three more telescopes, similarly geared for sight and sound, on the other three glass walls of the penthouse. He walked toward one of them, changed his mind, and returned to the chair.

"Oh, old age, I guess. I worry a lot, you know that. You listened in to the phone-tapes recently?"

"I have and it wasn't worth it."

"You checked yesterday's?"

Hanlon pulled open a drawer of his desk and stabbed a finger at the control panel inside. A hiss of blank tape sprang from the four corners of the room. There was a click and Frank Carradine's voice came on. A woman, clearly distressed, asked if he would come immediately to a house above the Old Harbor. Her son had a fever. Two days earlier the child had a tetanus injection and. . . .

Carradine sighed and said he'd be there. Click.

There were eighteen calls in all. Marvin Fish accepting a golf date; Carradine in conversation three times with Ben Olafsson about the affairs of the Rod and Gun Club; Jack Shawn lining up town committee meetings; Carrie Hanlon talking to Helen, Joan, and Grace; Helen taking a call from La Belle Alsacienne, her dressmakers on Fifth Avenue; Hanlon calling Carradine. Nobody called Margo.

Hanlon switched off the tape. "That gives you everything for the past forty-eight hours. Up to about two hours ago. You want more?"

Hanlon's secretary buzzed at the security door on the floor below and he freed the automatic lock. She came up the stairs in the far corner, laid out the alfresco meal on the desk, and left.

Hanlon pulled open the drawer again and touched the control panel. The perpendicular whitewood blinds on the glass walls turned and became a solid wall that shut out the light. He hit another key and the hidden loudspeakers gave off a high-speed hiss. When the run clunked to a halt, he pressed another switch.

From the centerpoints of the four walls, two feet above head height, four beams of light stabbed the darkness and splashed panoramic slabs on each wall. There was a flickering of numbers, then each wall filled with the grotesquely larger-than-life-sized figures of Carradine, Shawn, Fish, and Cater. Four soundtracks crashed out in a tidal wave of noise. Lamb raised both hands to his ears. Hanlon grinned in the stabbing light and turned off the sound.

The room was now an enclosed box on whose inner sides giant men came and went, opening doors, entering cars, laughing, pointing, looking sad, dressing, undressing, eating, drinking. Scene cut into scene without warning: from house to garden to office to street. Wives were pecked, stormed at, touched. Children were patted. Meals were eaten. Friends greeted.

Finally, three walls were blacked out and on the fourth there appeared an interior shot of Hanlon's own home. A card table was set up against one wall and Carradine, Fish, Shawn, and Cater played wordless poker.

Hanlon turned a control knob and the game surged into frenetic Keystone Kops high-speed.

"Okay, okay. You made your point," shouted Lamb. Hanlon

hit more buttons. The lights died and the window blinds revolved and the afternoon sun came in to dazzle them.

"Maybe we can level with each other now." Hanlon arched an eyebrow. Lamb looked away and fed a wedge of cheesecake into his open mouth with a tiny silver fork.

"What's to level about?"

"So you're satisfied."

"Who said I was dissatisfied?"

"You did. By turning up here off-schedule, looking like the last rose of summer."

"You're crazy, and I'm not so goddamned surprised at that." He edged forward on his chair and wiped his fingers on a crisp white napkin. "Tell me something, Sam. What in hell do you *really* know about those people?" He waved a hand at the silent walls.

"Oh, come on, Alec. What kind of a question's that after fifteen years? You know everything I know and that's total. *Total.*"

"Sure it's total. A billion percent total. And that's what's wrong with this whole damn picture show. We're bogged down in a sea of crap. There's so much detail there's no room for evaluation."

"Evaluation is your bag, Alec. I'm here to get the detail. Every last spit and cough. That's what I do."

"Yeah, I know. I get your reports. Beautiful. They tell me everything and they tell me nothing. What d'you expect me to say for fifteen years of nothing? Ask yourself a question: Why did Moscow seed Kingfish here in the first place? Go ahead; ask yourself."

Hanlon swung his feet onto a corner of the desk.

"Let me ask you one, Alec. Who's turning the screw? What's going on?"

Lamb stretched full-length in the chair and lit a king-sized menthol.

"Nothing's going on. And that's the precise problem. The Agency's under the microscope, man. Even you can understand that. We're on the rack. We don't get to play it carte blanche any more. The world's changing and we're being screwed to change with it."

Hanlon nodded slowly.

"Maybe it's about time we had some questions asked, Alec."

"What the hell do you mean by that?"

Hanlon raised his hands, palm up.

"In 1958, Moscow station turns up a defector. He spills a lot of garbage. Some we can check. Some we can't. *Most* we can't. Kingfish is one little piece, but the only thing he knows is four names and the fact that they trained out of the KBG's Americanization Unit. We're all a little uptight then; we'll believe anything then. Right?"

Lamb squirmed. "You're not making sense."

"Try me. So we have four names. Four last names, to be precise. And although our brave little defector doesn't know their first names, or their case officer, or their controller, or their targets, or their Russian names, he *does* magically know exactly where in the US of A they intend to seed."

"So?"

"So, Number One: we have an anomaly. A twenty-two-carat anomaly. Number Two: we act on the information and that means me. But our whole strategy still hangs on one man's unqualified word. Are you with me so far?"

"You're driving."

"Number Three: Moscow Station can't get this prime defector out because he's a big-time high classification KGB man. So they break all the rules and debrief him on the spot, as and when he can spare the time. And one day he doesn't turn up."

"He's dead."

"He's dead, they *said*. All I'm saying to you, Alec, is this: if that guy wasn't shot, if he's still alive, and if he was a plant, we've got a real dandy little sideshow running here, wouldn't you say? Agents, assets, a whole damn machine tied up in the ass-end of nowhere watching four perfectly innocent Americans."

34

Lamb stared at him for a long time.

"I wouldn't like to believe that kind of crap is dictating the way you handle this job, Sam. I really wouldn't like that."

"Don't worry, Alec. Doubts work two ways. But when you've lived with them as long as I have. . . ."

"Don't tell me. You really get to *know* people. And you know best."

Hanlon shrugged.

"Don't waste your time throwing curves at me, Alec. You know what I mean. There's a reasonable doubt."

"And you really believe that?"

Lamb grabbed the arms of the Italian chair and hauled himself to his feet. He walked to the head of the stairs, lifted down his coat, his briefcase and his hat, and frowned back at Hanlon.

"Do me a favor, Sam. Take a couple steps back from this and try looking at it from a different perspective."

Hanlon reclined his chair further.

"You mean look at it till I see it Langley's way?"

Lamb was on the fourth stair down. Only the upper half of him was visible.

"See it the way you always did. Just accept instructions and act on them."

Hanlon released his pressure on the chair and it sprang upright.

"And forget the evidence of my eyes and ears!"

"That's right," Lamb said evenly. "Until I decide the evidence is important. Until I decide it fits."

Hanlon came to the head of the stairs and glared down aggressively. "I want it in the record, Alec," he said tightly. "I want it on paper that I register disquiet about the whole background to Kingfish. I have a right to. . . ."

Lamb folded his lips into his mouth and bit on them. His patience snapped.

"There's no goddamn doubt, Hanlon. You're out of line. One

more step and I'll break you. That's *my* right." He clenched his teeth against the uncharacteristic spate of anger and released his breath.

"None of that was on the record, Sam, okay? If you're taping this you'd better wipe the track. And take it from me, that Moscow defector was real enough. I debriefed him."

Hanlon was genuinely surprised. He said lamely, "I still say you can't be sure he died."

For the first time Lamb smiled. It was an expression of relief, not triumph.

"I can. I put two bullets in the back of his head from a range of five feet. Believe me—he died."

7.

Daniel Carradine tightened the stock of the crossbow in the workbench vise and cranked the ratchet that drew the steel bowstring.

The room was an extension of the double garage, its walls a showcase for Frank Carradine's love affair with archery. As a collector, Carradine had scoured the world for examples of antique bowcraft. As a craftsman, he had learned from history and improved on it. In the past two years, he'd turned his passion for projectile accuracy to the crossbow. There were at least thirty examples of his work hanging from the roof beam above the bench.

Bobby Hanlon lay face down on an old trestle table across the room, his chin cushioned on his arms. He was totally relaxed but watchful. Bow-making was one activity where Dan excelled, but you couldn't say for sure what might happen when he started playing with sharp-edged tools.

"I can't see anything wrong with that bow," he called out. "Looks pretty good to me."

"You don't *see* flaws in a bow. You *feel* them. The balance is wrong. It'll affect trajectory by twenty percent over a hundred yards."

"You're the genius."

"No genius involved." Daniel looked up; his pale, intelligent face was serious, his deep-set eyes dark with concentration. "The principles involved are fundamental. The genius was the man who worked them out first. I'm just adapting."

"Like your dad." It sounded innocent but Bobby realized uncomfortably that he didn't mean it just that way. Daniel dropped his eyes to his work and cranked the bowstring full out.

"I mean, your dad is kinda hung up on bows, so it's natural for you to be, too. Like me and Sam go for the boat."

Daniel examined him penetratingly. "I never heard you call him Sam. Not to his face."

"Yeah, well . . ." Bobby's embarrassment was acute. "Someday I will. I'm just getting into practice." He turned temporary defeat into attack. "I guess you don't feel the same way about the doc, huh?"

Daniel bent low over the vise.

"My mother wouldn't like it. She's a traditionalist."

Bobby spluttered mock disbelief. "A what?"

"You know what I mean. Anyway, I don't want to talk about it."

Bobby swung himself into a sitting position, legs crossed.

"It won't go away because you don't want to talk about it. What happens when you go to college? She gonna move in with you?"

Daniel sighed but kept his eyes on the bow. "You seem to want to provoke something. Is that what this is about? Or are you just doing what," his face twisted bitterly, "*Sam* told you to do?"

Bobby stared at him uncomprehendingly. "Sam? I don't know what you're talking about."

Daniel's face burned a deep angry pink. "He wants to run everything, doesn't he? Anything doesn't conform with the way Sam Hanlon sees it, it's got to be changed. Like my father! Why d'you think he spends so much time around my father? Well, I'll tell you. He hates the way you and me stick together. Oh yes, he does! And I'll tell you something else. He wouldn't come straight out and say, 'Look, Bob, I don't want you hanging around the Carradine kid any more,' he just gets to work on my father to put pressure on us."

Bobby, bemused at first, was now astounded.

"I see. Just like that. Well, I'll tell *you* something, Mister Know-It-All, my dad wouldn't hate anybody that much. Not your father, not you."

Daniel's face continued to burn but his temper cooled.

"You believe what you like."

Bobby bounced off the trestle table onto the floor.

"Don't worry, I will. At least I'm free to think what I like."

"What's that supposed to mean?"

"I don't have to ask my mom for permission to breathe, that's what I mean. I don't let her use me against people, that's what I mean."

Daniel turned back to his work, but Bobby raged on.

"You know, some days I just don't understand you. One minute we're okay and everything's dandy. Then your mom starts talking to you in your head and right away you're going for my throat. You're two people you know that? Split personality— one's sleeping while the other's awake. And they come and go like crazy. But you expect me to stay the same, right? Well, hear this, genius: I'm sick of listening to your mom speaking through you. That's what she does. She's got you really brainwashed stupid. All that crap about Sam. Well," he gestured helplessly, speechlessly, for a moment, then made for the door, "well, to hell with both of you."

38

There was a click, the thrum of a released steel bowstring, and Daniel howled with sudden anguish.

Bobby turned and raced back to the bench. He grabbed Daniel's quaking left hand. The string had cut deep into the cushion of flesh below his thumb. Bobby reached for the medicine chest on a wall bracket over the bench and stanched the flow of blood.

"My God!" he gritted. "You aren't fit to be left alone for one minute."

8.

From: Dmitri Orlov, Director, First Directorate, KGB
To: Marshal Vasili Bunin, First Deputy Chairman of the Council of Ministers of the USSR

SECRET.

The KINGFISH cell has been activated. It is only a matter of time before Stefan Andreyev is aware of this. We must move quickly if we are to exploit the situation. I have written a note (copy attached) to the Praesidium, which will also be sent to the Premier.

To: Members of the Praesidium of the Central Committee of the Communist Party and the Council of Ministers of the USSR
From: Dmitri Orlov, Director, First Directorate, KGB

It is with the utmost concern that I must report a serious situation involving the First Directorate of the KGB, of which I am. head. It has come to my attention that a cell of deep-penetration agents has been activated under the aegis of my department but without my knowledge. These agents—*residentura*—are based in America, and the process of their awakening is irreversible. The reason for their awakening, under whose authority, and in what respect, are all unknown. A top-priority investigation has been authorized by me, but the files on KINGFISH have, strangely, been discovered to contain only the barest information. Four American code names are all we have to identify this group:

CARRADINE/FISH/CATER/SHAWN

They are merely cover names, and there are no corresponding Russian names or codes. The group's formation was conceived and executed some *twenty years ago*, and I have put all this information to Comrade Andreyev, Chairman of the KGB and my immediate superior.

It is, coincidentally, helpful that the Comrade Chairman was, in fact, Director of the First Directorate some twenty years ago and is therefore in a position to enlighten us further.

From: Aleksander Rostov, First Secretary of the Central Committee
To: Stefan Andreyev, Chairman, KGB
Copies to: Dmitri Orlov, First Directorate, members of the Praesidium

SECRET.

It is outrageous that the Soviet Union should be faced with a situation of such immense potential embarrassment at such a time! As Premier, I order an immediate investigation at the highest level. In the meantime, I also authorize and order that the four names of the so-called KINGFISH cell be passed on immediately to the senior officer of the American CIA, together with all other information that may help apprehend the group. I note also, Comrade, that it was skillful work by your subordinate Orlov that first brought this matter to my attention, and not yourself!

9.

Hanlon turned off Main Street into the square and loped around the ornamental pool with its fizzing fountain to the main entrance of the Center. He rang the night bell and Roy Barker shuffled out of his office on night-tired feet encased in carpet slippers. The old man grinned at Hanlon's tracksuit—because it was the embodiment of the legend that everyone talked about but rarely saw—and unlocked the elevator to the penthouse.

It was six-forty. Hanlon showered and shaved in the private suite below his office and put on a white turtleneck sweater and jeans. Then he played the telephone tapes for the last seventy-two hours. Nothing came across that he couldn't explain. He played them again.

The sun crested Mackie's Point, highlighting polished surfaces with gold and bronze, stirring the town to Saturday-morning bustle. Hanlon triggered the control panel in his desk drawer and keyed in for sound from the Carradine house. He had bugs located in every room—even *that* room—but, except for the rattle of pots and pans in the kitchen where Margo Carradine's Filipino maid was preparing breakfast, there were no sounds that couldn't be explained.

Marvin Fish slept late on Saturdays. He commuted to Boston every day and rarely returned from the money-go-round much before nine at night. It was a punishing work rate, and his wife had persuaded Frank Carradine to program Marv against an early coronary. His concessions to medical advice so far had been a Saturday-morning lay-in and an overweaning interest in hang gliding.

On Saturday mornings, Marv slept late. In the afternoons, he tripped out on the warm air thermals below Jonathan's Rock.

41

Doug Cater was in the shower, his cigarette-stained baritone rendering an off-key version of "Pennies from Heaven" against the background hiss of hot water.

The Shawn household was still dead to the world. On the sixth day, Jack rested. On the seventh he was in church at seven for his mayoral stint at morning eucharist.

Hanlon flicked from house to house and heard each man rise, stretch, and yawn. He heard them dress and argue and pass from one bugged room to another. He keyed in the Shawn house again and there was still nothing. He leaned back in the swivel chair, irritated. It was stupid to allow Lamb's goading to affect him this way, but he had a lot of ground to cover. Lamb had come up to Teague's Landing off-schedule, unexplained. He had come for something specific. Like what?

On impulse, he picked up the phone and tapped out Shawn's home number. He heard the phone ring in the kitchen, living room, and bedroom. Jack was available everywhere.

Helen came on brightly.

"Sam!" She had a way of making him feel that he was the most sexually desirable man alive. He wondered if it was genuine.

"Hi, baby." He slipped into character so easily that it was difficult to register the transition himself. "Can I talk to Jack?"

"Better than that, darling. You can talk to me. We're alone."

"Well, what do you know. You manage to get rid of him at last?"

"He took the car to Boston, I think. Something must have come up. At quarter of ten on a Saturday morning, I couldn't get too interested in the details. I'm—er—," her voice dropped a conspiratorial octave. "I'm still in bed, Sam. Arrayed in all my sexy silken splendor—you know?"

He played the game for a few minutes more, then hung up. He reeled back the bugged phone-tapes and listened again. There was no evidence of a late-night or an early-morning call to Jack Shawn, no indication of a breakdown in the line-tap either.

He felt pinpricks of panic at the base of his skull. If Shawn had gone to Boston he must have been contacted, received a message by word of mouth or by hand. There had been no telegrams, that much he knew. A note through the door? An early-morning caller?

He replayed the tape of the house bugs. Nothing. The bugs were voice-activated, including those installed outside the house and in the garage. The automatic starter of a car was enough to trigger the garage bug, but there was not a whisper on the tape. There had to be something wrong with one of the pickup mikes. A disconnection—possibly a deliberate one.

Hanlon picked up the phone decisively, but his finger hovered over the keyboard and then withdrew. He replaced the receiver fretfully. What could Alec Lamb do about it now, anyway?

He got up and roamed. In theory, Kingfish were out of his control when they left the Landing. Lamb's fieldmen took over the moment any of them ranged out of his area. In practice, Hanlon knew that Lamb couldn't hope to cover all of them all the time. And why should he? They'd done nothing wrong.

He found himself back at the desk; he leaned over it and stabbed out Lamb's New York number.

There was an interrogative groan from the other end.

"Alec? Sam. One of my dogs is missing."

Lamb appeared to have the receiver clutched to his face under the sheets. "So?"

"Shawn. He drove to Boston this morning."

"He's a big boy. He can look after himself."

Hanlon banged the receiver three times on the edge of his desk. Hard. There was an explosive oath from the other end.

Hanlon said, "You awake now? I said Shawn's out on his own. I got nothing on tape says he had any message."

"So it's probably nothing."

43

"He goes into Boston no more than a half-dozen times a year on weekends. I know about it when he does."

"So what's eating you?"

"I don't like sudden disappearances, Alec. And I especially don't like it twenty-four hours after you turn up here playing Dick Tracy."

There was a flapping sound at the end of the line as Lamb came out of his fetal tent.

"Look, Sam, I appreciate the service call, and I'm sorry if I overplayed Big Brother yesterday. I'll put a tail on Shawn. But I'm making no promises we'll find him. I'll call you back."

He hung up.

Hanlon studied the dead receiver blankly then put it back on its rest. Alec Lamb was nobody's fool. He was not noted for schizoid behavior, but yesterday he had revealed a facet Hanlon had never seen before. Now he made Shawn's escapade sound like it didn't matter. What the hell was he playing at?

PART TWO **AWAKENING**

10.

Jack Shawn lifted a soft leather moccasin and reined back on the metallic blue Lancia Scorpion, sensing it chafe impatiently as it fell into line with the string of Saturday trippers on Route 3.

The custom-fitted steering wheel was white and cool under his fingers as they played over its ribbed edge. The low, sloping vee of the hood was steady enough to balance a tray of martinis. Cars had always been a ruling passion with Jack Shawn, he was the first to admit. Cars and women. He blamed it on a too-rich diet of old movies, the plots of which he had long forgotten. The plots maybe, but never those white-walled tires, those ivory steering wheels, and the supremely satisfying—almost sexual— "thunk" of sedan doors slammed by B-rated-movie private eyes. In those days, of course, the blonde was a no-option extra, a statutory squeak and whimper in scented boa and black velour. Jack Shawn had spent the last eight years letting his love affair with cars communicate itself to an audience that was no match for his enthusiasm.

When he started as a salesman in Jacksonville in 1959, he had made it his business to know *everything* that went on under the hood of every car he touched or was likely to touch. It gave him satisfaction, but, as he came to realize, it was totally unnecessary.

Just as a chef can con the customers' taste buds with pursed lips, pinched thumb and finger, and high rolling eyes before they had even tasted the dish, so Jack Shawn could have sold every rogue car this side of Chicago if the mood struck him.

47

Luckily for the East Coast road-fatality figures he had played it straight, first with his own garage on a small patch of land off the main highway between Jacksonville and Daytona. Six years later he sold the lot for $60,000 and a good-will fee of twice that.

He moved to Boston, set up showrooms in a new city center development, won the Lancia franchise and with it his no-option blonde.

Helen Shawn had been wearing slash-cuffed jeans and a T-shirt when she applied for the job of secretary. It wasn't exactly boa and velour, but the way she wore it was damned near enough. They were married within six weeks, and to his, her, and just about everyone else's amazement, Jack Shawn had settled into a state of terminal marital bliss.

Doug Cater's wife, Joan, had gone to high school with Helen and, on the Caters' special pleading, they had moved to Teague's Landing in 1963.

With his dark good looks and easygoing manner Jack Shawn had, almost against his will, found himself propelled into a heavy social scene. In 1969 he ran for mayor. They still loved him.

Margo Carradine had once asked him, playfully, what there was left to live for: hadn't he got it all? The answer was his stock one, accompanied by a lecherous glance at Helen: a 180 mph waterbed.

He swung the Lancia off Route 3 twenty miles south of Boston and reached the town in twenty minutes. The Saturday crowds had already taken over and he could see the day was shaping up to be a scorcher. He began to wish he had brought along a spare shirt. Just setting foot outside the air-conditioned car would be enough to turn the gray/green-striped job he was wearing into a limp rag. Still, the Atlanta, where he was due to meet Marini, was only a step away from the multilevel parking lot.

He tweaked left, brought the car up to the cash booth, and

lowered the window with the touch of a button. The attendant recognized him immediately. Most people did. Once seen. . . .

"It's fuller up than a grain-fed goose, Mr. Shawn. If I'd knowed you was comin', could've saved a hole."

The black attendant pushed forward a pink bottom lip, shook his head, and showed the red flecks in the corner of his eyes.

"Shore is maaghty forgetful of you not to notify Machenry you was comin' in today."

Jack Shawn grinned and reached for his ticket.

"I'll settle for the eighth floor, Machenry. The exercise will do me good."

"Lawdy, lawdy," said Machenry, returning the grin.

Shawn had patronized young Machenry for two years now and the patter seldom changed. Old Man Ribber English, Uncle Tom deference, and a look that would have made Al Jolson eat his heart out. Mac was radical, Black Power, proud. When he waved Shawn through, he returned to the law book balanced on a shelf under the counter. Another year and some luckless attorney would be facing that deceptive deference across a courtroom.

The eighth floor had been an optimistic guess. On the tenth, Shawn waited while an owlish matron tried to do things with an aging Buick that a car was never built to do. Hands crucified across the steering wheel, diamond-studded flyaway glasses glinting, she pushed the heap in a series of coughs and jerks down the ramp to the floor below. Shawn parked in the vacated space.

It was five to twelve. The note said he should be in the lounge of the Atlanta at midday. An odd time for Marini. Odd day, too. Marini was the Italian representative for Lancia, and he believed in restricting business to business hours. With three young children, a mother-in-law, father-in-law, brother, not to mention his wife, all under the same roof, Paolo Marini viewed his family responsibilities as a martyr valued his tormentors; without them he would be nothing.

49

Shawn ran over the possibilities as he strode the two blocks
to the hotel, trying to ignore the message of his itching fingers
that he should unbutton the collar of his shirt. No way. The
Atlanta was not that kind of place. It could only be the HPE's,
the Lancia station wagons. Through Marvin Fish, Shawn had
been introduced to a rancher from Nebraska who needed only
ten minutes in the car to order five with the possibility of another fifteen, ". . . if it takes a shine to them old Nebraska
roads."

A number of minor amendments to the chassis and the deal
seemed set. Then, at the last minute, the Nebraskan phoned to
say his wife wanted a sun roof. On all of them. Marini refused
to see the funny side of it, but it wasn't an order you turned
down.

Chances were there was a crisis; maybe the cars were stuck
in a freight yard somewhere between here and Omaha. On their
way back. It had to be something big.

The lobby was cool and the martinis in the Cleveland bar
were as dry as ever. Shawn made his second drink last fifteen
minutes, then decided to check with reception. Marini, said
the clerk, had last booked in three weeks ago for two days. He
was not expected again for another week. It was a fixed, regular
booking. No, there was no mistake. He found a booth and
phoned Marini's office in New York. All he got was a machine
trying to sound like a human. Would he care to leave a message? He left a message. "Marini. Jack Shawn. I have switched
to Alfa Romeo. Please remove your cars from my showroom."
At least it would guarantee a return call Monday morning.

He wandered back to the bar and ordered another martini.
He needed something to settle the real anger his bantering
message had cloaked. Marini knew that Saturdays were special.
What was he up to? Or was it some crazy son of a bitch who
wanted him out of town for a few hours? He phoned Helen.
The line was busy. Debated another drink. Weakness won
hands down. He swallowed it guiltily and walked out onto the
street.

It felt like someone had focused a vast burning glass over the town. The citizens, like ants under scalding water, scuttled from shadow to shadow. Shawn tugged off his tie and stuffed it into his pocket as he made his way back to the parking lot. With luck he would be home within the hour and he and Helen could crash out by the pool. Even the thought refreshed him. That black bikini of hers with the drawstrings at the hips and breast; they operated like parachute cords. The warm, sculpted brownness, with its sheen of fine gold baby hair like chicken down. Long legs stretched wide, unashamedly offering themselves to the sun.

He took off his dark glasses and pressed the elevator button for the tenth floor. Two middle-aged women gave him an appreciative appraisal and got out at the seventh. He smiled as they exited. The martinis were beginning to soften his mood.

Tenth. Thirty paces from the Lancia he knew someone had jimmied it.

The driver's door showed the faint, telltale scratches where a picking tool had been inserted in the lock and had slipped: the top of the window was chipped where a jimmy had been prized in. He tried the door and it swung open. The radio had been a Panasonic. Forty channels, four watts—the legal maximum—variable squelch control, modulation meter, noise blanker, PA system, detachable mike, and a quick-release, reversible bracket to prevent theft. They'd all worked perfectly well the last time he used them, but he could no longer vouch for the quick-release, reversible bracket. It had been torn from its mounting by someone who was wasting his time stealing car radios; he had a bigger future in alligator wrestling.

Two packs of Philip Morris and a rolled gold Sheaffer pen had joined the collection *ex Shawn*. But that was all. It could have been worse. That's what Helen would say. It could have been worse. So could Watergate, Hurricane Annie, the "Late Hate Show," and the Bay of Pigs. It didn't make him feel any better. He sat himself behind the steering wheel and let the impotent rage rise and bathe his mouth with bile. He lit a cigarette. It was going to be one of those days. The way things were shaping up there would be a four-hour traffic jam on Route 3, a cloudburst over Teague's Landing, and it would be Helen's time of the month. He pulled the door, and by torturing the handle, managed to lock it with what was left of the mechanism. He started the car, swung angrily out of the berth, and jammed his foot hard on the gas pedal. The Lancia roared angrily along the rough concrete to the descending ramp.

Foot up.

Foot up, stupid!

The Lancia had touched 40 mph in that short angry burst. It was reaching 45 mph when, thirty feet from the ramp, Jack Shawn raised his foot from the pedal and touched the brakes. The car took no notice. The gas pedal remained glued to the floor and the brake squelched obscenely.

Twenty feet from the ramp he reached down and tugged desperately with both hands at the jammed gas pedal, but it was locked tight, as if held by a steel spring. He slammed his hands back on the wheel and swung the car violently toward the descent ramp. It screamed into a side-on skid. That was when Jack Shawn started to yell. The Lancia hit the low retaining wall sideways at 55 mph. Both offside wheels folded under the chassis on impact like bent bottle tops. A spume of gas hissed forward under massive pressure from the ruptured tank.

Momentarily, the wall held, bending outward like elastic. Then the steel reinforcing rods twisted their dynamic energy in on themselves and, with an apocalyptic crack, the whole section erupted, spraying concrete two hundred feet into the street below. Jack Shawn screamed at the yawning emptiness below and his bladder emptied in pure terror as the car began its agonizing spiral to the street.

A hundred feet above the sidewalk, the twisting metal bomb exploded as fuel cascaded over Shawn and the cigarette that had fallen from his mouth. A half-second later the whirling, blazing, threshing machine hit the street and chewed a path through cars and pedestrians, tearing clothes from bodies, skin from bone; turning screams to silence, welding victims to walls with their own blood.

And, as those who witnessed the carnage later recalled, the most freakish and terrible thing of all . . . a wheel, its tire liquid with red-black flame, was sent spinning through the air like a demonic Frisbee. It scythed across the street and, in one whirling flash of movement, decapitated a young man. He had just finished his morning shift in the parking lot and was taking his law book to lunch in the Paprika Pizza Parlor.

11.

Carrie Hanlon had spent the morning preparing a meat loaf. Normally it took her less than ten minutes to prepare the ground chuck, chop the onions and the bacon, and make it ready for anointing with oil, tomato, and horseradish, but then, normally, she didn't have her mind this full of Sam Hanlon.

There was something wrong with Sam; something was throwing him. She knew it instinctively, as she knew that whatever the problem was, he'd keep it from her come hell or high water. Sam didn't share things, except when they were going well. Good old reliable Sam. Expansive most of the time. Laughing from the belt. The guest who could charge a premium for coming to dinner. That was the public face. There was another. That one belonged to Samuel Reeves Hanlon, and Carrie knew very little about him. He wasn't a man you could really come to terms with. In her first few inquisitive years of marriage, when the contents of his jacket pockets, his wallet, and his office phone book were frighteningly intriguing, she desperately wanted to identify that other face. Not any more. It was the logic that keeps the hypochondriac from having his fears confirmed by a doctor. Living with latent unease is better than facing unpalatable truth.

First there were the telephone calls, some long after midnight. The "friends" he never invited home, even after fifteen
years. The "business trips" that finally engineered their two-day
estrangement just a year after they married. She had walked
out and stayed in a downtown Boston hotel until he traced her.
Two men, quiet, gray, and overwhelming, who called themselves
police but showed no identification, had picked her up and
taken her back home. One of them had called Sam "sir" as he
left. He didn't look the type who used that word lightly.

And so, the "explanation."

No, there wasn't another woman. It was work. A job. To do
with the army. Helping out, sort of. Communications, stuff like
that. A hangover from army days. Carrie had stopped listening,
hating the lies. He judged her response and they went to bed
and made love until she sank into a stupor of exhaustion, listening to his heart pounding in her ear, knowing he was awake,
knowing the lie was unburied.

Six months later she had found the gun and the shoulder
holster in a drawer in his study. She had said nothing then or
since.

Whatever it was, she decided, it was preferable to another
woman. She had accepted the fact that she would never have
all of Sam Hanlon, that not even in the most private moments
would a full and total transference take place between them.
Curiously, it no longer worried her. Except when the dark side
clouded the light and became so obvious that she couldn't hide
the truth from herself.

The upturned bottle of horseradish gurgled faintly and deposited its contents over two pounds of chopped meat; she came
out of her trance, swearing under her breath, glancing guiltily
over her shoulder in case Bobby was in the room.

The ringing phone was a welcome distraction.

She wiped her hands, appraised herself automatically in the
hall mirror, patted her hair into place, and moistened her lips
with her tongue.

It was Marvin Fish, Supermarv. For the past year he had been into a health kick that was driving everybody crazy. All Bran, ginseng, jogging, horseback riding, skiing, and now—God help him—hang gliding off Jonathan's Rock. If he was trying again to get Sam to go play with him, she would give him the answer she gave him last time: Sam takes off, I take off.

But Marv Fish was in no mood for even his favorite topic: himself. His voice was missing its customary bounce. He asked for Sam.

"He's at the office, Marv. Anything wrong? You sound as if you spent a day on the Exercycle and put on ten pounds."

"I don't want to bother you, Carrie . . . it's, well, have you listened to the radio?"

"No, Sam has been meaning to fix it. . . ."

He cut her short. "It's Jack Shawn, Carrie. It's on the news."

"Jack? He's dropping by the house toni. . . ."

Marv's silence communicated itself like a douche of cold water. For a moment they shared it, then he said:

"He's dead, Carrie. Car smash. I wanted to tell Sam so he could . . . well, maybe tell you himself. The telephone—it's so cold." Pause. "It's going to hit us all hard, Carrie. All of us."

She felt a nerve in her cheek pulse uncontrollably. The air in the hallway was suddenly as thick and heavy as a hothouse. Sucked dry of oxygen. Smelling of damp velvet.

"Carrie?"

"I'm all right, Marv. I just couldn't grasp it. Does Grace know?"

"Yeah. She's lying down. The doctor's here. Frank. He gave her a sedative. She was the first to hear—about twenty minutes ago on the radio. She didn't know it was Jack. Then the police called me right after. Christ." He fell silent.

"Thank you, Marvin," she said crisply. "I'm glad you phoned."

"It's just that with Grace not feeling so well I can't leave. I promised Joe Ruban—the chief—one of us would tell Helen."

55

"No! The police would have told her already . . . wouldn't they? Oh, my God, Marv, somebody has to get around there!"

"I phoned. There was no answer."

"I'll call Sam. When Grace feels better tell her to call me at Helen's. I'll get in touch with Joe Ruban."

There was always so little to say.

The blank face, suddenly shrunken by shock, suddenly more fragile than skin and bone could be, eyes flickering into every corner, desperate for a scrap of hope. Hanlon had seen it too often.

As a one-time administrative assistant on the Army Intelligence Staff, he had arrived on a dozen doorsteps like a black-bordered telegram, orchestrating heroism for the weeping newly widowed. After the first few confrontations he had resorted to a cold formula: "Your husband was a brave man. He died a hero's death. His last words were for you and his mother. His country can be proud of him."

And then the practicalities. After a decent pause a mention of the Company's insurance plan. At about that point, the handkerchief stopped twisting. Or was that just his imagination? After six months of it he hated himself so much for thoughts like that that he applied for active service.

All in all Helen Shawn had taken it well. If that was the word. She breathed deeply, shuddered, and simply said, "I see." She poured herself a drink, a shopping bag still hanging forgotten at her wrist. Hanlon left her with Carrie and Doug and Joan Cater and warned them privately that in a few hours she might well collapse from the delayed-action effects of shock.

But Frank Carradine would know all about that.

Hanlon had given no thought to the shock *he* was feeling. Now, back in the insulated calm of the penthouse, he began to peel off, layer by layer, the emotions that were clouding his judgment.

One: Jack Shawn had been a close friend, and Helen was

perhaps closer to Carrie than anyone she had known since her school days.

One: Jack Shawn was a professional spy working on orders that might one day have called for the destruction of God knows how many people. His wife was camouflage.

Two: His own shock at the news of Shawn's death was a natural reaction after so many years of social contact.

Two: He had allowed himself, at a crucial moment, to forget what twenty years of training had made instinctive. He was getting old. And soft.

Three: The death of Jack Shawn was an accident that could have happened to anyone. People get themselves killed. Cars crash every day.

Three: The death of Jack Shawn was an "incident." Sleepers, spies, agents, high-risk Intelligence operatives, never died *accidentally*. Occasionally one might pass away peacefully in his sleep at the age of ninety, surrounded by weeping relatives, but it was against the odds. "Accidental death" and "natural causes" were not common coinage in the espionage trade.

Hanlon poured himself a Chivas Regal and stared out over the rooftops of Teague's Landing. Coincidence had never impressed him as being a valid philosophy either. To accept it was to substitute superstition for thought. He glanced at the telephone, walked across to the console, and pressed a button. The tape hissed to the start of the day's run. He listened to the playback. There had been only two phone calls. One was from Alan Farrar at Langley, giving the usual weekly update on minor Company events at home and abroad that might vaguely concern him. Nowadays they reflected his status in the eyes of the Langley mandarins:

The Russian Premier is frequently absent from Central Committee meetings and diplomatic functions, and this is giving rise to rumors of a possible reshuffling of the Soviet hierarchy. It might also be taken as an indication of illness.

President Tito is still refusing to be coerced into any agreement that would weaken his personal political control in Yugo-slavia. The possibility arises of a Soviet-inspired coup to oust him under circumstances not favorable to a countermovement in his name. Rumors of a sexual nature are believed to have been sown by Soviet agents.

The presence of Soviet forces in Mozambique is . . .

Hanlon stabbed the button savagely, sending a splash of Scotch onto the console. The tape spluttered a high-pitched gabble as he ran it forward until a buzz marked the next call. It was from Alec Lamb. He put down his drink, pulled up a chair, and crouched over the machine.

"Lamb. I'm traveling up to Teague's Landing tonight. Book me in at the Coach House. Usual room. I'll call you when I get there." Pause. "Don't forget to wipe this, Hanlon."

He ran the tape back and deleted both messages. Unconsciously, his finger traced a pattern in the spilled Scotch on the teak casing. According to the monitoring meter, Lamb's call had been made less than four hours ago—at least *one hour* after Jack Shawn had died. It was now six o'clock. He reached for the remote-control monitor and switched on the television set. Selecting a news channel, he pushed the videotape slide lever to RERUN and found the five-o'clock news.

The flames were still licking greedily when the TV news team arrived. Firemen and police were holding back the crowds. Jack Shawn's car was unrecognizable—a few pieces of charred metal fallen from the back of a garbage truck.

The camera panned across the faces in the crowd and up to the gaping hole in the parking lot, ten stories high. Then, it retraced the midair dive to the street below.

Hanlon reached for his drink. He was in command now. He had been too long out of practice as an operational strategist, but he had an old-fashioned suspicion that his cynicism was functioning in overdrive and he didn't like what it was telling him.

If the television teams had enough time to film Jack Shawn's death scene, then Alec Lamb would have known about it ten

58

light-years before them. So why was he chatting about booking him in the Coach House that night as if nothing had happened? There could only be one reason. For the next hour he tried desperately to think of another.

12.

The Coach House, according to its publicity brochures, had once been just that, although there was nothing left to prove it. It was a solid brick-built monstrosity, three stories high, with a pseudo-Athenian portico and a battlemented roofline, acquired in the 1880s by a well-to-do Boston family as a fortress to contain their homicidal-maniac son. The publicity literature left that period of its history unsung.

It was now a hotel; gaunt, poorly-lit, and overstuffed in the manner of the twenties, but comfortable. Lamb walked down from the station and phoned Hanlon to join him. He was pouring himself a Chivas Regal as Hanlon came into the suite.

Hanlon braced himself in the middle of the room, feet apart. Lamb looked at him and sniffed. "It's going to be like that, is it?"

"It's going to be straight this time, Alec," Hanlon said quietly. "Any more bullshit like last time and I quit—I'm out, finished."

"Why don't you sit down and relax."

"I'd rather curl up with a boa constrictor."

Lamb swirled the whisky in his glass and watched the play of light in the tawny liquid. "If you're expecting me to apologize for letting Shawn kill himself . . ."

"At least you recognize that it might have been avoided."

"Shit! How d'you avert an Act of God?"

"You don't. But if you get the word well in advance, you can try to avert an Act of Man."

"Speculation—and lousy speculation at that. He took off through a wall ten floors up. Who knew he was going to be there? Did you? What kind of a nut goes for complex accidents when he can do it with a gun or a knife?"

"Someone who needs to make it look like an accident. Are you telling me you see no connections *anywhere?*"

Lamb took a long slug from his glass. "Sure we have to look for connections. I have. All afternoon. I've had our people go over every inch of ground. I've checked every move Shawn made. It was an accident."

"How could you know?"

"We checked his car. He went to the Atlanta Hotel. He had three drinks—martinis. He waited a half-hour. He left. He went back to his car and . . ." He made a flowering shape with his hands.

Hanlon studied his case officer's face for the slightest hint of tension. He was clean. Perhaps it *was* cold professionalism that persuaded Lamb not to reveal Shawn's death when he talked on the phone earlier this afternoon; but there was nothing professional in pretending the death of a Kingfish was just another statistic. Unless . . .

Hanlon said easily, "So we just forget about it, do we?"

"We don't forget, Sam. We double up on security all over, but we accept the reality of the situation. People die. People have accidents. Even spies."

"What's the word from Langley?"

"They are thinking about it."

"That's nice. Are they thinking this is the first thing in fifteen years to happen to Kingfish? Are they concerned that it might happen again?"

Lamb flashed a brittle smile. "Maybe they take the view that one less Commie bastard is no bad thing."

"But you say you're stepping up security anyway."

Lamb put down his drink and folded one leg over the other. He nodded mechanically.

"We won't be taking the same chance next time, if that's what you mean, Sam. We're bringing in a second cover. You have yourself an assistant."

Hanlon blinked; this was something he hadn't anticipated.

"How's that again?"

"Don't be coy, Sam. I said 'an assistant.' I mean it. Next time one of 'em takes off alone—*if* there is a next time—you'll have someone on his heels every step of the way."

"I don't need assistance."

Lamb shook his head wearily. "Be consistent, will you? Anyway, you have no choice. Nor do I. Langley wants in."

"Who is he?"

"I'll tell you when they tell me."

"When?"

"Few days, I guess. I'll be in touch."

Hanlon drove away from the hotel and turned onto the Ridge road. Five hundred yards from the Shawn house he stopped the Mercedes, got out, and stood on the shoulder looking down on the town. Two fishing boats were putting to sea from Old Harbor, their navigation lights shivering like naked torches in the sea mist. At the foot of the hill below the station the Coach House was ablaze with neon. On Main Street, a string of cars climbed homeward from the square, their headlights fingering the pine woods.

Hanlon dropped his cigarette into the dust and ground it to shreds. He had made his decision. From this moment on, nothing would persuade him to trust Alec Lamb again.

He got back into the car.

There was a corollary to that, of course. Lamb had obviously made up his mind not to trust *him* either. By accident or design, they were probably telling themselves at Langley, Hanlon had lost a dog. And if he could do it once. . . .

He laughed out loud. For the first time in years, he was actually scared. It was not an unpleasant sensation.

13.

At the turn of the century, Joseph Leiter, the son of a Chicago businessman, decided to use his vast wealth to build the home of his dreams. He chose to spend the rest of his days among the rolling hills and forests of Virginia's Fairfax County, at a spot where his guests could wine and dine and enjoy breathtaking views across the Potomac, where only the hoot of an occasional owl disturbed the balmy evenings.

He called his pleasure dome the Glass Palace, and it stood in epic grandeur until Leiter's death in 1932. In 1945 it was destroyed by fire, but its splendor had long since departed. Since the Government had by then bought the land, no one wasted energy on caring for the grand old house. For sixteen years there was nothing but silence, an eerie almost tactile silence, possessed of places where gaiety and grace had once had their day.

The silence was broken by bulldozers. In 1961, a vast new building, shielded by groves of trees and in its own way as magnificent as the old Glass Palace, was erected at a cost of $46 million—a sum that would have impressed old Joseph Leiter himself. The 125-acre site was designed to house some ten thousand people.

It was to be the new home of the Central Intelligence Agency —known by those who work for it, or against it, as the Company.

It was a storehouse of classified information without parallel in the civilized world. A fact warehouse that gorged itself daily on obscure data. Like any organization that builds around itself a wall of secrecy, it was a hotbed of gossip and scandal. Sam Hanlon was counting on that.

If anyone knew what was going on it was Alan Farrar. Farrar had worked with Hanlon years before. They had been on the road together. They had seen little of each other in the past decade, but there was an unspoken understanding between them that had grown stronger when they were both put out to pasture. Farrar had been sidetracked into a desk job in one of the Company's "libraries," the sifting centers that collected the raw material of Intelligence on microfilm and in computers. There were over 40 million punch cards at Langley.

Hanlon used his priority call number and got through immediately. Farrar sounded as if he were talking through a blanket.

"Tuna on rye," he explained. "Sticks to the plates." He masticated energetically for a few seconds. "Right. Obstruction cleared." It was one of their family jokes. The phrase had often been dispatched by the team of Hanlon and Farrar in the days before Intelligence had bought itself kid gloves. It had conveyed the successful completion of a mission—the forcible removal of an obstruction in the shape of an enemy agent.

"Right. Shoot, Sam."

"Nothing vital," said Hanlon. "Just a couple of checks you might run over sometime. A rerun on Marvin Fish and Doug Cater. Newspaper mentions in the last year, anything like that. No sweat."

"Will do, Sam. You want it on tape or a print-out?"

"Tape will be fine."

He knew that Farrar was getting the message. He had received a print-out only three weeks before, and they had discussed it at the time.

"When are you coming up again, Al? The fishing's better than we've had in years."

"Me?" Alan Farrar had never set foot in Teague's Landing. "Last time was time enough. Took me a week to catch up on the work here. Seriously though, Sam, I'd like to make it again, but you know how it is. The pressure's on."

63

"Sure. The boys okay? And Sylvie?"

"Can't grumble. The boys have got themselves jobs for the vacation. With my being tied down here so much this summer they're taking over as the men around the house."

"Ferdie still into teaching?" Hanlon asked, feeling his way.

"Is he *into* it! When he's not burning up the neighborhood in that old Dodge, he's turning the place into a bookstore."

"You should worry! I can remember the days when you bored the pants off every dogface at Camp Peary. Readings from Chaucer, then a quick flip down to the shooting range."

"Those were the days, Sam. Still . . . a mighty maze! But not without a plan, as the poet said."

"Tennyson."

"Crap!"

"He's the only poet I know."

"You've spent a lifetime trying to hide behind your ignorance," said Farrar. "Try Pope, 'An Essay on Man, Epistle 1.' He's even better than Rod McKuen."

Hanlon laughed a little too loudly. "You should've taken it up professionally, Al. Laying 'em in the aisles with couplets at fifty paces. Anyway, I can't spend the day gabbing. Just you get yourself time off and get your ass up here. I'll give you a few lessons in landing big cod in a rough sea. It beats poverty every time."

"I'll check it out. Thanks, Sam. Seeing you."

"Ditto, Al. Over and out."

It was the crudest and possibly the most stupid gamble he had taken in many years, and he despised himself for putting Alan Farrar in the position of a sitting duck. It was a measure of the man that he had played. One mitigating factor lay in the surveillance methods on incoming and outgoing calls at Langley. With the kind of bureaucratic idiocy that stamps so many overweight organizations, calls were analyzed according to the importance of the caller or the recipient. By the time some communications analysis clerk had got to the Hanlon/

Farrar call, a debate on kids and poetry would rank way down the scale of priorities.

Next day, he sent his secretary for a list of books from the local library: Davidson, Slovo, and Wilkinson on Southern Africa; the Vintage Mencken edited by Alistair Cooke; and the collected poems of Alexander Pope.

> *An Essay on Man*, Epistle 1
> Awake, my St. John! Leave all mean things
> To low ambition and the pride of kings.
> Let us (since life can little more supply
> Than just to look about us and to die)
> Expiate free O'er all this scene of man;
> A mighty maze! But not without a plan.

Farrar had made it clear that something big was on the fire at Langley by his reference to the hours he had been working. The Company, with a budget of millions, was notoriously penny-pinching when it came to overtime payments. It would require a World War III to justify extra work in the records division. Now, if he had been left with any doubts, they were eliminated. The sentiment expressed by Alexander Pope was a worthy one. But, in this case, the merit of his poetry lay in Farrar's interpretation of it. Alan Farrar had fed him just one key word in all that clumsy double-talk over the telephone. It was contained in the line that began the section.

"Awake."

14.

Marv Fish squeezed from the car and sidled crabwise to its tail, his briefcase held at arm's length above the roof. The garage was too damn small and Grace agreed. Her VW Beetle lived in the driveway and would probably die there of a pulmonary embolism or whatever passed for arterial neglect in the internal combustion engine.

Fifteen whole years ago (and may there be fifteen more, please, God) Marv had gotten Joe Sayer to come around with his jointed measuring stick; together they'd drawn a damned fine plan to double the size of the garage and link it with the wall of the house by the utility room. The idea was to get this big spatial deal where cars and tools and bric-a-brac slept snug together under one roof. They never made it. Grace had to have the pool because Helen was building herself a pool; then in 1968 Marv was out of work for nearly a year, and although Frank wouldn't have taken a cent if he didn't think they could afford it, the medical bills still made holes in their savings.

Then, last year, young Tom Hoffman told him about the hang-gliding bit and that did it for 1977. Fisheye 1 had required an entire wall of the garage and, even in its dislocated state, with wings, frame, harness, and guidance system all neatly packaged flat for traveling, he had to pull the car well over to the opposite wall to make room. Fisheye 2 was bigger and better and a wonder to behold, and she lived in fairy robes of plastic sheeting behind the workshed at the bottom of the garden. A baby's swing, suspended from a triangular blue frame, had stood on that spot for ten years. The little girl they tried for tacitly refused the invitation, but they had kept that swing oiled and polished and rust-free until Frank told them they were wasting their time. They were still wasting their time, he and Grace, but meanwhile the swing lay in sections along the wall of the garage and Grace's Beetle still stood weather-stained in the driveway, and he still sidled crabwise from his car every night.

So who had that much continuity in life? At least they were consistent.

He let himself into the house, hung his coat and hat in the hall closet, removed his black business shoes and stowed them on their frame for cleaning. The Friday-night ritual; end of another week; birth of a whole new weekend. He enjoyed ritual and, as an obsessively neat and ordered person, worshiped those who felt as he did. Grace apart—and how could a goddess be judged otherwise?—his closest friend was Doug Cater. Neither of them had exactly rejected social contact in the old days, but they weren't celebrated as the playboy type either. Grace (God bless her) had cured him of most of his social short-comings, but he had stuck to old Doug like iron filings to an electromagnet. Even their golf outings were ritualized to allow for their egocentric habits, their total lack of coordination, their mutual horror of losing. One week Doug won, next week Marv won. They never played with anyone else and they never competed.

Marv checked the notepad in the kitchen. Grace had written: "Back at ten-fifteen. Margo's juvenile session. Don't eat till I get back. Love you."

He sniffed. He didn't like Margo and, God knows, he'd tried to for Grace's sake. And for Frank's. Still, Margo was doing something for Grace right now that he couldn't do himself: taking her mind off Jack Shawn's death seven days ago. You had to hand it to the woman; she'd cut through the guilt and the sentiment and the self-serving agonies that people call mourning and jolted the women back to reality. Not just Helen but Grace, Joan Cater, and even Carrie Hanlon, who wouldn't have accepted the time of day from Margo if she could avoid it.

Marv Fish went to his bedroom, stripped and showered, and slipped into a soft cotton safari suit. Grace described its color as crushed mushroom. It had hand-carved horn buttons, and he tied a dark brown polka-dotted silk scarf around his neck. He was in the course of the long and delicate process of parting his hair high on the crown to hide a slight graying at the temples when a movement in the garden below caught his eye. The sun was setting and its last flickering rays were so dazzling that it was impossible to identify the shape. He shaded his eyes and squinted, nose to the window pane. Who . . . ?

He finished brushing his hair, slicked a soft cloth over a pair of brown moccasins before putting them on, checked himself in the long mirror, and went downstairs. He told himself that he had not been wasting time at all but merely giving himself the opportunity to think and to judge his reactions, but that was a lie. He didn't want to go into the garden. He didn't want to know who and why. Where the hell was Grace? Oh, yes.

When he came around the corner of the house, onto the patio above the pool, his shadow raced ahead of him, elastic-thin in the dying sun. His legs ducked down across the cerulean blue water, his hips fell across the rosebeds, his trunk lay like a black pencil on fifteen yards of shorn turf, and his head threw a blob of shadow that registered squarely on the end wall of the workshed.

The figure straightened up immediately and turned. Marv's heart rose to his throat, so he put one hand into his trouser pocket and tried to look relaxed.

"You looking for something?" he called. Dumb question!

The figure shaded its eyes against the stabbing sun. "Is that you, Mr. Hanlon? I knocked at the door, but I guessed that no one was in." The figure set out briskly toward Marvin Fish, covering the ground in a lithe, rising, ball-of-the-foot movement that would have been a swagger in someone less sure of himself. The figure hurdled the anchored end of the springboard as if it wasn't there and took the steps up to the patio three at a time.

Marv was already relaxed. Huh! Just a kid. Nice kid, too, if God was still making eyes as windows of the soul. Not one of the long-haired, grass-touting dropouts, either. Clean, clipped, neat. Conservative black shoes, black pants, black shirt—looked like it was silk, too—black/green-checked raincoat over his arm.

He held out his hand. "Gee, I'm really glad I was able to see you tonight, Mr. Hanlon," he said eagerly. "I mean, turning

68

up at the Center first thing in the morning, well. . . ." He colored and lowered his eyes. "It's kinda cold, I guess. I thought if we could meet and say hello. . . ."

Marv took the hand and shook it warmly. "Hold it, old son," he chuckled. "You've got the wrong man. Sam Hanlon lives up the hill there. White house with green shutters. You can see it from the driveway.

"Oh." The color in his cheeks deepened. Marv slapped him on the shoulder. "Look, I'm sorry I stomped all over your property, sir," the boy said. "I thought, if there's no one in the house, maybe they're working in the. . . ." He trailed off unhappily.

"Forget it." Marv was feeling much better. He knew the youngster had taken in the quality of the suit, the obvious taste the clothes revealed, and he thought he detected real respect in those quiet intelligent eyes. Sure. Respect it was.

"It's very kind of you to take it this way, sir."

Marv planted a fatherly hand on his shoulder and they turned into the sun. "Sure it is. Kindness personified, seeing as how we execute trespassers up here in the Landing."

The boy threw back his head and hooted with laughter. It was a most attractive sound. His features crinkled and his white teeth flashed, and Marvin Fish placed it on mental record that, had he and Grace married a couple of years earlier and dreamed of a boy instead of that reluctant girl baby, the kid might have grown up to look roughly like. . . .

"I couldn't help seeing the kinda kite-thing back there by the shed, sir." The boy jerked his head behind him.

Marv beamed happily. This young man, whom Grace would love on sight for his looks, his elegance, and his good manners, also seemed to know instinctively what would appeal most to a complete stranger he had met by the purest accident.

"Hang glider, son," he explained. He turned to look back at it, but it was a solid wall of winking sunspots under its plastic sheathing and he flinched away.

"You mean, the things you jump off cliffs with—that kinda thing?"

"I can think of a few people who'd prefer it to be put a little more elegantly than that," Marv said drily. "But that's near enough, I guess."

"And *you* . . . ?" The boy made a plane of his right hand and flew it against the pink-fluffed sky.

"That's right." Marv had his eyes closed because of the sun and his arm coiled lightly around the young man's shoulders; he knew he had never experienced this kind of—yes—jubilation in his life before. Sam knew it. Maybe Frank, too—once. This was stupid, of course, but they were *aware*, he and this boy. The respect in the kid's eyes was magnified by real admiration, *Admiration*. He could feel the boy looking at him.

"It sounds pretty scary, sir. I've seen it on TV. You have to have a hilltop or a cliff, and you just—well, jump off."

"And you're thinking to yourself—who does this middle-aged nut think he is? Superman?"

The boy protested hotly. Marv enjoyed the embarrassment in the voice, the borderline hysteria as the kid, like all kids who talk without thinking, wallowed in his own uncertainty. God, this was a boy he could get to like.

"Hey, I'm kidding you, son. Relax. It's not an offense yet. Now, you say you want Sam Hanlon, right?"

"Yes, sir." *Sir*, yet. When did kids in this day and age call their elders sir?

"Okay." He stopped in front of the garage and pointed above the treeline where Sam Hanlon's house stood proud against the sky. "You turn right out of the gate and it's a half-mile further up the hill."

The youngster held out his hand. Marv took it and clamped his own around it with more firmness than might have been understood in a cynical, sexually perverted world. He pulled his hand away quickly.

"You aiming to stay here in the Landing?"

"Hope so, sir. If it works out tomorrow, I'll have a job with Mr. Hanlon at the Center."

Marv winked at him conspiratorially. "If Sam's giving up a Saturday morning, you must be good. Tell him you ran into Marv Fish, and tell him for me he's a dummy if he doesn't tie you to a twenty-year contract."

The boy grinned. "Thanks, Mr. Fish, I really appreciate that, but I think I'd better not say anything this time around. If I get this job, I want to get it on ability. It's . . . important." The face was deadly serious. Marv felt something melting in him around the environs of his heart.

He slapped the firm muscled shoulder. "Okay, boy. Go to it and give him hell. You'll make it." The young man made off down the driveway. Marv watched him and tried desperately to think of something to say to make him stop. He yelled, "You have any time to kill tomorrow afternoon, get someone to tell you how to get to Jonathan's Rock. You can watch me in action, okay?" He held out his arms and planed from side to side. "Supermarv!" he yelled.

The boy stopped at the gate and waved.

"I'll be there, sir," he shouted back. "You can count on that."

When the young man reached the road, he ducked his head and doubled back to the gates. He peered carefully through the slit made by gate and gatepost and saw Marvin Fish turn slowly back to the house. When the door closed on him, the young man climbed the grassy bank alongside the gate and plunged quickly into the hedge that topped it. There was a rustling and, briefly, a low growl that stopped almost at once.

The young man turned in the direction of the sound, stepped around a clump of flowering shrubs, and met the dog head on. The strong silver chain was locked to a conjunction of root and branch at the heart of a thicket. He crawled in and released the chain. The dog, black and orange and panting, tongue extended, as if from some great chase, sat in front of

71

him as he kneeled and watched his face for orders.

He gave none. He clipped the chain to a wide circlet on his wrist and lay the raincoat over his arm to hide it. Then he crawled back to the hedge, inspected the road, and scampered back down the bank.

There was no sign of Marvin Fish from the gate, but the young man bent double and did not straighten until he had found the cover of the far hedge on the downhill side. For a moment he looked up toward Hanlon's house outlined against the darkening sky. Then he turned his back on it and set off down the hill toward the town, his mind racing.

Marvin Fish: five feet ten—maybe ten-and-a-half. Weight: a hundred and seventy pounds; seventy-five maximum.

Occupation: stock analyst.

Disposition: mild to apprehensive.

Weaknesses: middle-aged vanity and hang gliding.

The file had said all that and more. So had the file on Jack Shawn. But no file ever gave the true *feel* of a man. It was *feel* that guaranteed results.

15.

From: Marshal Vasili Bunin, First Deputy Chairman of the Council of Ministers of the USSR

To: Aleksander Rostov, First Secretary of the Central Committee

I have spoken, as you directed, with the American Secretary of State. His internal security forces are alerted and in operation. Our offer of use of the centralized computer services to help pinpoint the location of the KINGFISH cell was rejected. The Americans claim that the identities of the CARRADINE/ FISH/CATER/SHAWN cell are known to them—that the

cell was known to them within a short time of its formation
and that they have maintained continuous surveillance for many
years! They are, of course, amazed at the circumstances leading
to this unprecedented situation.

I am equally amazed to discover that our security is sufficiently
lax that the existence of Residentura can be so easily ascer-
tained by hostile agencies!

In this case the outcome is, to say the least, favorable, but it
must not obscure the fact that once more we have before us an
example of blundering and incompetence. The situation must
be dealt with ruthlessly and, I suggest, calls for a full-scale re-
thinking of the structure and command of the KGB.

I am also disturbed to learn of the missing files concerning the
KINGFISH group and the involvement of KGB Chairman
Andreyev in its initial formation and dispatch. As you instructed, I have demanded a full explanation from him and
will report directly when it reaches me.

From: Dmitri Orlov, Director, First Directorate, KGB
To: Marshal Vasili Bunin, First Deputy Chairman of the
   Council of Ministers of the USSR

MOST SECRET.

The dogs have been loosed and it is now a matter for the American Counter-Intelligence agencies to try and recapture them!
They are not as all-seeing as they have permitted themselves to
believe.

I understand that Andreyev has been asked by you for a full
explanation of events . . . events I know he cannot explain.

As requested, the Special Investigations Department has passed
on to me the file on Andreyev and is continuing its investigations into sensitive areas concerning his past. As Director of the
First Directorate I have, as you are aware, power to call a
plenary session of the Collegium at which members of the
Praesidium may be invited to attend. As this is a matter which

73

concerns the security of the State, I am bound to call such a meeting.

My report to them will undoubtedly be a watershed in our campaign, and I will need all the assistance you can offer. Pressure will be brought to bear on the KGB. It is vital that we ensure it falls on the right shoulders.

To set your mind at rest, Comrade Marshal, and in answer to your recent telephone call, the handing over of the four names is not all it may at first appear and does not compromise our efforts in any way. How and why will become clear.

16.

Jonathan's Rock was a natural finger of eroded sandstone, the high point of a long curving ridge that sheltered Teague's Landing in its crooked arm. In a romantic sense, it was a fitting memorial to the piratical talents of the man whose name it bore.

The Rock was also the best kite-flying venue in a hundred miles of coastline, and for the past year the native gulls had been forced to crouch on sheltered ledges on weekends while human beings launched themselves into the sky.

Jonathan's Rock, the addicts swore, had been created by the Almighty for the specific purpose of hang gliding.

"Get it UPPPPPPP!"

With a banzai yell one of the birdmen caught the updraft, lifted off from the cliff edge, and found a thermal. The yellow-and-gold dart rose like a primeval bird as its ribbed wings rippled, then snapped tightly against the air.

"Looks bad," said Marvin Fish as his wife strapped him into the harness of Fisheye 2.

"It looks nothing of the sort," said Grace Fish firmly.

"But with Jack hardly . . ."

"Jack would have wanted it. He was never a grieving man."

74

"Well, maybe. It's just that . . . oh, what the hell. I suppose you're right."

Grace Fish usually was. She was physically strong, beautifully built in a Wagnerian way, and in her marriage had revealed an unflinching strength of mind when her husband's interests were at stake. Cajoling, urging, weeping, she had used every device in the book of womanhood to shake her man free of his suffocating self-doubt, his unnatural diffidence, and the stammer that characterized both. It had taken her just six months to correct the stammer, nearer sixteen years to transform Marvin Fish into a witty, outgoing, entertaining extrovert. The result had been to push him to the other extreme: he was now a man of passions and crazes. Nobody knew how she had done it, but most put it down to the fact that the Fishes' bedroom light went on early and stayed on late.

"Marv, there's a mist comin' in off the sea. If you're goin', go now." Tom Hoffman, the club organizer, pointed to the thin layer of white gauze wreathing across the water.

"Okay. Ready to go," Fish yelled back. Grace tugged at his tight-fitting windbreaker and smoothed it over his chest.

"Don't be long."

He pecked her cheek. Two of the club members held the tips of his wings and helped him into position. Hoffman was right; he could feel moisture on his face, the taste of salt on his lips.

"Come on, grandpa," grinned one of the wingmen.

Fish angled up two fingers and grinned back. He was a good ten years older than anyone else in the club, and the leg-pulling was now almost mandatory. Nobody joked once they had seen him in the shower, though. He was a match for most of them when it came to physique—another thing Grace was responsible for.

He bounced around experimentally on his toes, waiting for the current, as a surfer anticipates the perfect wave. It came.

"Hi ho, Silverrrrrrrrr."

The wind snatched him up like a shuttlecock, throwing his body into the horizontal, and blew him high on a funnel of warm air. He turned, saw Grace waving, and waved back nervously. He adjusted his center of gravity and the glider settled into a steady sweeping curve out over the Atlantic.

"He'll only have fifteen minutes at most," Tom Hoffman murmured to Grace Fish as they squinted up into the misty sun. "It'll be wetter'n a fish's back out there." He closed his eyes at the unintentional pun.

Grace smiled and waved an arm at the sea mist. "Why doesn't the wind blow it away? The mist, I mean. Why does it hang out there like that when you can fly around as if it was blowing a gale?"

Hoffman put on his dark glasses and helped Grace slip a windbreaker over her tight polo-neck sweater.

"It's not the wind that keeps it up, it's the thermals. That mist is being formed by the same warmth of the sea meeting the cold air that's keeping the gliders rising. It's the damp that gets you, though. Goes right through. Takes the fun out of it."

Grace nodded absently. Marv had disappeared into the rapidly rising mist.

"He's moving beyond it," explained Hoffman. "Probably clear as a bell on the other side." He drew the zipper up Grace's jacket. She had figured prominently in the dreams of the young men of Teague's Landing for years, and Hoffman was no exception. She smiled her thanks and finished the last, critical five inches herself, pulling the nylon material away from her body as she closed it over her breasts. Hoffman's eyes lingered. "Why don't you do it?" he said.

"Do it?"

"Glide. Why don't you? You're in good shape, anyone can see that. I could maybe run over a few points with you sometime. You'd pick it up in no time."

"Thanks, but no thanks," said Grace. "I need to lose ten pounds before I'd trust so much as a balloon taking me out there, and even then I wouldn't."

"You look fine to me," said Hoffman, lamely.

"And that's the way I intend to stay. Fine. I can live without

76

ridges on my bottom and biceps like a weight lifter." She patted his cheek and pursed her lips in a look of mock chastisement. "If I didn't know you better, Tom Hoffman, I'd think you were propositioning me. Special lessons, indeed!"

The boy colored. "Mrs. Fish, I . . ."

She giggled and punched him playfully in the midriff. "Don't be silly, Tom. Don't get so uptight."

She shuddered and glanced at her watch. The curtain of mist was thick now and its fringes were brushing the Rock itself. She felt beads of condensation like perspiration on her brow. Hoffman was staring out to sea, cloaking his embarrassment with professional concentration.

"There he is. No, that's 'Stumblebum.' There! See? To the right. He's coming in, I think."

"Thank God for that," said Grace. "I could do with a hot drink. And I do mean brandy."

The mist rose high and sent feathery fingers downward to touch the entire headland, dampening every sound, isolating the watchers like headstones in a graveyard. Fisheye 2 began its slide down the back of an updraft, appearing and then disappearing as it moved in and out of the haze. Grace waved, knowing he couldn't see her. From way out on the very lip of the Rock's threshold above the sea, someone turned and called, but the sound was swallowed up in the wetness. People were waving.

Grace saw someone running, pointing up at Fisheye 2 as it swept in over the Rock. A black-and-orange dog raced out of the mist, barking and leaping, snapping the air as it joined the chase beneath the glider.

Grace shouted at the dog and picked up a stick for it to fetch, but she did not throw it. Marv's glider drifted lazily in out of the mist at tree-top height. The dog barked twice more and then someone called it and it sped away, tail down.

Everyone was looking at her. Why were they looking at her? Why didn't somebody call out to him?

77

Fisheye 2 passed fifteen feet above Grace Fish's head. She raised a hand to wave—and froze.

Marvin Fish, his neck grotesquely angled, hung like a broken doll from the gallows of his harness.

17.

Hanlon lay on the sofa and stared at the ceiling, eyes wide and unblinking, like a drunk anchoring his dizziness. Taut and pale, a nerve pulsing irregularly at his temple.

Anger.

Think about something else.

Fishing. Early morning, a weak sun rising over the edge of the sea, the lap-lap, lap-lap of the boat rocking with the tide; droplets of mist dancing along the anchor warp like spider trails.

Mist.

The face of Marvin Fish. The nerve settled into a rhythm and its pulsing spread.

"Jesus Christ." Softly.

"JeSUS!" Smashing the side of his fist deep into the cushions of the sofa.

"JESUS!" Sitting up suddenly, one foot stamping down, grinding the carpet with his heel.

Less than an hour ago Joe Ruban had come by to tell him about Marv.

An obscene death up on Jonathan's Rock as the weekend crowds watched. A clip had "given way" on the harness, and the unequal weight displacement had torn one of the vital restraining straps in half. Marv Fish should have fallen into the Atlantic. He didn't. Some freak of circumstance had entangled his body in the remaining straps, and as he plummeted downward on the frame, one had caught under his chin. He had strangled slowly, unable to reach up for the control bar.

Terrible, Joe Ruban had remarked. But they had been expecting an accident like this ever since that damn fool craze started.

"Accident," said Hanlon.

Ruban had shaken his head, pushed back his cap, and scratched his head as police chiefs seem obliged to do when reflecting on the frailty of human nature.

"Sorry, Sam," he said. "I know he was a friend. I thought I oughta stop by." He got into his car and drove away, red light flashing, leaving Hanlon on the porch.

It was then that the anger came. He needed to keep his head clear, but he was engulfed by it. First Jack Shawn. Now, exactly one week later, Marv Fish. Lightning striking twice. But even that wasn't bothering him now. The real question now was not how the lightning had struck, but who had switched it on. Who was rubbing the clouds together?

He called Langley and asked for Lamb. Sorry, not here. Strauss? In a meeting.

The A.D? Dull pause. He could visualize the operator sliding back his headset, drumming his fingers, waiting for a convincing amount of time to elapse before he came back with the lie.

Sorry.

"Listen, dummy—either you get me his secretary or next time I'm over there I'll make a special journey to your cubicle and slide five inches of that talking tube down your throat."

A murmur of indignation. Click, click. The AD's secretary answered—a fur-lined voice that gave nothing away.

"This is Hanlon. I want—must—talk to the AD. I know, you're going to tell me he's in a meeting, talking to the President or planning World War III, but I'm telling you I want him now. So be a good girl and go in there and tell him it's his golf club on the phone and we've just cancelled his membership. If he'd like to talk about it, this is the time."

"The AD left for . . ." The girl caught herself in time. For one second her job hung in the balance. To reveal that the AD even existed was a sin that outranked the Ten Commandments.

"He isn't available, Mr. Hanlon. That's the truth. I can get a message to him, but that's all." She was telling the truth.

"Forget it," he said.

The back door slammed and Carrie called out from the kitchen. She had been shopping with Bobby and was in a good mood. She had taken Jack Shawn's death hard. Too hard. Now . . .

Bobby burst through the door and Sam fixed on a smile. It was a frozen asset by the time he entered the kitchen. Carrie unloaded her parcels and recounted details of her expedition as if she hadn't set foot outside the house for a year.

He helped her pack the freezer, admired the new pastel green dress she had bought, and pulled a generation gap face at the cover of Bobby's new LP. A convincing performance.

What in hell's name had Fish been up to? If Alan Farrar was right and an awakening message had gone out to Kingfish, then it made no sense. Fish would never put himself in a position of danger just days after his group had been switched on. Maybe the message hadn't reached him. Maybe Jack Shawn hadn't passed it on. Maybe Fish had pulled out. Could happen. Life with Grace was a powerful inducement to forget old allegiances.

Yes—and maybe at the end of the Yellow Brick Road was the Big Rock Candy Mountain.

Fish had been prepared too well. There was more chance of a Jesuit condemning the Pope. He noted wryly that if nothing else, Marv had become Fish.

Good or bad?

". . . have you?"

He shook himself back to what Carrie called reality.

"I said, you haven't been listening to a word, have you?" she nagged.

"Every one," he said deeply serious. Then, catching Bobby's eye, ". . . two, three, four, five, six. . . ."

She punched him affectionately.

When he drove to the Center a few minutes later, he still hadn't found the courage to tell her. He thought of going straight back, of going over to see Grace, of calling Frank Carradine. No deal. Stand back and take it as it comes. Even Carrie.

18.

The crowds ebbed and flowed but never quite evaporated. Joe Ruban, the police chief, and his deputies had been joined by three state troopers. Together they roped off a crescent-shaped slice of ground that isolated Joanthan's Rock and the scene of Marvin Fish's accident from the growing crowd.

Midafternoon bulletins had already spread the news across the state, and by four-thirty the first rubbernecks were trickling in from villages and towns upstate. Joe Ruban gave his team another half-hour to take their measurements, finalize on-the-spot statements from witnesses, and remove the broken hang glider to town. He didn't like crowds.

The pleasant-faced young man in the black/green-checked raincoat strolled casually from one end of the roped enclosure to the other, watching the police activity but taking care, like a good citizen, not to impede it. Heads turned to stare at him as he passed, and this appeared to embarrass him in a nice old-fashioned way. He was not tall, but he moved with a natural grace that men associate with athletics and women with brimming masculinity. His light brown hair was cut conservatively short. He could have been nineteen years old or twenty-nine; there were no obvious clues in his smooth, inoffensive features.

Beside him the dog loped passively, its eyes on the ground.

The observers who turned their curiosity to the young man also turned away instinctively when their eyes fell on the dog. It was black and orange and frighteningly muscled, and around its jaws was a polished leather muzzle. From a large steel ring on its wide black leather collar ran a length of bright steel chain that disappeared into the sleeve of the raincoat.

When he had completed his walk, the young man moved away from the crowd to the edge of the cliff and ordered the dog to sit. For a few minutes he observed the crowds watching the police, not in a critical way, but with the detachment of a student. Then he brought the dog to its feet and walked briskly down to the belt of pines.

There were no heads to turn to watch him there. The soft boyish features were still inoffensive, but the expression in his eyes was one of acute satisfaction.

19.

Carrie reached an uncertain hand for the cigarette box on the table beside her and sent her whisky glass flying. The contents pooled on the white sheepskin rug and she stared at the mess stupidly.

Hanlon whipped a handkerchief from his pocket and dropped it on to the brown liquid. "Don't you think you've had enough?" he growled.

"Oh boy, oh boy, oh boy, oh boy." She was four-doubles drunk. Another half-hour and she was going to be very, very sick, but for the moment she was head-high and rising.

Hanlon had been at the penthouse, reviewing again the life patterns of Kingfish, turning over every continuing contact they had, reevaluating them for meanings, undertones, implications that might have escaped him. And in the back of his mind, he had waited for her to call. Someone would tell her. He was right. When her call came, it was strangely prescient.

She said, "They've killed Marv. They've killed poor Marv."

He drove back to the house but she was already two drinks ahead of him, and he hadn't the heart to try to stop her. She shook uncontrollably as she spilled out the news of Fish's death. When he asked her what she'd meant when she said, 'They've killed Marv,' she put her face in her hands and sobbed till the tears ran through her fingers and down her arms.

Slowly, achingly, he'd drawn her back over the edge of hysteria. For a full twenty minutes she'd nestled childlike in his arms, her cheek on his chest, and when she was quiet at last, he had propped her in a cushioned corner of the couch and gone into the kitchen to brew some good black coffee.

When the phone rang he had leaped for it, but he was too late. Carrie listened without speaking as a doctor at the hospital asked her to help him find Grace Fish. He'd treated her for shock and left her resting in a room at the hospital. When he returned later, she was gone. He'd checked at the Fish house without success. A neighbor told him Grace had taken the car. He'd called Helen Shawn too, but she hadn't answered. Would Mrs. Hanlon have any idea . . . ?

Hanlon ran to her as she cried out. He took the phone out of her hand and replaced it. He reached for her and she fought him away, screaming, sobbing hysterically. He called Frank Carradine, but there was no reply from the house or the office.

Then Carrie had started drinking in earnest.

Hanlon turned the handkerchief over and swabbed the pool of liquor. He said, "Okay, baby. It's all right."

She found the cigarette box, took one, and pressed it between her lips, but her trembling fingers broke it in two. Hanlon lit one for her and she took it from him sulkily.

"I'm glad it's all right, Sam. You're all right and I'm all right

83

so that makes *everything* all right. All right?" She twittered idiotically. The smoke made her cough and the cough slid inexorably into tears again.

He forced his arms around her. "Look, you've got to cut this out. You want Bobby to see you like this?"

The cigarette was tear-stained to within a centimeter of the ash. Hanlon took it from her and ground it out in an ashtray. Carrie let her hands fall into her lap and studied them obsessively.

"Why do things happen like this, Sam?" She was making a major effort to control herself, but her voice shook dangerously.

"I don't know, honey. Accidents. . . ."

"Oh boy. Accidents! You don't listen good, do you? Remember when Grace gave that party for the PTA and Helen told Marv he could kill himself on that kite thing? Marv said, 'Accident is just another word for bad judgment. I'm a mathematician. I don't believe in accidents.' You remember that?"

Hanlon nodded vaguely. "I remember."

"You remember what Jack Shawn said?"

"No."

"Because you don't want to. Well, I'll tell you anyway. Jack Shawn said. . . ." She rubbed her face with both hands, her memory slipping away from her. "He said . . . he said. . . ." She shook her head angrily. "Well, Jack knew cars all his life. He was always careful. Freaky careful. Jack wouldn't ever. . . ."

The effort was too much for her. Her eyes fixed unseeing on the far wall.

"I don't want anyone else to die. Please, Sam."

Hanlon felt his fist bunching until the pain across the knuckles became acute. "Sure. Sure."

"Promise?"

Hanlon was wondering how soon he could leave her and raise Alec Lamb. Seven days; in just seven days Kingfish had been decimated under his nose.

"Promise?"

84

"I promise."

He got her upstairs, persuaded her to take a sedative, and put her to bed. Her eyes closed almost immediately, but he sat beside her on the bed until her breathing fell into the resonant rhythms of deep sleep.

He scribbled a note for Bobby: "She's asleep. Don't wake her. I'm at the Center for a half-hour." Then he went out to the car. A young man in a black/green-checked raincoat was walking up the driveway to the house with a dog at his side—a Doberman Pinscher.

Hanlon slipped into the car but held the door open.

"Yes?"

Bright smile. Good-looking boy. Clean.

"Afternoon, sir. I guess I've come at a bad time. I could drop by later?"

Hanlon said impatiently, "Do I know you?"

"No, sir. We haven't met." He looked around swiftly, taking in the house, the car, Hanlon's fingers drumming on the window sill. "I guess I should've phoned." He half-turned to leave. "Six o'clock be all right with you, sir?"

Hanlon didn't need confirmation, but he asked anyway.

"What d'you want, son?"

The youngster flashed an embarrassed grin. "I have to report to you, sir. Name's Merrit Leitch. Mr. Lamb said you'd know who I was."

Hanlon slid out of the Mercedes. What was so familiar about Merrit Leitch? Why was he telling himself he'd seen that face before? That kind of face. Roughly, he took Leitch's slim brown hand in his. He found what he was feeling for; the unmistakable raised ridge of hardened flesh on the leading edge of the right hand. It was more a weapon than a physical tool, developed with painstaking deliberation over years of practice on the karate chopping post. He got back into the car abruptly.

"Tomorrow," he said with deliberate coldness. "I'm busy right now."

85

20.

Frank Carradine turned in the bed, freed his cramped right arm, and rubbed the circulation back into it. From her bed, Margo groaned audibly and pushed herself up on one elbow.

"What is it *now?*"

"Oh, nothing. Go to sleep."

Margo was no martyr. She never resorted to traditional feminine wiles. "I can't sleep with you rolling and bouncing around in that bed like a banshee. Why can't you take a Valium or something?"

Carradine pushed himself into a sitting position. "You know I can't. I'm on call tonight."

"Then for heaven's sake try to relax yourself. I thought we'd agreed that you sleep in the guest room when you're on call. I've got a long day tomorrow, you know that."

"I know." Dammit, why did she always make it so hard? "Maybe I'll read for a bit."

Margo's head came off the pillow again. "Not in here, you don't. If you want to read, go downstairs. I'm tired."

She began to breathe deeply. Carradine sat in the darkness and wondered how he could have learned so little about the woman he'd married that after twenty years he was still discovering her faults. Had she really cared so little about Jack and Marv that their deaths failed to keep her from sleep for an instant? Did she feel nothing for Helen and Grace? Did she care where they were? What had happened to them?

Stupid questions. Margo had never pretended friendship with anyone. When Doug Cater came by to blubber his version of Marv Fish's death up on Jonathan's Rock, Margo had displayed

86

no emotion, no remorse, and when Cater finally lost control of himself and the tears came, she had left the room.

She had asked only two questions when Cater left: Had anyone actually seen Grace Fish and Helen Shawn leave together in Grace's car, and did anyone know where they'd gone? The answer to both questions was no; a technical No, anyway. But everyone knew they'd left together. It was obvious, wasn't it? Two women who had clung together in happiness would be inseparable in crushing mutual bereavement.

Margo had gone back to her office to make a couple of phone calls, but if they had revealed anything about the girls, she had kept it to herself. He'd said no more about it; there was no circumnavigating Margo's absence of feeling, and questioning it was just plain destructive.

And bad for Daniel. My God—Daniel!

In the end it all came back to Dan. All his ambitions crystallized in Dan. All his mistakes came back to haunt him for the way they might one day rebound on Dan. All the secret, unpronounceable, long-ago errors lay fermenting behind the artificial façade of his life, waiting to be visited on Dan. The sins of the father. . . .

If only it were possible to go back and undo the wretched blunders—to clean the slate. Margo knew what it meant to him, but she had struck it off her mental record long ago, expecting him to do the same.

Marv Fish, Jack Shawn, and Doug Cater—all of them had understood because all of them. . . . But only Doug was left now, and he was a liability. Doug was still a small-town storekeeper. His fortunes had changed, his business clout had taken him from one cramped store on Main Street to a string of supermarkets from Plymouth to Providence, from Falmouth to Provincetown, but he had the mentality of a fishwife.

There was Sam Hanlon, of course, but Sam was 100 percent American, secure, untroubled, and honest. His friendship was based on what he thought he saw in Frank Carradine. What

87

would he think if he knew the name was really Andreas Szabo?

"Margo?"

Grunt.

"Margo, please. Will you listen to me?"

Mmmmmm.

"I think I'm being watched."

There was a long silence, but he knew she was listening. He said, "I know it sounds ridiculous, but I'm not imagining it. I *am* being watched."

Margo said nothing, but he heard her turn to face him.

"I don't know who. I mean, I can't give you names. Sometimes the sensation of being," he fumbled for the right word, "*pursued* is almost physical." He sighed. "I can't explain. You have to experience it to know."

Margo spoke very slowly and deliberately. "Who would want to watch you, Frank? Who would be interested in knowing what *you* do and why?"

Carradine fretted in the darkness. He couldn't tell her. Not because he was afraid of diminishing himself in her eyes, but because she would use anything he said to further compromise his relationship with Daniel. Everything came back to Daniel.

"I can't tell you that." He knew he'd already gone too far. She would never allow him to forget this night. Oh God, why was he so weak!

Margo waited thirty seconds before she delivered an opinion. "The paranoid can never explain. A persecution mania is never specific."

"Damn yooouuu!"

The words came out of him in a muffled hiss of hatred. An incomprehensible dizziness overtook him, and he leaned back into the headboard for salvation. Margo was unruffled.

"I take it you have evidence to support what you're saying?"

His anger was too great, too suffocating, to answer her.

"Or are you inventing this nonsense to explain why Shawn and Fish killed themselves?"

88

That was too much for him.

"Killed themselves! "You . . ." He held a hand to his burning forehead. When he spoke again he was in control. "You're the coldest, most heartless woman I think I've ever had the misfortune to know. I've been sitting here thinking I made a mistake wishing my friends on you when you had no capacity to accept them. I was wrong. You have no capacity to accept *anyone*. You're totally without feeling, without human compassion or understanding. You don't *care*. You *can't* care. You fill me with . . ." Again the words wouldn't come.

"Oh, don't be so melodramatic. And keep your voice down, please. I wouldn't want Daniel to hear his father making an utter fool of himself."

Carradine closed his eyes and saw the face of his sleeping son. "If he doesn't hear I'm sure you'll make a point of telling him."

"And you attack *me* for suggesting you're paranoiac! First you're being watched—*pursued*. Now I'm turning your son against you. My God, Frank, pull yourself together."

"Isn't that supposed to be the classic callous response? The partner who won't recognize symptoms she doesn't want to see?"

"Very well."

Margo's voice was cool, professional. She was in consultation, and he was a suitable case for treatment.

"If you want my opinion, I'll give it. Shawn and Fish are typical examples of the intensive stress suicide. Shawn spent his life seeking personal aggrandizement. When he achieved some semblance of it in business, he found it hollow and unrewarding. He wasn't prepared for that because it left him with nothing but what he started out with—a massive inferiority complex. So he ran away and killed himself where the people he'd tried to impress couldn't see him doing it.

"Fish was just a weak man who caved in to pressure. I wouldn't be at all surprised if Shawn's death wasn't the trigger

89

he'd been waiting for. He needed an example. He was a natural follower.

"As for you," she suppressed a dry laugh, but not successfully. "You've hidden your character weakness from yourself by burying it in the weaknesses of your friends. Now you've only got Cater and Hanlon, and they're not much comfort, are they? That's why you want to believe someone's following you, watching you. You need a nice cozy phantom to direct your fears against. Well, you can hide from them, but you can't hide from me, Frank. And if I ever think for one moment—one *second*—that this obsession is affecting Daniel, I want you to know, here and now, that I'll take him out of this house, away from you, as fast as I can. Is that understood?"

He nodded numbly, dumbly, in the dark.

"Did you hear what I said?"

"Yes."

In the next room, Daniel Carradine took his ear from the wall and stood shivering in the dark.

There were tears in his eyes.

21.

Carrie was up and clattering around in the kitchen when Hanlon returned from his morning swim. She had on the new pastel green dress and a brittle "try me—I'm over it" smile. Her makeup was immaculate.

Hanlon showered. As he began to dress he heard Bobby yelling excitedly from the orchard and a reprise, somewhat faint, that had to be Daniel.

He began to shave.

So this is where it all finished. Kingfish dies a little at a time while their keeper stands idly, helplessly, on the sideline, watching the massacre. And approving it. The thought stung him. No, *not* approving it. He stopped shaving in midstroke. Face it—in this situation, doing nothing implies approval.

Alec Lamb was "temporarily out of reach" according to his recorded answering service, and since Marv's death, he'd made no attempt to call Hanlon himself. Ditto George Strauss. *Ergo*— the word from Alan Farrar was 100 percent copper-bottomed fact: Langley was into a high-level crisis that involved Kingfish, and they were taking what they would later describe as AEA—Appropriate Executive Action.

He nicked the skin on the angle of his jaw and a drop of dark blood ballooned and burst and dribbled down his neck. He tore a corner from a piece of Kleenex and slapped it onto the wound.

So he was finished, too. They had deliberately excluded him from the operation—the field officer most directly concerned. There were two officially recognized reasons for taking such action: when involving the agent could compromise his cover, and when the agent himself had been *suborned* by the enemy.

Had he been suborned by the weak, submissive Carradine? By Marv Fish, a man who owed his sanity and his career to a strong wife? By a failure-psychotic like Jack Shawn? By fumbling, bumbling old Doug Cater, a drunk who didn't dare drink, an epileptic terrorized by scenarios of his own death?

The door chimes saved him from further confession. He heard Carrie at the door and a second voice too softly pitched to identify.

"Sam!"

"Right!" he shouted down to her. "Five minutes."

When he came down, Merrit Leitch had peeled off his raincoat, rolled up the sleeves of his black silk shirt, and was whipping a creamy yellow mixture in a cooking bowl. He used a handwhisk with the speed and dexterity of a master chef, and as he whipped he talked. Carrie stood beside him at the kitchen table, engrossed.

91

"Right." He put the bowl to one side. "That's your dessert for lunch. Leave it and pour when you're ready to bake. Now for breakfast. . . ."

He snatched up a towel and wiped his hands briskly. He saw Hanlon from the corner of his eye, turned his head, and flashed a grin of total disarming good will. "Hi, sir."

He turned back to Carrie. "The *pièce de résistance*. Have you any ramekins, ma'am? I guess you'll need four, okay?"

Carrie was captivated.

"Wouldn't dream of living without them. What the hell is a ramekin?"

Leitch cupped his hands. "Tiny dish, maybe three inches across, inch-and-a-half deep. They usually have fluted sides."

"Oh, *those*."

Carrie bent to forage in a cupboard and Leitch looked around again at Hanlon. "We were talking food, your wife and I, sir. I suggested *oeufs en cocotte*." He made Hanlon feel like an interloper.

"Ah." He took the small dishes from Carrie and raised the lid of a bubbling saucepan. He smoothed butter into the ramekins, plopped a spoonful of cream into each, and set them into the hot water. He and Carrie stood over the saucepan watching intently. Leitch dipped a finger in the cream, removed the dishes, then, with superb facility, broke an egg, one-handed, into each of the ramekins. He poured the rest of the cream over the eggs and topped each with a pat of butter.

"Right. Moderate oven, middle shelf. Bake for, let's say, eight minutes."

"How will I know they're done?"

"The eggs'll be just about set, but they'll tremble when you take out the ramekin. Okay?"

Carrie followed instructions and Leitch watched her as though he intended awarding marks for performance later. Carrie straightened up, flushed, eyes shining.

"Are you married, Merrit?"

The young man blushed. "No, ma'am, I guess I never had much success around girls."

Carrie placed her hands on his shoulders. "Name the girl of your choice, Merrit, and I'll have her eating out of your hand in five minutes. What you need is a good agent." Leitch colored again.

Hanlon was fidgeting visibly in the doorway.

"You wanted to see me?" he growled pointedly.

"I just thought I'd drop by in case you wanted to . . ." The green eyes flashed a warning. ". . . to discuss my duties, sir."

Carrie's eyebrows arched a question. "What duties?"

Leitch was in like a flash. "Aaaah, well, ma'am. I guess maybe I'm being a little premature. Mr. Hanlon's giving me a week's trial at the Center. Executive Assistant."

"You didn't tell me, Sam." Carrie liked to be told, whether she could understand or not. But she was smiling.

"Yeah." Hanlon put together the lie smoothly. "It was supposed to be a surprise. I've been interviewing over the past month. Leitch here is . . ."—he glared at the young man—". . . a real prize."

Carrie checked the kitchen clock. "Then he'll stay for breakfast. You've got exactly six minutes to talk turkey, and then I want both of you back here to eat."

Hanlon closed the door to the den. Leitch fell into a chair, and when Hanlon turned from the door, the sight of the young man's sprawling figure triggered something in the back of his mind. "Where's the hound?"

Leitch angled his head. "Out front."

"You mean you left that thing . . . ?"

"He won't move till I tell him. He wouldn't move if you held a cat under his nose—bound, gagged, and deep-fried. Believe me, sir, there's absolutely no reason to concern yourself."

Hanlon hissed, "I've got two kids out there who think all dogs are man's best friend. Get out there now and. . . ."

Everything about Merrit Leitch radiated honest dismay. Except his voice. He said, "I said the dog will do what I tell it, sir. The boys are safe."

Hanlon unrolled his fists. "All right. What d'you want?"

"Wouldn't you rather sit down, sir?"

Hanlon did so automatically and cursed himself for even subconsciously seeming to obey this relaxed young slob. Before he could speak, Leitch said:

"It'd be a shame to spoil the *oeufs en cocotte*, sir, and I figure you want to keep your wife's suspicions cold, so let me say this: Mr. Lamb is effectively off the case, and I'm working on instructions out of D.O.D. Washington. That's as much as I'm able to tell you, sir. You want more, I'm instructed to say you have to call the DDCI's office direct."

Hanlon's mouth formed a hard, tight line. That was it, then. The Domestic Operations Division was an arm of the Directorate of Operations, the largest area of the CIA and better known as Clandestine Services. But D.O.D. conducted its covert operations inside America, not abroad. Its civilian chief had muscle equivalent to a three-star general, and he operated from an office in downtown Washington just two blocks from the White House. His influence was very nearly presidential; his network was nationwide, and there were D.O.D. bureaus in every major American city.

The DDCI, Deputy Director of Central Intelligence, was a political appointee. If he was coordinating Kingfish, the orders were coming directly from the White House.

"What am I expected to do?" Hanlon found it suddenly difficult to talk. His mouth was dry.

"I'm instructed to say, sir, that you are to continue exactly as you always have. If I need assistance, I'm to ask for it." He looked really apologetic. "I won't ask if it's not essential."

"What happened to Shawn and Fish?" Hanlon sprang it on the boy. The unlined young face didn't flicker.

"I really don't know, sir. That's not in my brief."

"And what *is?*"

"To prevent it from happening again, sir. To keep Kingfish on ice until Division knows who's responsible and why."

"And they want me to stand in a corner and mind my own business?"

"I don't think they see it that way, sir. I think . . ."

The barking shocked them both. It came from the sunken garden beyond the pool. Hanlon was at the window first, but Leitch was at his shoulder instantly. Hanlon's heart danced into his mouth.

Bobby and Daniel stood at opposite ends of the wide lawn, about twenty yards apart, tossing a baseball from one to the other in long high arcs. Between them the black-and-orange Doberman whirled and raced and leaped for the ball, the silver chain streaming from its collar, long pink tongue salivating, unmuzzled jaws bared, its barking high-pitched and excited.

Hanlon shouted, "For chrissakes . . ." but Leitch was already halfway to the door.

Before he reached it, Carrie's voice came to them from the kitchen.

"Come and get it or I throw it away!"

At that moment, Bobby threw his arms around the neck of the leaping Doberman and rolled with it into the grass. He was screaming—with laughter.

22.

The sign at the entrance to the long gravel driveway read Hiawatha's Pine Lodge Motel, but to its habitués it was "Julian's" after the angular little albino queer who ran it. Julian's stood on a rocky promontory jutting out like a wedge of ginger cake above an inlet south of New Bedford. From its patioed overhang the view was Olympian.

Margo parked her car in the shade trees one hundred yards short of the reception complex. The motel was discreetly veiled by close-growing pines that washed it with a permanent and all-pervasive perfume as though the pool had been infused with bath oil. She stopped, dug into her capacious handbag, located an atomizer of eau de cologne, and hissed short bursts of it behind her ears, on her throat, and on the inner wrists above the line of her white kid gloves.

Everyone had heard of Julian's, the way everyone had heard of the Mafia; in Teague's Landing, respectable people maintained the same moral distance from contact with both. No man brought his wife to Julian's, or his friends. Innocence of what happened there for those who had the money to pay never lasted beyond the second visit. Julian's existed to relieve the sheer unrequited agonies of moral rectitude, and it did so with appalling efficiency. Arnie Wellman, the Landing's pastoral shepherd, occasionally took it as his text for a virulent sermon on earthly hell and damnation. Julian's was a long, long way out of his area of influence, he admitted. But so was the Devil's Inferno.

Julian himself had made only one gesture in recognition of society's universal condemnation of his life style. He had created the Hellfire Delight. Three-fifths fire to two-fifths brimstone. He also renamed his Crystal Lounge the Paradise Club.

Julian was a real wit.

Margo straightened her white linen jacket and crossed the air-conditioned twilight of the lobby. The heat rebounded off the stone patio to meet her, and she stood uncertain for a moment, scanning the listless bodies around the pool.

Helen Shawn was not the type to be easily lost in a crowd. Margo spotted her at once and her irritation was instant. Anyone seeing Helen for the first time in this setting would have gathered from the attitude of the waiter serving her drink that she was hardly a stranger to the place. Helen was part of the furniture. It showed in the way she draped her body on the sun lounger; the way she managed to conceal the fact that she wore a bikini; the way men unconsciously licked their lips, and the way she knew they were doing it without once looking at them.

She had her reasons. At least, that was the story while Jack Shawn was alive. But even at his funeral she'd carried her widow's weeds with more flagrant sexuality than a strip queen. In Teague's Landing, that was dangerous. Arnie Wellman was not alone in his feeling of outrage that Helen could not even begin to pretend a sense of loss. Jack had not only been a hard-working mayor, he had been a universal uncle, a figurehead with a fixed grin, a kind, unremittingly open confidant, and a civic asset who gave his time as if it didn't cost money. The fact that he also had a reputation as a philandering Lothario was never held against him; in fact, it bolstered his extrovert image because he encouraged it. "A man with something to hide hid it" was the attitude of Teague's Landing's inner coterie. Jack plainly had nothing to hide.

For that reason alone, and much against her moral judgment, Margo had ordered Helen to check in at Julian's. It was a pity that it had to be this way but . . .

Helen raised a red polka-dotted kerchief and waved vigorously. Margo walked around the end of the pool, flinching under the passing inspection of men's eyes, and stopped.

"Not waving, but drowning," she said acidly.

Helen frowned, her upturned nose blooming with freckles under the influence of sun and tanning oil. "What?"

Margo shook her head dismissively and sat herself primly on one end of the lounger. "Nothing. Doesn't matter."

On the other side of the white-painted table, Grace Fish lay behind a pair of enormous sunglasses, a long mint julep glass rolling in her fingers. She offered Margo no greeting, no flicker of recognition.

Margo said, "Don't you think it would be better if we found

ourselves somewhere more . . . private?" She turned her head and the lolling pool bums stared back and grinned encouragingly.

Helen raised her sunglasses an inch and focused on Margo, then she swung her long legs to the ground and took the glass from Grace's hands. The spectators stiffened with anticipation.

"Margo's right," she said matter-of-factly. "It'll be cooler inside, Grace." She cupped Grace Fish's elbow in her hand, and the other woman responded immediately to the touch, as if blind behind her glasses.

Margo strutted quickly around the pool to reduce her embarrassment, but Helen swayed after her with exaggerated nonchalance. The men sat up to watch her, and their whistles followed her until all three were inside. They took the escalator to the Lodge Bar. Along one wall a vast sheet of black glass looked out over the sea, its single sliding door open to the pine-scented breeze. They sat at a polished pine table, alone in the big room. A waiter got up from a chair at the far end and started to greet them, but Helen waved him away.

Margo leaned across the table and plucked the dark glasses from Grace's face. "You don't need these in here," she said reprovingly. "There! Now we can see you."

Grace was in no state to be seen by anyone. Her eyes were bloodshot and ringed with the dark bruising of exhaustion, pain, and despair. She drew a hand across them, pinching the bridge of her nose to bring her eyes into focus. She blinked, first at Helen then at Margo.

Helen began, "She won't do anything I. . . ."

Margo interrupted. "What's wrong, Grace?"

Grace Fish's eyes widened in disbelief, then she choked the beginnings of a laugh but checked it and bent her face to her hands.

"I'm sorry, dear." Margo's attempt at sympathy was pathetically inept. "But it would have been worse if you'd stayed in town, you know that."

"I wanted to be there when they. . . ." Grace muffled her sobs in her tightly wound fingers.

"I know. I know." Margo rested gloved hands on her arms "But you know what that would mean, don't you? We've been through this before, you and I. I understand, believe me I understand, but you mustn't think about it. Frank is going to take care of the funeral and. . . ."

Grace Fish crumpled onto the tabletop, her cheek damp on the polished wood. Margo forced her up. "Listen to me!" She tightened her grip on Grace's slim forearms.

Helen looked around her uncomfortably. The waiter had returned to his invisible perch at the end of the bar. She said, "I had one hell of a time getting her to leave. It was all very well you saying, 'Get her out of there,' but she was absolutely. . . ."

"Shut up!" snapped Margo.

"Oh, thanks heaps," Helen drawled. She angled up her glasses and positioned them on her yellow hair.

"I'm sorry, Helen." Margo touched her hand apologetically. "What else could I do? Answer me that. If you'd been a little more understanding, perhaps she'd . . ."

"Understanding? Hah!" Helen exploded. "I'm the one who makes the accommodations every time. It's always me. Poor little Grace has to be understood. My own husband was in his coffin three days—three days!—but do you ask if Helen needs understanding? Do you, hell!"

"I said I'm sorry. I meant it. You've been through hell, both of you. That's why I wanted you out of the way. At least up here you're. . . ." She didn't know how to finish. Helen smiled.

She flicked her blonde hair off her face and touched Grace on the shoulder. "I'm going to have to tell her, Grace." She turned to Margo. "She took some pills. A lot." Margo tensed angrily. "Oh, it's all right," Helen sighed. "I got to her right after she did it. We didn't have to call anyone, did we, Grace?"

"What kind of pills?" Margo snapped.

Helen reached into a toilet bag and placed a small green bottle on the table between them. It was empty. "I don't know how I did it, but I pulled her through. She said they were sleeping pills, so I kept her on her feet. I spent hours walking her around and around that room. My God, Margo, you don't know what I went through."

Margo took the bottle, sniffed it, and studied the label. Helen watched her. "I made her sick, in the end," she said. "I stuck my fingers down her throat and made her sick."

Margo closed her eyes comfortingly. "You did the right thing, dear. I'm very grateful."

Helen dabbed at the perspiration on her throat with the polka-dotted kerchief. "She'll be all right now, won't she?"

Margo slipped the empty bottle into her bag and took out an identical one. It had a white paper seal over its cap. She placed it in the middle of the table. "That one's full, Grace," she said evenly. "Fifty tablets." With studied precision she broke the seal and unscrewed the top.

She said to Helen conversationally, "I first prescribed these for Grace a year ago, for a skin complaint." She allowed a dozen pills to pool in her hand. "A kind of eczema. Hypertension often induces that kind of effect. We went into psychotherapy together and the pills supplemented the treatment."

She turned on Grace. "Without the pills, the eczema comes back, doesn't it, Grace? But these are very special." She upended her palm and the pills rattled onto the table.

"That's why I. . . ." began Helen.

Margo cut her off with a flick of a hand. She said, "Go ahead, Grace. Take them. Take them all. That'll be two bottles of oblivion. It ought to do the trick." She picked up one of the white pills and popped it into her mouth and crunched down hard. She added another. And another. A fourth. Helen rose in her chair. Grace continued to fix on infinity.

"You could chew these all night and they wouldn't give you a mild headache. They're nothing, Grace. A placebo."

She sat back in her chair, pausing for effect, then she said slowly, "You're really very strong, Grace. Do you know that? You just like to feel vulnerable because you think you have a right to. You shared your strengths with Marv Fish, you built him up, you made him strong, you cared for him, you solved his problems. And what did he do for you? Did he say, 'What can I do for *you*, Grace?' No. He didn't—did he? You weren't his wife. You were his surrogate. It was the ventriloquist who got the sore throat, but everyone insisted on asking the dummy how *he* felt. Right Grace? These pills . . . You had to believe in them, didn't you? A support, a crutch—anything would do. Except . . ." She leaned forward on the table, her tone persistent, softly demanding, "Except all you've ever really needed was to believe in yourself. You've forgotten how."

Margo shook her head as Helen stretched out a comforting hand to Grace Fish. She said, "It's all right, Helen. Grace knows what I'm talking about."

A quicksilver tear trembled in the corner of Grace's right eye and quickly vanished as though absorbed by a sponge. She turned to Margo, looked down at the pills.

"You bitch," she said slowly. "You lousy . . ." Her fingers curled over the table edge, knuckles white.

Margo prepared herself for the onslaught she had engineered and Helen Shawn, seeing the storm gathering, got to her feet and pattered across to the bar. Margo's eyes were riveted on Grace's as though waiting for a sign. It came.

At the bar, Helen made a fool of herself to divert the bartender and the waiter from the torrent of invective that issued from Grace Fish, but her giggling sycophancy didn't fool either of the men for a moment. When the guilt and the anger and the pain and the fears had been released, Grace slumped back in her chair and fixed her eyes again on the hard white sky.

Through the branches of the pine trees, the sun made passes at her across the unbridgeable distance, and she tasted old names on her tongue to make sure they were real. Carradine and Fish and Shawn and Cater. Friends, according to the book of years, but now bonded inextricably by a chemistry more powerful than routine and familiarity and neighborliness. What was happening to them all?

They were dying, that's what was happening. Two of them dead, two to go.

Margo stared fixedly into Grace Fish's eyes. Grace dropped her's first and ran her fingers through the pills littering the tabletop. Her tears had still not come but lay dried in crackling smudges of grief behind her eyes.

Helen returned to the table clutching a pale yellow drink adorned with mint and lemon. She tugged at the straps of her bikini and measured herself unthinkingly in the reflecting surface of the black glass window.

"It's not easy for any of us," Margo said with judicial sincerity.

Helen leaped in anxiously. "Exactly. What about Jack, Grace? It's not as if it was just you."

"Anyone could see you are heartbroken," Grace sneered.

Helen burst out, "Christ, Margo! If she's going to . . ."

Margo slapped the table hard. "This isn't a game! Be quiet, both of you. You're under stress. You're saying things you'll both regret. I want you to relax and do as I tell you. This thing's completely out of proportion."

"Tell that to Joan Cater," snapped Grace viciously.

"And what's that supposed to mean?"

"Figure it out for yourself, Margo. First it's Jack. Then Marv. Who d'you think is next? Go ahead, spot the next man most likely."

Margo flashed out a gloved hand and took Grace by the wrist. She said firmly, "You're talking nonsense again, Grace. You're trying to make us feel as sorry for you as you are for yourself. Well, it won't work." She tugged fiercely at Grace's arm. "Don't look at me like that. I'm telling you the truth. It was coincidence. That's all."

"Coincidence!" The word burst from Grace like an obscenity.

"Two men are killed in one week. Yes, *killed!* They've been friends for twenty years. Both of them have something to hide."

"And they were married to us," Helen slipped in from behind her glass.

"Very well," said Margo, coldly. "They had something to hide. They were illegal immigrants. We've all lived with that ever since it began—the three of us and Joan. If we're honest with ourselves, we'll admit we knew someone would find out someday." She looked from one to the other searchingly. "Well?"

"Tell that to Doug Cater. And your own husband," Grace said. "Wouldn't you say one of them is next, Margo—or don't you care? Maybe you know something about them we didn't know about Marv and Jack."

Margo's anger rose no farther than her eyes. When she spoke her voice was dispassionate and perfectly pitched. "There's nothing to know, my dear, except that the American Government doesn't kill people who fail to declare themselves when they enter the country. Nor does anyone else."

Helen shifted in her chair and emptied the glass. "You know what you're saying, Margo?" she drawled casually. "You're saying there's some other reason. I can only think of two. One —suicide. Two—if it's not an *out*sider it's an *in*sider. One of us, maybe—huh?" She was almost smiling.

Grace let her have it. "Don't even let yourself think that— at least about Marv," she flashed. "I saw what happened to him up there on the Rock. He did what he's done a hundred times. The harness snapped and. . . ."

Helen raised the empty glass to her in salute. She was more than a little drunk. "Attagirl, baby! You tell her. So who cut the harness, Grace? Me or Margo or Joan?" She giggled stupidly and Margo cut in savagely.

"I won't put up with this, d'you hear!" She placed her hands palms down on the table and breathed deeply. "They

103

were accidents, nothing more. All right, you're upset and you're worried. But don't go reading signs that aren't there."

She placed a hand over Helen's and renewed her grip on Grace's wrist. "I think it would be best if you two separated. No!" She raised a hand as both of them tried to protest. "Wait a minute! Listen to me. Grace needs help from me, not you, Helen. I'd rather you stayed here for a day or two. Later on, when things quiet down and I know what's happening, we can all get together again."

Helen fiddled petulantly with her bikini strap. "Dammit, Margo, I feel, too, you know. Maybe not the same way as Grace but certainly not the same as *you*." There was more venom in the last word than she had intended.

"Then that's *your* problem, Helen," Margo retorted.

"Chrissakes," muttered Grace to herself. "Chrissakes!"

"Take it easy and be sensible," Margo crooned, smoothly. "Now, just leave it all to me. Tomorrow I'm seeing Joan Cater and maybe I'll talk with Frank in case he knows anything we should know about Jack and Marv. I'll get you a place to stay, Grace; in fact, I think you'd better come with me now. I'll keep in touch with you, Helen, at least twice a day."

"And meanwhile?" Helen Shawn's lips were pursed in the shape of a gleaming red-black cherry.

"I don't understand," Margo said.

"If there's a maniac loose in the Landing," said Helen carefully picking her words, "how do we make sure he doesn't do it again?"

"I've told you, Jack and Marv died accidentally. That'll be the coroner's verdict; take my word for it."

She got to her feet and the others followed suit uncertainly.

Grace's throat swelled with sudden emotion and with a sweep of her hand she scattered the pills from the table to the floor. The waiter, leaning with the bartender at one end of the bar, started forward in a reflex of professionalism but saw their faces and stopped.

Margo stepped around the table and put her arm across Grace's shoulders. "I know. I know you loved him, Grace. I really do."

The lump in Grace Fish's throat bobbed awkwardly, and she covered an involuntary sob with a cough. She dropped two of the white pills from her hand. They bounced on the floor and rolled away. Margo watched them roll.

23.

He arrived at the office as the cleaners cackled and shuffled their way out.

His throat felt as if it were lined with sandpaper and his shoulder ached. The night had been a washout. After an hour's sleep he had awakened with his head spinning and his lips moving in wild argument. He left a note for Carrie and slipped out. He'd had all day and all night to get Merrit Leitch out of his system, but the cool young bastard was still there. The swim should have straightened him out. It didn't.

He poured himself a glass of orange juice from the refrigerator and winced as the ice kidney-punched him. Twenty-five thousand dollars' worth of electronics and no damn way to make coffee. He unlocked the desk drawer, pressed a red key, and let himself into Doug Cater's life.

Doug sounded as if he were fielding an épée to Joan Cater's claymore. The row was past its formative stage and had settled into a series of deep lunges and sweeping cuts. Doug was in the bathroom, Joan in the bedroom. Hanlon heard the familiar intake of breath as Doug splashed his face with Brut. Joan would be lighting her first of the day: Pall Mall Gold 100's ('Not too strong, not too light, not too long, tastes just right'). Only Hanlon and Doug knew she smoked in bed. But then Hanlon knew everything about the Caters.

"I don't give a damn about what you've got planned. I'm not staying and that's final." Rustle of satin sheets.

Doug pulled on his Brooks Brothers shirt and buckled an alligator belt around his mohair pants.

"Listen, honey . . ."

"Listen shmisten! I tell you I won't be here. Fuck it, how many times do I have to tell you?"

Joan Cater's clip-voweled Boston accent curled around the obscenity like a chamois glove around a sledgehammer.

"Honey . . ." Click as the cabinet opened. Doug unscrewed the top of a bottle and swallowed his daily dose of high-potency, stress-formula vitamins. Joan sucked on her Pall Mall. It was 0750. Doug would be buckling on his Porsche waterproof chronograph ($475 from Rafael) and tying his Yves Saint Laurent tie.

Hanlon tried to backtrack the argument to its source. There didn't seem to be one. Joan had it in her head to leave, spend four days with a girl friend, and to hell with what Doug wanted, had planned, or promised.

Chances were it had begun in the twilight hours when the first birds were singing and a man, half-waking, half-sleeping, feels the stirring of his youth. Doug Cater had never accepted his wife's frigidity as being a psychological illness, a deep-seated malfunction. It had to be a passing phase, the result of misuse. If only he could find the trigger, everything would be all right. He had spent six years looking and wouldn't admit it was no longer there to be found.

Poor bastard; if he knew, it would kill him. A girl friend out of town—hen parties she called them. There were always nights of clawing frustration before one of Joan's visits with her little blonde friend. Doug had to suffer so that she could suffer— at least enough to seal off her guilt. Crazy dike!

"I'll see you, honey. I've got to dash. This evening. We'll grab a meal in town and then, maybe . . ."

"Forget it, Doug. Everything's fixed and I can't change my

plans. Not for you, not for anyone." She was calming down. She'd won again.

A kiss on the cheek from the vanquished. Door drawn carefully shut to avoid any suggestion that it was slammed. Joan Cater stretching on the bed; a deep weary sigh. Waiting for her escape. . . .

Hanlon switched off the monitor and watched through the telescope as Doug slid back the garage door and backed the car into the driveway. It was new. No more than six weeks old. A Plymouth Volare, small, black, and elegant with its distinctive T-bar roof where the two smoked-glass panels could be slotted in when the weather broke.

It was going to be hot and the Plymouth was the nearest thing to a convertible. He pulled out of the driveway and turned north toward the Main Ridge Freeway.

Hanlon watched him to the end of the street where the car disappeared. He swung the telescope back to the Cater house, set it on the driveway, and locked it. He turned away. Spun on his heels. Grabbed the telescope. Focus, damn you!

The car was a small, white, open-topped English MGB. It pulled away from the curb and followed in the wake of Cater's car.

Hanlon crashed the office door behind him and sprinted for his car. He knew it was a race he couldn't win.

24.

The pines on the Main Ridge Freeway were oozing early-morning chlorophyll as the sun gathered strength, throwing their shadows across the road in broad regular bands.

Doug Cater felt the tension ease out of him. Women! He selected a cool music channel and settled back with Mancini.

He had been driving for only sixteen months and it was still a new experience. By driving he meant *really* driving, not just tooling around like some old broad up to the freeway and back. Now he could really let himself go, listen to the wind in his ears, the steady rising hum of the tires. After three years of treatment, the epileptic attacks had suddenly stopped. "It's like asthma or any other allergy," the doc had said. "You're one of the lucky ones. We can control it."

The doc.

Frank Carradine.

Doug owed him a lot. Like freedom.

He put his foot down and sped along the deserted freeway trying not to think of Joan and the fact that she wouldn't be there when he got back. Another spate of phone calls, explaining away her absence, smiling, shrugging, trying to wisecrack, pretending they weren't talking behind his back. Did they know? Sam Hanlon did. He'd never said a word, but he couldn't hide the fact that he knew.

The rear-view mirror was a miniature movie screen in which the retreating road flickered like a silent film in the alternating bands of sunlight and shade on the freeway.

The small white sports car appeared from nowhere and was chopped into racing fragments of light as it settled dead astern and slowly grew larger.

25.

It was, of course, insane, Hanlon told himself for the tenth time. Blind and unbalanced, sick and senseless. No, not senseless. It made sense all right.

The Marquis de Sade's idea of sense.

Unless he had guessed wrong. Maybe Leitch was merely

doing his job, keeping tabs on Cater. Or was that really his job?

Bricks without straw. It served no useful purpose to conjure scenarios out of circumstantial evidence. So why was he turning on to the Main Ridge Freeway at eight o'clock in the morning when he should be dipping his nose into a cup of coffee and leaving it to his "assistant"?

Answer: Because.

He gunned the engine of the Mercedes. The road ahead was deserted. Cater and Leitch had a good five minutes' start and by now would be approaching the banked turn that took the freeway off the Ridge before it passed Jonathan's Rock. Once on that stretch, the road was as straight as an arrow for four miles. Leitch would have been less obtrusive in a chopper with a loudspeaker. But then, maybe he didn't mind being seen.

26.

As Doug Cater took the wide curve off the Ridge, the white MGB pulled out from the inside lane and began to pass him. He could hear the blaring of a tape playing rock music. The sound was snatched up in gusts and whirled away as the car drew alongside. He glanced across. The driver was wearing dark wraparound glasses and smiling straight ahead as if in deep communion with the music. Doug Cater lifted his foot and the Plymouth fell back.

The MGB fell back.

Cater shot him another look and this time the young man turned and smiled, a short, almost perfunctory smile as if he were sharing a joke. Then his shielded eyes went back to the road.

Cater shrugged and gave a little wave, wondering if the other driver was in trouble. He accelerated. The MGB accelerated; they were doing 84 mph.

Cater dropped the speed to seventy-five. He was tired of the game. The MGB was getting to him and the rock music was going down badly with Mancini. Not only that, he had the beginnings of a headache. He reached into the glove compartment, pulled out his vitamin C capsules, and swallowed a handful.

The MGB began to pull ahead, the sun glinting on its trunk. Cater didn't recognize the license plate. Out of state. He squinted as the reflected sunlight momentarily caught his eyes. The dark glasses he normally wore were gone from alongside the pills in the glove compartment. He guessed Joan had taken them again. The MGB settled down in the adjacent lane, keeping religiously six feet ahead of the Plymouth. The thought flashed into his head that it had something to do with Joan. A lover perhaps? He let the thought die in its own gall. He waved an arm high above his head, flicking the hand forward as if waving away a cloud of midges.

"Okay, you've had your fun!" he shouted into the wind. "Now get out of here before somebody gets hurt."

There was not the vaguest chance his warning would be heard. The crashing waves of hard rock blew back into his face from the white car.

"Okay," he said. "Okay."

He pushed it to a hundred. The MGB stayed in front.

Then he thought of Jack Shawn. Marvin Fish. And the taste of copper filled his mouth as his stomach contracted.

The young man in the dark glasses checked the speedometer needle as it hovered on the hundred, then returned his eyes to the rear-view mirror. The mirror was tinted and angled so that he could see the front half of the Plymouth. Above it was an extra mirror, untinted and twice as wide as the one in which he had framed the car. He reached up and moved it until he found what he was looking for.

As the first flash of light hit him, Doug Cater instinctively swerved the car. He only just managed to pull back into line before he ran out of road. He wanted to reduce speed, but first the flashing light had to be stopped. It glittered maddeningly from the MGB, reflecting sunlight in a single stabbing beam.

Stab.

Stab.

Flicker.

He raised an arm across his eyes, but the car swung dangerously and he was forced to grab the wheel double-handed again.

Flicker.

Using his rear-view mirror as a guide, the driver of the MGB was flashing reflected sunlight backward into the Plymouth with the regularity of a metronome.

"For God's sake!" screamed Cater. "Cut it out!" Flicker. Flicker. Flicker.

"Cut it ou. . . ."

The fingers of his right hand began to burn as if thousands of tiny needles were tattooing them. Like brushing against stinging nettles. The steering wheel developed a soft rubbery feel and a green glow circled the inside of his eyes.

Flicker. Flicker.

"Joan," mumbled Doug Cater. A fleck of white foam blew from the corner of his mouth.

"Joanie. Help me."

He closed his eyes and the light still flickered, only now it was coming from inside his head. A great burst of powdery light exploded softly and rained snowflakes. He couldn't move his neck.

The first spasm gripped him and he arched back into the seat, his foot hammering the gas pedal. The car surged forward, its engine bellowing in protest.

Cater opened his eyes wide in pain and bit through his tongue.

The last thing he saw was the white car slipping away behind him, the young man at the wheel, staring dead ahead; a black-and-orange dog pulled itself up from the small back seat and sat erect, its ears twitching in the wind.

It stared at him quizzically as he lost control.

27.

In the last few days of the war Hanlon had been stationed in France, traveling from village to village to coordinate what remained of the underground, trying to establish some semblance of order that might be useful in the peace. There was an air of desperation and unreleased tension wherever he went. A dormant violence he could almost taste.

One morning he had witnessed a scene he would never forget. A young girl, barely sixteen, was dragged to the steps of a drinking fountain in a village square. Her hair had been cropped and her breasts bared. She stood accused of informing the Germans of black-market traffic in cigarettes. The smugglers used the village as one link in a chain that stretched from Marseilles to Paris. It was true, of course. There *was* a chain and she *had* informed. She had wanted to frighten her boyfriend who was a member of the cigarette ring and was threatening to leave her for another, older girl.

Hanlon watched as she was shoved and jostled and spat upon. Someone mixed the fountain water with dirt and rubbed mud in her face. She spat it back at them.

One man tugged at the hem of the girl's dress and for a moment Hanlon thought they were going to rape her. Powerful peasant hands spun her like a top into the waiting crowd. She fell against a grizzled old man, and he grasped her by the shoulders, shaking her until her breasts bounced. She dug her teeth into his cheek and he roared with pain.

His son, standing alongside him, reached for the girl and drew the blade of his penknife across her throat. She slid to the floor and lay there as the crowd drifted away, the sport over. For several minutes Hanlon was rooted to the spot, disbelieving.

For months he had tried to reject what he had seen. It was a long time before he taught himself to accept that it was the only thing that *could* have happened. It was the way of the world.

The memory raced in and out of his mind.

Even before he heard the dull explosion and saw the plume of smoke rising from beyond the freeway, he knew that to have expected anything else was an act of gross folly.

He reached the scene two minutes later, drew the car off the road, and parked it behind the white MGB. He climbed the embankment beside the deep ruts dug by Doug Cater's Plymouth. At the top he looked down and saw Leitch and the dog. He was standing well away from the blazing wreck talking to a motorcycle cop who had driven over the field from one of the small slip roads below the Ridge. He walked down to them feeling the heat rising from the twisted metal to meet him, tasting carbon and rubber on his tongue.

Leitch looked at him bleakly. "I was following him," he said coolly. "He went off the road." He nodded at the flames. "He was driving so fast I could hardly keep him in sight."

The dog tugged at the chain attached to Leitch's wrist, and without looking down, he shook the animal into submission.

"You were following him," said Hanlon. "And he went off the road."

"That's about it," said Leitch.

"Just like that."

"Just like that. By the way, don't stand too near the dog. The fire makes him nervous." Leitch gestured apologetically, cast one more glance at the blaze, then raised his dark eyes in a blatant challenge.

"Waste of a good car, don't you think?" he said.

28.

Dear Assistant Director in Charge of Internal Intelligence: Having worked for your organization for twenty-eight years I have thought things over and decided that, owing to circumstances outside my control, I wish to quit. Please may I tender one month's notice. Let me know if there's a refund on the luncheon vouchers.

Yours, as ever....

Hanlon sat with the typewriter in front of him and the sheet of paper as blank as it had been an hour ago. He ran his fingers across the keys as if playing jazz piano and wrapped them around the glass of Punt e Mes, the first bottle he had come to. It tasted like mouthwash that had traveled badly. He poured himself another. So how do you resign from the World's Greatest Intelligence Machine, wise guy?

No trick questions. But I'll tell you how.

How?

I told you, no trick questions.

He looked at the paper again. It read:

Nothing. The typewriter keys were welded into a tight bunch one inch from the paper. It should have read: asdfghjkl;? —but typewriters, like people, didn't always function as they were expected to, especially when you played them like jazz piano.

Hanlon tried to blink away the nonsense in his head but had no heart for it. He felt drunk and that was how he wanted to stay. Jack Shawn, Marvin Fish, Doug Cater. That was one fine reason for staying drunk. That and Frank Carradine.

Carrie opened the study door and smiled softly. "I thought you might like something. You've been in here for hours."

She placed coffee and cookies next to the typewriter and rested a hand lightly on his shoulder. He clasped his hand over it and looked up at her. He could smell her perfume. "It's a bad time," he said.

"Yes," she said. "It's not good, Sam." She hesitated and rearranged the cookies on the plate. "Sam?"

"Yes?"

"Nothing. Don't be too late."

One hour later, the paper still blank, the phone rang. It was Leitch. "Mr. Hanlon. Sam Hanlon." It was not a question.

"Sam Hanlon, Leitch."

"I think we ought to talk. Soon. Today. I think we ought to air a few common problems, Mr. Hanlon."

"Okay, Marlon Brando, we'll talk. Which reptile house are you using today?"

A deep sigh from Leitch. "Mr. Hanlon, do you *want* to talk or do you *not* want to talk?"

"Fine, Leitch. Sorry if I upset you. I've had a busy day, chasing corpses. Something you get used to. But then, I'm telling you . . ."

"Quit the jokes, Mr. Hanlon. I'm talking business. And don't you ever forget that. Sir."

"In one hour. No, check, a half-hour. My office at the Center. Okay?"

"Right. One half-hour exact. Thank you, sir." The phone went dead. Hanlon carefully screwed the top back on the Punt e Mes and stowed it in the refrigerator. He took a sip of the coffee and it felt good. Carrie was reading in the bedroom. He made the usual excuses and kissed her.

"Be careful, Sam," she said.

"Sure."

He slipped on a jacket and stepped out into the warm night.

For the first time in ten years he was aware how heavy a .38 really was.

29.

From: Stefan Andreyev, KGB Chairman
To: Dmitri Orlov, Director, First Directorate, KGB

S E C R E T.

At the meeting of the collegium I was deeply shocked at the evidence you presented concerning the KINGFISH cell. None of this was presented to me before the meeting as well you know it should have been. I feel it better for all concerned if you detach yourself from the current investigations. The matter need not concern you further. I have instructed the Director of the Illegals Directorate (S) to relieve you of the task of investigating your own Directorate.

From: Dmitri Orlov, Director, First Directorate, KGB
To: Stefan Andreyev, KGB Chairman

I am aware of the delicate nature of the inquiries currently taking place and, in particular, the embarrassing position in which you find yourself. A position that must be of grave concern to you. I have tried to act with my country's interests at heart and with concern for my colleagues high and low. Obviously that has been misinterpreted. Concerning your suggestion that the Director of Directorate S assume control of the investigation, I must inform you that Marshal Bunin has personally asked me to prepare the final report for the Praesidium. In view of this I have instructed the Director of Directorate S that his services will no longer be required and feel sure you will concur. I am, as a matter of course, forwarding a copy of this note, together with yours, to the office of the Special Investigations Department, where it will be sealed and filed.

30.

Hanlon closed his hand comfortingly around the butt of the .38 and stepped out of the elevator on the floor below the penthouse. He raised the flap on the wall beside the security door to his suite, whirled the combination lock, and, when the door clicked open, reset it.

The old revolver was more a comforter than anything else. He'd carried it through his war, hefted it in the Cold War undergrowth of East Germany, Czechoslovakia, Poland, and Romania. Its muzzle velocity was laughable by modern standards and it still kicked high-right, but its butt somehow countersunk itself naturally in his fist and the molding-line down the trigger had been worn to nothing by his forefinger. They were old campaigners, he and the .38. They knew each other's faults.

He reached the head of the stairs and Leitch turned from the telescope pointing down into Old Harbor.

"Hey, this is real powerful, sir."

Hanlon stopped abruptly.

"How . . . ?"

Leitch's now-familiar expression of injured innocence asserted itself.

"I assumed you'd want me to be here, sir, when you arrived."

"How'd you get in?"

"The old guy let me in the street door. I got the combination for the security lock from D.O.D. I thought maybe they'd told you that, sir."

Hanlon came into the room and threw his car keys onto the desk. No one knew the combination of that door. There was a low rumble from the far corner and Hanlon spun on his heel. The Doberman's hackles bristled. Through the muzzle, saliva dropped in glistening trails.

Leitch spat three words and the dog went quiet. It sat down and stared fixedly at the floor. Hanlon recognized the commands, but his Latin was too rusty for an exact interpretation. Leitch eyed him, expecting comment. Hanlon turned to his desk and checked the drawers and the control panel.

"If I *had* touched anything, sir, I don't think you'd know anyway," Leitch said softly. "For the record, I didn't."

Hanlon controlled his temper with a massive exercise of will. He kept his voice low but it trembled. "Let me tell you something *for the record.* You're finished here, sonny. I'm calling DDCI personally, and when I'm through, you'll be on your way out. For good."

Leitch swept a swatch of hair off his forehead and shook his head uncomprehendingly. "Why, sir? I don't understand?"

"You don't understand? You wasted Doug Cater. You sat and pushed him till he blew it."

"You've got a real sense of humor, sir. I sat on his tail, all right. That was the order. But the rest. . . ." Leitch's forehead crinkled. "How could I stop him, sir? The guy was an epileptic. He'd been warned not to drive a car fast. There're two people who saw him drive off the road. We've had the brakes, the steering, the gearbox—everything—checked out. Nothing wrong with the car. The coroner's report says Cater probably died in spasm. Epileptic spasm. And you know yourself, sir, I was right behind him. You were there."

"How far behind him?"

Leitch shrugged. "I did the best I could. He's a—he was a professional, sir. If I'd not tailed him real tight he'd have lost me."

"I don't think D.O.D. is going to see it that way."

Leitch tried his apologetic look again. He opened his arms wide, disclaiming responsibility for what he was about to say.

"D.O.D. sent in their own men to check the car, sir. They also had two medical consultants up from New York. I got the word from Washington tonight. They've already listed Cater as a four-two-fourteen-three."

Hanlon's teeth closed on his tongue and trapped it painfully. A 4-2-14-3 was numerical Company jargon for DBNC—Death by Natural Causes. In an organization devoted to the belief that Death only visited professionals by appointment, a four-two-fourteen-three was as irrevocable and as final as original sin. By the very nature of the system that arrived at that opinion, it wouldn't, couldn't be changed. Doug Cater had given immortal shape to one of those accident scenarios he feared for years—and posterity, if it cared, was stuck with it.

He sat back on the desk top and chewed his lip, forgetting his companion. Leitch was not easily disposed to being ignored for long.

"You're taking this pretty hard, sir." The tone was not ingratiating, but the effect of the words was.

"What's that supposed to mean?" Hanlon rapped.

"Only that it's hard to be part of men's lives for years. Hard to feel . . . untouched when they die." His air of innocence was almost saintly.

"Spell that out the way you mean it."

Leitch raised his hands defensively.

"I swear to God, sir—just that. Your job was to get under these people's skins, and the way I see it, that means they're bound to get under yours. In time."

Hanlon felt the blood drain from his face and his knuckles tighten on the edge of the desk. He couldn't help himself. Leitch was needling him and doing it strictly according to the book. Hanlon had been taught the techniques himself as he'd been taught so much else at the Farm, the CIA's West Point near Williamsburg which operated publicly as a military base called Camp Peary.

To know the method was to beat it. It was just a game, after all. Offensive and counter-offensive. Living chess.

He relaxed.

"You're right." He sighed openly, loudly, and derived satisfaction when Merrit Leitch pitched up a sympathetic grin. "It took seventeen years to get Kingfish under my skin. It took 'em three days to get under yours."

For the first time, Leitch reacted uncertainly. "I don't get you, sir. How d'you mean—under *my* skin?"

"You read the file on Cater before you came in?"

"Yes, sir." He was walking on razor blades.

"And Carradine?"

"Yup."

"Anything in there point to their being active?"

"Not for me to say, sir."

"Exactly."

Frown "I don't get it."

"There was nothing in either of the files to suggest they were active. D.O.D. pumped you in and left you to prove yourself. That left you only one way. You decided to sit on Cater. *Hard.* You left him to make his mistake. Deliberately. You knew he was epileptic. You knew a car drive might kill him. You pushed him over the edge."

"That's not logical, sir." Leitch couldn't quite dampen a slight tremor in his voice. "I had no choice."

"Oh, sure. No choice. Anyway, what kind of a choice is it? Let a known enemy agent die or keep him alive till Washington chooses to have him wasted."

"That's way out of line . . ." Leitch bit off the anger quickly. "With respect, sir."

"But not unreasonable."

Leitch shrugged. "I'm not into speculation. But as you say, sir, it's a reasonable thesis . . . morally speaking."

120

"Reasonable enough for a bright young career officer to act on?"

Leitch glanced out of the window at the scudding clouds coming in from the Atlantic. They were full of rain. Unconsciously, he weighed the raised ridge of hard flesh on his right hand in the palm of his left. He was designed for physical reflex, not mental game-playing.

When he looked again at Hanlon his cheeks had a faint blush of pinkness in them that hadn't been there before.

"Unlike you, *sir*, I work to order. Right down the line. I don't play games with facts—I accept them. I use them any way I can to achieve an objective. That's the way it goes these days. I guess you'd call it a dehumanized way of working. They tell me you're big on humanity. That's a pity. You canceled yourself out of this operation because you're so goddamned human, sir. You were hired as a field surveillance officer, not a missionary. These men are organized Communist agents working against the United States in our own backyard. What d'you expect them to do—advertise on television! Okay, so I failed. A man died. That's one to me—two to you."

Hanlon pushed himself off the desk. He made himself drop his head and said quietly, "Right. You're right, Merrit. I'm sorry."

He walked across the room, his hand out. Leitch raised his own expecting the handclasp. Hanlon closed with him and, as their hands hovered within inches, changed direction. His right hand swept upward through the open neck of Leitch's shirt and found the carotid artery. He locked it between his thumb and the forefinger knuckle and squeezed.

Leitch's teeth came together with a crunching sound and tears spurted into his eyes but no sound escaped him. Slowly, Hanlon increased the pressure and the first convulsive sob of exploding breath burst out of him. Hanlon pressed down and Leitch's legs buckled. He fell to his knees and Hanlon held him there, enjoying it.

121

He saw the bulge under the stretched cloth of the raincoat, reached inside, and unholstered the gun. It was a Magnum .450. At twenty feet it could have killed a charging rhino.

Hanlon suspended it by the trigger guard between his finger and thumb. The safety catch was off. He clicked it to "safe" and tossed it onto the carpet. Then with a final twist of his hand, he threw Merrit Leitch onto his back.

"I'm sure you can find your own way out, son," he said.

He crossed to the stairs and stopped. He'd forgotten the dog. Christ! He looked quickly over his shoulder. The Doberman sat statue-still, eyes on the ground, but it was quivering all over with the electricity of kinetic energy.

Hanlon said, "Congratulations, son. That's one hell of a dog." He closed the door before Leitch could prove it.

31.

"Let her go!" yelled Daniel Carradine. "Now!"

Bobby felt his arms beginning to tremble as he squinted along the crossbow sights. It was now or never.

"Go!"

The bolt leaped from the bow in a streak of silver, whistled across the lawn, and buried itself deep in the fiberboard target.

Daniel ran forward. "Good one," he called over his shoulder as he tugged it free. "Still a bit high. But strong."

Bobby strolled across. His shoulder was starting to ache, and even as it hung relaxed by his side, his left arm still trembled. He looked at the deep gouge left by the bolt in the board.

"Not bad. Not fantastic, but not bad." He handed the bow to Danny. "Did your dad make it all? I mean, all the steel pieces, too?"

"Everything," said Daniel Carradine. "I helped shape the stock and polish it. That's important."

"I'd like to see him hunting with it," said Bobby. "You think he might let us go along with him someday?"

"Maybe. He hasn't done much hunting lately. There are seasons for it. Y'know, like fishing. Special months. He shot a moose once."

"Deer."

"Moose."

Bobby aimed along the empty bow at a cat skulking along the perimeter of the garden.

"You can't shoot moose. It's illegal."

"A moose. He shot it. Up in Canada, a long time ago. Honest."

"How did he know?"

"Know what?"

"It was a moose. How did he know it was a moose, not a deer?"

"Because," said Daniel, rolling his eyes in exasperation, "they're different."

"How?" Bobby switched his aim to the silhouette of his mother in the next garden. She hated him playing with things like guns and bows. He had even had to appeal to Sam to be allowed to keep his bowie knife.

"Well, dummy," continued Danny, "instead of its horns— antlers, I mean—sticking out like this," he stuck two fingers out from either side of his forehead as Bobby watched with consummate interest, "they sort of go around and around like this, only not just around, wide too, sort of like this . . ."

Bobby couldn't contain himself any longer. Widening his eyes he wrinkled his nose and pushed his face against his friend's. With a badly suppressed giggle he stuck his fingers out from his forehead and began to advance, as Daniel, fingers drooping, retreated . . .

"Hey, you flipped, or. . . ."

"Moose," said Bobby. "Mooooooooose!" He prodded Daniel in the chest with his "antlers." His friend began to grin and backed away faster.

"You're a nut, you know that . . . a . . . Lay off . . ."

They ran around the lawn giggling, Daniel adjusting his antlers, turning on his assailant, locking fingers, butting away until they both fell to the grass, panting, laughing out loud.

"You're a nut," repeated Daniel, throwing a handful of grass cuttings at his friend.

"Mooooooose," trumpeted Bobby, lying back on the grass, shielding his eyes from the sun.

Daniel squatted beside him, looking down the sights of the crossbow.

"Couldn't hit a barn door," leered Bobby. "Or a moose come to think of it."

Daniel raked the houses with imaginary bolts and swung the bow down to the driveway, focusing on the rear of the parked car. Bobby was right, of course. His eyes weren't that good; he was still supposed to wear his glasses for at least half the day, but unless his mother insisted, he no longer bothered. Not only that, the bow was heavy. Now, one of those Fiberglas pieces . . .

The blurred shape fixed itself at the end of the sights and he blinked it into focus. Then his whole body began to tremble.

"Bob," he said, his lips barely moving. "Bob."

Bobby Hanlon pulled himself into a sitting position and clasped his arms around his knees. He followed Daniel's gaze down the driveway and his arms locked as if steel handcuffs had been slipped over his wrists.

At the end of the driveway stood Frank Carradine. He was wearing a cream linen summer suit. It was torn, smeared with blood and dirt. He stood swaying by the car, one hand resting for support on its hood. His face was streaked with blood.

"Get your mom, Danny," he said quietly. "Get your mom, quick."

124

32.

It wasn't difficult to persuade Carrie to go to bed early. She had been complaining of persistent headaches since the day of Jack Shawn's death; her way of crying out for help, but she wouldn't take sleeping pills or even half-grain Librium because drugs implied mental corrosion.

So she went to bed early and tossed and turned in the dark for a couple of hours until her brain switched off from sheer exhaustion.

Hanlon sat in a chair with Thomas Carlyle's *Reminiscences* on his lap and waited for midnight. Carradine had called him a little after seven. The story of the hit-and-run maniac was all over Teague's Landing by then. Bobby had seen to that.

They agreed that to meet at either of their homes would be unwise. Neither chose to explain why. Carradine suggested Hanlon's boat. At midnight.

In high summer security was tight on the floating pontoons of the marina because boat-rustling was fast becoming a national sport, but Hanlon knew the four-man night team well. He was president of the marina corporation and commodore of the yacht club. He chatted with the supervisor until Carradine stomped up onto the boardwalk. Then they walked in silence to where *Babalou* lay on her mooring and climbed aboard.

The boat was a Grand Banks deepwater cruiser; forty-two feet of beamy comfort equipped with twin 280 horsepower GM diesels that gave a handy range of a thousand miles. It smacked a little too much of the gin palace for Hanlon's taste—too much interior mahogany and leather, too much deep carpeting—but those were the concessions Carrie had demanded as a condition of her joining him and Bobby afloat.

The two men stood together in the dark on the bridge deck watching for movement on the pontoons. There was none. Carradine's hand fell onto the polished mahogany of the spoked wheel.

"It was no accident, that thing this afternoon," he said quietly.

Hanlon had not switched on the bridge-deck light, and in the darkness a muted voice seemed mandatory. They both felt it. Hanlon tapped absently at the face of a dead instrument dial. "Who says?"

He felt Carradine bristle beside him. "He came at me like a tank. Two wheels on the sidewalk."

"He?"

"Whoever it was."

"You saw the driver?"

Carradine slumped over the wheel, leaning on it for support. "It was too fast. I had other things on my mind. The car came off the corner, I saw it and. . . . I think I jumped. That's all I remember."

"You recognize the make, the license plate?"

"I was on my back!"

"Okay, okay, Frank. Relax. What d'you want me to do about it?"

Carradine eased off the wheel and lowered himself into the pilot's seat. He didn't speak for some time, but when he did his voice was harsh.

"What really happened to Jack and Marv and Doug—can you tell me that, Sam?"

Goose flesh formed along Hanlon's arms. He rubbed it away with a shudder. "You tell me. You're the doctor."

He looked down at Carradine. The man's fingers were interwoven tighter than a garroted throat, one hand throttling the other.

"Three men—my closest friends—get themselves killed in stupid accidents. Maybe that's credible over a space of ten years, but in a space of a few *days?*"

126

"Is that supposed to make sense, Frank?"

"*Sense!*" Carradine's head went down into his hands and his lungs discharged a strangled hiss of despair. "Dear God, you expect any of this to make *sense?*"

Hanlon laid a restraining hand on his shoulder "You'd better tell me what this is all about."

Carradine nodded dumbly in the half-light. He raised his head and clamped his hands firmly on his knees to hide their shaking.

"They want *me*. That's what this is all about. They're saying, 'First we take your world apart, then we take you.' It's . . . a way of exacting retribution, Sam. They believe there has to be retribution. No matter how long it takes."

For a moment Hanlon was too confused to form a reply. He'd expected a *cri de coeur* from Carradine. At least that. But outright confession!

"Who's *they?*" he asked mechanically.

"They." Carradine echoed the word hollowly. "After it happened, when I'd got myself home and cleaned up, I had to talk to someone. You, Sam. There isn't anyone else I could trust. Now I—I dare not tell even you."

"I came here to help, Frank. I'm volunteering."

"That's why I can't tell you. I don't have the right to involve you. You're clean. Stay that way.

"I said I'm volunteering. Frank. I'm your friend. That gives me certain rights, too." The lie left a taste in his mouth.

Carradine was racked with another shuddering release of breath. "No one has rights," he rasped. "A few people get lucky enough to live their lives without interference, that's all. But they have no rights. Any time, for any reason, the State comes along and says, 'Okay, buster, we want you'—you do what you're told. You don't have the right to say, 'No thanks, I'm busy.' They just pluck you up and smash you down."

Hanlon tensed with anticipation. It was all coming out. Everything. If only he had a tape deck on the boat. Years of perfectly coordinated silence and Carradine unbuttons for the oldest, most craven reason in the book: a threat to his imperfect neck.

"Who plucked you up, Frank?"

Carradine got to his feet, walked aft to the saloon, and unlocked the big glass hatch door leading to the sun deck. Hanlon followed him and lit a cigarette in his cupped hands to avoid showing too much light. The moon sailed through mountainous white cloud, beating a pattern of fractured light on the sea. The air was warm, still, velvet-gloved. The Ridge reared above the town, cocooned in misty piety.

Hanlon tried again.

"What are we talking about, Frank? Is this something to do with Marv and Jack and Doug?"

Carradine took a cigarette but made no attempt to conceal the flaring Ronson. "Something to do with them, I suppose. That much I'll tell you. I don't have the guts to tell you the rest. I'll keep it that way, Sam, for your sake."

A long black shadow crept from the yacht basin two hundred yards astern of *Babalou* and turned toward them. A searchlight sprang to life from a deckhouse mounting and hurled its shaft in long probing runs over the moored craft along the outer pontoons. Carradine's nerves jumped.

"It's okay—the security launch," Hanlon said automatically. "We'd better go inside. No point in advertising."

The launch burbled by, its light raking *Babalou* from bow to stern and back again and, when it passed, its wake delivered a series of waves that rocked the cruiser against her warps.

"So why are we sitting here, for chrissakes? Don't try to tell me you think I'm good for a sympathetic ear and no questions asked?"

Carradine nodded. "Yeah, that's what I think, Sam. For the time being, anyway."

Hanlon was momentarily grateful for the darkness inside the saloon. His tolerance was at the breaking point, and he couldn't afford to let Carradine see it.

"All right." Hanlon waved his hand dismissively. "It's your funeral. But tell me one thing. Why kill Shawn, Fish, and Cater? Why not me? Why not. . . ?" He stopped abruptly. He had been about to name Margo and Daniel. He added, "Why not people you work with? The staff at the hospital? Anyone?"

Carradine said evenly, "They have a sophisticated sense of purpose, Sam. You just wouldn't understand. Me and Jack and Marv and Doug had something in common. We were a tight little group, you know? Oh, you were a part of it in some ways, but you're an outsider, too. You were *my* friend. That's the way the other guys looked at it. *My* friend."

Hanlon's palms were sweating. Nearly there. One more gentle push.

"I never felt that."

"You wouldn't. It wasn't a visible line. We didn't encourage people to takes notes. We had different reasons, I guess, but it came down to the same thing. Something to hide."

"And you're telling me three men had to die because of it? That's crazy, Frank."

"Huh!" The attempt at laughter came out stillborn. "That's Margo's line. She says I'm paranoid. If she ever gets to think about divorce, she'll use it in court, too."

"You've told Margo?"

"I tried. Waste of time. My wife's a realist. She has a value system as adventurous as peanut butter. She told me to take a pill for it."

Hanlon felt it slipping away from him again.

"Let me get this straight. You told her that Jack, Marv, and Doug were dead because of you?"

"No. Not exactly like that."

"But that's what you believe."

"I believe."

"And after them—you."

"You can bank on it. Look, Sam, this is stupid. Let's go, shall we?"

Hanlon pulled back the bridge-deck door and beckoned Carradine into the air. He stepped down onto the pontoon and waited for Carradine to join him. They began to walk back along the heaving boards to the security office at the pierhead.

Hanlon said suddenly, "I want you to get out, Frank."

"Huh!" That explosive nonlaugh again. "They have world-wide connections, Sam. Where can I run?"

"I know a place. Belongs to a friend of mine. Just outside Fuengirola."

"Spain?"

"That stretch of coast is crawling with tourists this time of year. The villa is off the road, behind the town a few kilometers. No one's going to bother you there."

Carradine stopped in his tracks. The moonlight illuminated his face. There was hope in it. Daredevil hope. Then it died.

"No use, Sam. They'll be watching me, the house, the car, the station, airports. They won't let me walk onto a plane . . ."

Hanlon grabbed his elbow and squeezed it viciously. His anger was partly directed against himself. He had heard everything he ever wanted to hear from Frank Carradine's mouth and now he was deliberately plotting his escape.

Why?

Don't answer that.

He ducked his head to within an inch of Carradine's face and breathed savagely, "What d'you want me to do—let them turn you into another goddamned blood sandwich like Doug Cater? Oh no, I wouldn't give 'em that much satisfaction. I'll get you out okay. Believe me."

"How?"

"I've got an idea. Give me time to work it out. Come on, you'd better get home before Margo starts asking questions."

Hanlon drove Carradine back up onto the Ridge and watched him get out in front of his house.

Hanlon shouted, "Wait a minute. One thing I need to know. About Shawn, Fish, and Cater. What makes them so damned different?"

Carradine turned slowly. "They were immigrants, Sam. East Europeans. Like me."

He was nearly there—Provoke! Provoke!

"That's horseshit! Who'd care a nickel in this place whether you're. . . ."

"I didn't say people would care one way or another, Sam. I said we didn't declare ourselves. There's a difference."

"But why? What . . . ?"

"We had our reasons. I've still got mine. Makes no sense to you, maybe, but it could finish me. One day, I'll have enough. . . ."

The porch light snapped on in front of Carradine's house with heart-stopping suddenness, flooding the driveway and the lawn with harsh yellow light. Carradine spun on his heel as the door opened.

Margo's voice cut like a buzz saw across the night.

"Who's that with you, Frank? Who's out there?"

33.

"I want to know why."

Carrie glared pugnaciously across the breakfast table, her fork pointed at Hanlon's chest. He reached for her hand but she withdrew it quickly.

"D'you want to know because you're concerned or because you're curious?"

She straightened in her chair. He could see the frost forming around her eyes. "Don't patronize me, Sam. I want to know, period."

"He's in trouble."

"Oh." That threw her. She lowered the fork to her plate. "Serious?"

"I dunno. He won't tell me. But I'd guess it's pretty damn serious. Well?"

"Well, what?"

"Will you help me help him? Without asking questions?"

Carrie stirred her congealing scrambled eggs. "I'm not sure. Not because I don't want to help Frank," she added quickly. "I just don't want things going bad here, for us and Bobby, if we help him."

"It won't affect us."

"You can't be sure of that. And what about Margo and Dan?"

"They'll stay here."

Carrie studied her plate for several minutes. When she looked up again he knew she had made her decision.

"What do I have to do?"

Hanlon reached inside his jacket and took out a folded paper. Carrie opened it and looked at the name, the address, the details of flight number, times of departure and arrival. "So?"

"I made the calls from the office early this morning. It's all fixed. I want you to drive out onto Route 3 one hour from now. You stop the car two hundred yards this side of the Brandling turn. Frank will be waiting in that belt of trees. You drive him to Boston. He'll leave you in town, get a cab, and go to the airport."

"What about luggage?" she asked matter-of-factly.

"It's in the trunk of the car."

"*Your* car?"

"That's right."

"And then what?"

Hanlon was growing irritable. "Look, the fewer people who know what happens. . . ."

"All right then," she said placidly, folding her arms. "No information—no cooperation."

He sighed loudly. "You win. He'll be joining a club charter to Malaga."

Carrie was seriously concerned now. "And you think he'll be allowed to fly away without anyone putting the arm on him? I mean, if he *is* in trouble, maybe it's police trouble."

Hanlon reached for her hand again and this time he caught it. He leaned over the table and kissed the tips of her fingers. "Does it matter? Would it change your mind about helping him?"

She smiled at him, softly, enticingly. "I guess not."

"Good. This club charter is the best chance he's got. There're three hundred and thirty-two passengers on that plane, all bound for the same place for the same reason. They call themselves the Knights of Santa Christobal. All I know is they're Spain-freaks. Some kind of historical-religious group. They go over there all the time. In a group that big there isn't going to be too much poking around by Immigration. I'm counting on that."

She thought for a moment.

"What does he do when he gets there?"

"That's up to him."

She was silent again. Then, slowly, "Does this have anything to do with . . . the others?"

Hanlon tightened his grip on her fingers. "I don't know that either, baby. All I know for certain is he's in trouble, and we're the only people who can help him right now."

She pulled his hand across the table and kissed the tips of his fingers, gently, one by one.

"Okay, mastermind. Whatever you say."

Whatever I say. Hanlon washed the phrase around his brain and waited for it to permeate the cells and convince him, too. Carrie got up and cleared plates and forks and knives and he envied her her simple faith in his solutions. If Hanlon says it's okay, it's okay.

All right—recap. And this time make it good. In one hour it'll be too late for second thoughts and frail intuitions.

"You want more coffee?"

133

He heard her the third time and grunted. She eyed him speculatively, thought about starting in on the whole thing again, changed her mind, and moved away. Sam Hanlon had checked out again. Samuel Reeves Hanlon was in the chair.

What was he doing? Simple—he was going ape. He was letting himself believe that, contrary to Langley's Law, Frank Carradine was a reluctant spy, a manipulated innocent or a 100 percent turncoat who wanted out. So he was giving him out.

Not good enough. Try again.

He felt Carrie's fingers on his arm and glanced up at her. She said, "It *is* something to do with Jack and Marv and Doug, isn't it? You think Frank's next, don't you?"

Out of the mouths of babes!

He shook his head and pretended a grin—a superior grin. "Bullshit," he said. He strained up and kissed her cheek.

Of course, she was right. They wanted Frank dead and he had no intention of letting it happen. Now all he had to do was prove he was right.

34.

Leitch lowered himself into the deep chair across from Hanlon's desk. He had given no hint on the telephone that he had cause to regret their last meeting. He was polite, relaxed, and brimming with plastic good will.

He reached down and scratched the throat hairs of the black-and-orange Doberman squatting at his side. The animal's tail beat a tattoo of pleasure on the carpeted floor.

"I figure you've got an apology coming to you, sir," he said lightly. "You had me on the ropes the other night. I should've known better. I hope you can overlook that."

Hanlon furtively checked his wrist watch. Eleven twenty-six.

Carrie should be within a half-hour of the Boston city limits. The plane was scheduled to take off at one-fifteen.

"I was out of step, Merrit. I wouldn't like that to get back to Langley. You want to shake on it?"

Leitch turned cold eyes on him. "Sure," he said. He made no attempt to hold out his hand.

Hanlon plastered what he hoped was a friendly grin across his face. "We should be working together, you and I. It's no fault of yours we're not. Okay. I intend to remedy that. This time of the morning I usually go over the tapes. I thought you ought to sit in on it."

Leitch shifted in his chair. His expression of youthful enthusiasm had undergone a subtle metamorphosis as Hanlon spoke. There were flashes of open suspicion in his eyes: uncertainty. "That's fine, sir," he said guardedly. "But is it strictly necessary? I'd feel safer if I was sitting on Carradine's tail."

"You can pick up Carradine on that telescope if you want, if it'll make you feel any better." Hanlon waved to one of the instruments. "He'll be in his office now."

Leitch rose from the chair and walked to the window. The dog rose to follow. Leitch spat Latin and the dog froze.

"I don't see Carradine," Leitch said, raising his head from the eyepiece. "Just the building."

Hanlon nodded. "Take a look in the parking lot. See his car there?"

Leitch obeyed, then straightened. "You know your people well, sir."

But he didn't return to the chair. He looked around the room as though he were seeing the penthouse for the first time, then his eyes lit on the dog and finally transferred to Hanlon and locked on. "Suppose, just suppose, Carradine decided to use another car?"

Hanlon felt his pulse beating like a gong in his temple.

"Suppose he had some reason to move on foot. Suppose he isn't in there. Suppose he's . . . taken a ride?"

135

Hanlon followed Leitch's gaze down to his own hands. He had picked up a long, slim, silver letter opener. His fingers were turning it, end over end in rapid, nervous arcs. Hanlon dropped the knife and with it went his self-possession.

"Oh, come on, Merrit. You're just work-hungry. What d'you say we have a cup of coffee down in the Center then walk across to Carradine's together? I could introduce you."

Overdone. *Overdone!*

Leitch shook his head firmly. "No thanks. I think I'd rather be out on the street. I don't want to take too much for granted, sir."

He snapped his fingers. The Doberman rose, growling.

35.

Aboard the plane, thinking.

There hadn't been enough time, nothing like enough. All the years he had spent living with the thought that it might happen, lying awake wondering what he would do, trying to prepare for the knock on the door, the explanations to Margo who wouldn't see it as anything but an attempt to disrupt her life, trying to explain to Daniel. He had worked out the scenario years ago; how he wouldn't argue, wouldn't run, wouldn't duck the inevitable, wouldn't hit back with a last, futile gesture.

It had all been worked out. Now, when the moment had come, it was nothing like that. A snatched shirt, a spare suit, a toothbrush and shaving kit thrown into a suitcase.

After all that, there had been no time to say or do anything.

He leaned forward in his seat and looked down at the gray-green of the Atlantic, cold as flecked marble. To stay would have been madness. As long as he was moving it drew them away from Daniel and Margo. At least he owed them that.

He walked to the toilets, washed his hands and walked back,

letting his eyes take in as many faces as he could, moving as slowly as he dared. What was he looking for? A snap-brim fedora? A trench coat and dark glasses? He swallowed the miniature of whiskey and tried to put his mind in order.

There wasn't much to play with. Three people had died and they—the murderers—had tried to kill him, too. He never thought it would have been done like that. An attempt to frighten him; yes, that was part of established pattern. But not this. Softening him up by executing the others. Nothing as savage as that. Doug Cater, Jack Shawn, Marvin Fish. Even Hanlon obviously accepted the idea that they had died because of him—the common denominator. If they were playing the game that rough, there were no bargains to be struck. Still, he had submerged himself for twenty years in America. He could do the same in Spain. Then, maybe, they would grow tired—forget. Maybe.

A white eiderdown of cloud scudded beneath the window, breaking the sea into a jigsaw. Carradine slipped on the headphones, closed his eyes, and pretended to listen.

Curious, the way Hanlon had seemed to take so much for granted. What did he know? There always had been that little bit of mystery about Sam. He was too controlled.

Peggy Lee serenaded him into a fitful sleep.

36.

From: Aleksander Rostov, First Secretary of the Central Committee
To: Stefan Andreyev, KGB Chairman

TIMED 1300 HOURS.

I have been asked by the American President to allow my Intelligence forces to cooperate with the Americans in the pursuit of the man Carradine. I have agreed. I shall expect your recommendations on a course of action on my desk within the next two hours.

From: Stefan Andreyev, KGB Chairman
To: Aleksander Rostov, First Secretary of the Central Committee

TIMED 1450 HOURS.

It is with regret that I do not enclose recommendations for KGB cooperation with the American Intelligence Forces. I do, however, strongly recommend that we *ignore* their request. Accepting the need to apprehend Carradine, we cannot allow ourselves to destroy the delicate network that we have created in Europe over the past decade. Many lives are at stake if we reveal the names and locations of our agents abroad. The case of Carradine can, I believe, be resolved by our own agents working independently and I urgently request—as I have before—a meeting whereby we may discuss this.

From: Aleksander Rostov, First Secretary of the Central Committee
To: Dmitri Orlov, Director, First Directorate, KGB

TIMED 1530 HOURS.

I have been asked by the American President to allow my Intelligence forces to cooperate with the Americans in the pursuit of the man Carradine. I have agreed. I shall expect your recommendations on a course of action on my desk within the next hour.

From: Dmitri Orlov, Director, First Directorate, KGB
To: Aleksander Rostov, First Secretary of the Central Committee

TIMED 1615 HOURS.

I have been formulating a contingency plan which would involve the alerting of agents in key European cities, in anticipation of your request. I am confident that, within twelve hours of their activation, a satisfactory conclusion can be reached. An approach can be made within hours of your orders and selected men can negotiate in the strictest secrecy with representatives of the CIA.

37.

Carradine checked into a heat-stained pension off Malaga's Plaza José Antonio. It was a cramped, poorly lit structure with a peeling façade and a neurotic red-and-green neon sign that flashed its name in crackling spasms across the gloom of a cobbled cul-de-sac. Inside, the lobby was a brooding mélange of chocolate brown and tobacco yellow. It was clearly not well patronized. In Malaga, in high summer, that was a crushing condemnation.

He ordered a bottle of wine sent to his room and tried to sleep, but it was an idle hope; he knew his mind had no intention of allowing itself to be switched off. Guilt was an emetic; it plunged a drillhead deep into the subconscious and released black crude under pressure. He smoked a string of loosely packed Spanish cigarillos and composed quiet, rational explanations for Life's crushing inequalities. After an hour, the reflected splutterings of the neon sign outside gave rhythm to his thoughts and the exercise became an imaginary conversation with Margo. He was on the defensive, of course, and a loser from the start. Why had he run away? Why had he implicated her and Daniel? What would happen to them if they were followed? What was their future, if any? How would they live? Survive!

It was too much. He switched on the single lamp by his bed, found a sheaf of onionskin, and began to write. It became another kind of explanation: an exposition, a release. He set it down, all of it, so that Daniel would know one day that the reasons, at least, were valid. If things ended as he feared they would, then maybe someone would find the sheets and pass them on to the police or the security people and ask questions. Hope springs eternal! Nobody cared and they would care less if he died.

He worked through the night, heedless of time, and when he finished at last the sky was baby-blue and gold and pink; the street below bustled with life. He rolled the papers into a tube and stuffed them into the lining of his suitcase. He washed and shaved, changed into slacks and a short-sleeved shirt, and walked into the plaza.

The day had to be killed somehow and he attempted to set the pace for it by lingering over a breakfast coffee at a sidewalk café. It was a mistake. He found that a small cup of dusty Spanish brew could be consumed in three minutes, no more. He ordered a fourth, contemplated it, and admitted defeat. He had expended eleven minutes precisely. He had twelve hours more to dispose of.

Safety in numbers, he decided, was not only a sound credo but potentially time-consuming. People could be watched, observed, examined—and provide valuable cover. He found crowds of them in the Calle de Grande; mingled, window-shopped. Shops proved beautifully wasteful, as did churches, museums, monuments to the civil war, and apartment blocks. Between the Palacio Obispal and the gothic façade of the Sagrario church on the Calle de Molina Larios, he frittered away a record two hours and fifty-three minutes. At that point, lunch presented itself as a timely break and he devoted more than an hour to selecting a suitable venue. He patrolled the pavements, wrinkling his nose speculatively at the bouquets of tomato, garlic, and onion in the birth pangs of *gazpacho*, at the pungent odors of *Chanquete fritos* hanging like escaping gas in the open doorways, where baby squids sizzled invitingly in their pans. He dismissed all but three, then walked around them again to find the most crowded. Three hours.

When he had given Carrie Hanlon the tickets for Margo and Dan, he had spelled out the program exactly. The early plane from Boston to Madrid. The shuttle from Madrid to Malaga. Ten hours in all. They would arrive about seven in the evening. In case—just in case—someone somewhere decided to follow, he would meet them at the Hertz office in town, not at the airport. Too public out there. If they were being followed, he would melt away. If not, he would rent a car and drive them up the coast to the villa at Fuengirola.

Carradine strolled at three forty-five to the Paseo del Parque. In the space of six hundred meters it contained more than a thousand varieties of trees and plants. He counted them.

At seven he posted himself across from the Hertz office. At nine he phoned the airport. The flight was in. No Carradines aboard. He returned to the pension, packed and phoned the Hertz office. A red Simca was delivered to the door.

It was nearly midnight when he drove into Fuengirola on the long stretch of road that paralleled the beach, but the town, huddled at the far end, like a victim of a shipwreck, was ablaze with neon and shaking to the beat of a dozen amplified tape decks. In the cantinas and bars, unnaturally bronzed Europeans nursed unnaturally cheap *vino tinto* and joined in tuneless choruses of American pop tunes. Hundreds more promenaded in the narrow main street, postponing sleep until the last moment.

The night was cool, refreshed by a soft Mediterranean breeze, but the sweat began to trickle from his temples and became a trembling pearl beneath his chin. It was a long way from the cutting Atlantic crispness of Teague's Landing.

Beyond the town he turned off the coast road and pushed the protesting Simca up a sloping dirt path. Fresh tire marks stretched way ahead of him in the dancing headlights. It had to be Margo and Daniel. A taxi from the airport, probably. For the first time he began to feel the tension slipping away. The knot of muscle at the back of his neck began to unwind, releasing its hammerlock on the nerves running up to his brain. It was all working out just as Sam said it would. Margo would be difficult at first—tired, argumentative—but tomorrow they might even begin to treat the whole thing as a holiday. To start with, anyway. A day or two in Granada or Seville. A trip along the coast to Alicante. Why not?

The villa stood at the summit of a sloping headland that ran down to a beach, its outline discreetly masked by palms, sub-tropical plants, and a six-foot-high ornamental wall.

A tall pair of wrought-iron gates were wide open and tied back to securing posts. Dogs—or kids—had got in among the shrubs and, even by moonlight, the garden looked as if an entire football team had been training on it. The shutters over the windows were closed but the front door was half-open.

Carradine set down his suitcase in the small paneled hall-way. He nudged open a door. He stopped breathing. There was a huge jagged hole where the shuttered windows had been, as if a heavy rock had been thrown through from the inside.

There was a bed, its metal frame bent, its springs distorted, leaning against a wall which had been daubed with—red paint? Nothing in the room was whole. Drawers lay in splinters; a bedside table had been axed to matchwood; light fixtures hung from the ceiling and walls like drawn sinews.

He dared not breathe, trembling at the thought of making a sound. He turned and tiptoed silently into the hallway. Another door. Gently! The man stood with the sledge hammer frozen at the peak of its swing, paralyzed. They stared at each other stupidly. The hammer sank in slow motion to rest on the fellow's shoulder. He tore his eyes away from Carradine and stared at the floor where tiles lay shattered into crazy patterns.

He came to his senses at last, dropped the hammer, and dived for the window. His head and arms crashed through glass and wooden shutters and he landed headfirst in the garden.

Carradine stood uncertainly for a second then swung after him over the low window sill. The man raced across a bed of flowers yelling in a strange, yawning croak. A voice answered from behind the villa.

Carradine's quarry sprinted through the double gates, turned right, and ran to a car parked further on around the bend in the road. Carradine crashed into a heavy wooden garden bench, jumped up on it, and, using it as a springboard, launched himself at the runner. They collapsed in a hydrangea bush, the man —thin but strong—clawing at Carradine's face and kicking wildly.

Carradine managed to hook a leg around his knees and, using all his strength, twisted the man's head until his face was pressed into the soft soil.

"That's enough!"

The newcomer stood, feet braced, knife held lightly. It was a beautiful Moorish blade shaped like a short scimitar. He held it as if he were preparing to shave.

Carradine rolled away from his captive and lay back on his elbows, the bloodlust replaced by instant nausea. The man with the knife prodded his companion with a foot. He picked himself up, snuffling and snorting. The knifeman waved him to the car with a twitch of the blade. Carradine recognized the signs. So that was why the man hadn't heard him enter the house. He was deaf, of course.

He pointed and raised a hand to one ear. "*Sordo?*"

The knifeman nodded and waved the weapon.

"*Y usted sera sordo, Mr. Karradin.*" His fingers moved from ear to lips, to eyes. "Deaf, dumb, blind. You comprehend?"

"I think so."

"Be sure so, Mr. Karradin. You see nobody, hear nobody, say nothing. It would be easy for me to make sure of that." He moved the knife in a small circle. "But I was not asked."

He backed away, reached the car, and slipped behind the wheel. He rolled down the window.

"*Buen suerte, amigo,*" he said.

Carradine levered himself upright and limped back to the house. They had known his name. That could only mean one thing. He stumbled from room to wrecked room. Margo and Daniel would have one suitcase each, at least. Where? Unless they'd been taken out to the car.

And food. Margo would have bought food, if only as a precaution. He jolted to a halt in the door of the kitchen.

Knife.

He clutched his throat as the muscles contracted.

Hammer.

Knife.

The neat white room ran red with blood—walls, furniture, floor. In the struggle it had even spattered the ceiling. In the sink it was coagulated in a solid pool around a mound of butchered flesh as big as a human torso.

He fainted.

"Will the señor be staying long?"

"Tonight. No more."

"Certainly, señor. One night. Would you sign here? Thank you. Is there anything else?"

"No, nothing. Yes. A telephone."

"Of course, señor, over here."

"No, in my room. Can I send a cable by telephone?"

"Naturally, señor. The señor can ask the girl at the switchboard and she will do all you require. It will be added to your bill in the morning."

"Thank you."

"José. Manuel José Juarez. José, señor."

"José. If anyone asks for me by name, anyone at all, either on the telephone or here at reception, you have no guest called Carradine."

"Of course, señor. No one will disturb you unless you wish them to."

"Good. Thank you. I'm very tired."

"The señor looks tired."

Carradine stared bleakly at the young man and slid a 500-peseta note across the counter.

"That's for being observant, José."

"Señor."

In his room, Carradine sat on the edge of the bed and began to shake. He had no idea how he had made the journey from the villa to the hotel on the beach road. At two in the morning, the night clerk was not easily persuaded to give him a bed. The scenes at the villa came trickling back like voices in an operating room heard through anesthetic.

He picked up the phone by the bed. "I want to send a cable to the United States of America," he told the girl.

There was only one man who could help him now.

38.

If Lamb had been on ice he would have been performing figure eights. As it was, the confines of Leitch's room at the Coach House limited him to crossing and recrossing the floor from corner to corner. He paused in the center of the room.

"I'd like to tell you exactly what I intend doing with you—but I can't. That's going to be the Controller's pleasure. By Christ, if I could throw away the rule book for thirty minutes, I'd. . . ."

Words deserted him and his blood pressure responded accordingly. He walked to the window and looked out, hands clasped tightly behind him, damming the flood. He said to the window, "I wanted to make something clear to you when you came here, but it couldn't be said. Now it can." He swung around. "I don't like this. I don't like you. There's something missing in what you pass off for a personality. You *enjoy* it. Well, you got it all fouled up, sonny."

145

Leitch sat by the door and met Lamb's fury equably. He said quietly, "Mr. Hanlon also insisted on calling me "sonny." I guess it's something to do with the generation gap, sir."

"Don't smart-ass me!"

"I was just making an observation, sir. You and Mr. Hanlon have the same kind of credentials."

Lamb pulled himself together with an effort. Any Career Trainee at the Broyhill Building at Arlington would have reacted more coolly to this kind of baiting.

He forced a wolfish smile. "Clever boy. You lose your man and the first thing you look for is someone to blame. Well, sonny, it won't work. You're nailed and you'll stay nailed if I have to haul you in front of a court of inquiry myself."

Leitch folded one leg carefully over the other. "I'm not blaming anyone, sir. You can only attach blame to a colleague who makes a mistake. Mr. Hanlon isn't a colleague and he didn't make a mistake."

"Come again?"

Leitch raised the palms of his hands upward. "As I told you on the phone yesterday, sir, Carradine wasn't in his office. He hadn't been seen since the previous evening. Mr. Hanlon made a very poor attempt to conceal that fact from me. It was obviously quite deliberate because Mr. Hanlon had already made sure Carradine wasn't around."

"Are you sure of that?"

Leitch falsified a smile. "I haven't got it on tape, if that's what you mean. I don't have a signed confession. But it was Hanlon all right."

Lamb turned back to the window and thought dully: you're right, you little slob. You're dead right. Everything was in the open now. The word was out world-wide on Carradine: get him and wrap him up tight. According to George Strauss back at Langley, it was more than just a CIA exercise now. There were other interests involved, too sensitive to mention. Lions were lying down with lambs. The dove was sharing the eagle's nest.

He whirled back into the room and pointed an accusing finger at Leitch. "Come the time, you can put it down in writing
and they'll use it as evidence. Right now, you're out of the ball
game."

Leitch stretched in the chair to get a hand into his raincoat.
He withdrew a long white envelope with the TWA crest across
its front. Inside was a travel wallet.

He drew out two ticket booklets like a magician performing
a card trick. Lamb strode across the floor and snatched them
from his hand. The tickets were made out in the names of
Margo Carradine and Daniel Carradine. The destination was
Malaga, Spain. The date: today. Take-off: eight forty-five.

"Where did you get these?"

Leitch's innocence was indelible. "I called you, if you remem-
ber, sir, yesterday as soon as I discovered Carradine wasn't in
his office. You told me to wait for you here." He shrugged.
"That seemed pointless. You couldn't get up here till today.
That left me time to check around. Hanlon didn't leave the
Center. I called on Mrs. Hanlon, just to be sure. A neighbor
said she'd taken off in the car at about ten in the morning.
Lot of women taking off in cars around here lately. I thought
I'd better hang around and check her in, at least."

Lamb flopped into a chair. "Go on."

"She drove back to the house at three twenty-five. I waited
a couple of minutes, then I went in. She was—er—taking a
shower upstairs. Her bag was on a table in the living room.
That's where I found the envelope. I'd say she drove Carradine
to Boston to get the Madrid flight. That's an hour and fifteen
minutes each way. She was away five and a half hours."

Lamb studied the tickets again, keeping his face averted from
Leitch's. Hanlon, you stupid, pig-ignorant, son of a bitch!

"Of course, I accept your accusation, sir," Leitch prodded
gently. "I disobeyed your orders. I guess I'll have to pay for
that. But, with respect, we've drawn a few conclusions we
couldn't have before. I don't think there's much doubt where

147

Carradine is, do you? And we also know Hanlon's working with
Kingfish. He's been turned. That's a pretty fair profit for one
day."

He waited in vain for a reaction, then went on: "As I see it,
we have two choices. You let me take Hanlon out—another accident—or. . . ."

Lamb snapped, "No! The Controller has orders from upstairs. A long way upstairs. No more blood."

Leitch dipped his head in a little bow of acquiescence. "I
think that's intelligent reasoning, sir. My alternative is that we
get those tickets back into Mrs. Hanlon's hands. I can jam them
down behind a seat in the car or put them in the glove compartment; she'll never know the difference. My guess is Hanlon
will hear from Carradine any time now. If we played it right,
we could make things hot enough for Carradine to get really
upset. My guess is, if he gets very hung up, he'll ask Hanlon to
help him out. It's only a guess, but I think it'll work."

"What about Carradine's wife? His kid?"

"Do we care? If they follow him, we follow them. Either way
we'll get *him*. Hanlon, too. And the big bonus is: we get them
both a long way from home. No more blood on the doorstep,
just like you said."

Lamb slid his briefcase from a table and made notes on a
blue-lined notepad. Then he held the tickets and the wallet out
to Leitch. The youngster eased himself gracefully from the chair
and took them.

"What do I do now, sir?"

Lamb didn't want to look him in the face. He busied himself
with the notepad. "Get those back now," he snapped. "Don't
ask me how. After twenty-four hours, Hanlon isn't going to believe she just lost them. Then keep yourself out of my sight for
the rest of the night."

Leitch retreated to the door, turned the handle, and paused.
"D'you mind if I ask you a question?"

"Well?"

148

"I'd say you're taking it hard—the way Hanlon turned out, I mean. Is that . . . *personal*, sir?"

Lamb's head snapped up, his eyes bulging.

"Get out of here you *punk!* GET OUT!"

39.

Hanlon spent an hour on the telephone in the bedroom after he received Carradine's cable. They were transatlantic calls and he kept them short and vague. In an ideal intelligence situation, his phone would by now have been monitored, but he knew bug technology well enough to be certain that Lamb had not yet got around to it. He had a perfect ear for interceptions.

When he'd completed his calls he went down to tell Carrie she'd married a liar.

There was no way of avoiding that now. Lamb may have been slow in running a tap on his phone, but he was smart enough to make sure he was informed of any overseas cables Hanlon received. And Carradine's cable had put him directly behind the eight ball.

"Your deal unavailable stop Storage area destroyed stop Rebasing anticipation *vendimia* as you advised stop Urgently need advice and assistance stop The boys are clipping my wings—Daniels."

The Ancient Mariner on the command deck of the Forrestal! Lamb wouldn't have to bother Langley Codes and Ciphers to interpret that one. If this was the code Kingfish used, they were still carving memos on tablets of stone.

Deal unavailable—Carradine couldn't use the villa.

Storage area destroyed—Just that, or "destroyed" as a viable safehouse? No way of knowing.

Rebasing anticipation *vendimia*—Going to Jerez, the sherry

149

capital of Spain. The fall-back area they had agreed on. The sale of the grape harvest (the *vendimia*) was celebrated in September.

The boys—He would use one of the boys' names (presumably Roberts since he'd signed himself "Daniels").

Clipping my wings—The phrase Hanlon had given him for the Hotel Los Cisnes where a clipped-wing swan was in permanent residence in an ornamental pool in the courtyard.

He couldn't have made his intentions universally clearer if he'd spelled them out in sky-writing.

Carrie was lying down on the couch, a sleeping mask over her eyes. She said, "Is that you, Sam?" when he opened the door but made no attempt to get up. They hadn't talked much since the blowup over the tickets last night. His fault. He'd lost his temper when she told him Frank had insisted on buying tickets to Malaga for Margo and Daniel, and he'd really flipped when she found they were no longer in her bag. They'd searched high and low. Everywhere. And then, this evening, a whole day later, she'd found them where he had already searched. She'd somehow allowed them to slip down the back of the driver's seat of the car.

Lamb! Playing with him—catch-as-catch-can.

He perched on the lounge chair beside her and ran his fingers across her brow. She had a temperature. "Look, I'm sorry about last night," he said clumsily. "I was. . . ."

"Brutal," she retorted from behind her mask. "You were scared, too, I could see that. You were scared and you had to take it out on someone. You've never done that before."

"There's plenty I've never done before, Carrie. A lot to be sorry for."

She pushed the mask up on to her hair and blinked to bring his face into focus. "What is it, Sam? For God's sake, tell me."

He got to his feet and turned away into the room. In a glass-fronted case on the wall in front of him, his sporting guns gleamed dully in their summer hibernation suits of oil.

He said huskily, "Are we okay—you and me?"

She sat up, her face pale, the bruised circles of pain and sleep-lessness around her eyes yellow-brown, disfiguring.

"What d'you mean?" Alarm bells.

He planted himself in front of the gun case, concentrating on the oldest weapon in his collection—a pump-action Winchester. "There's something you have to know. You're not going to like it. When I've told you, I'll be leaving . . ."

"Leaving?"

He turned to her. She sat stock-still in momentary shock as though movement of any kind would confirm the worst. He forced his eyes back to the guns. "I love you. Just remember that, will you? I love you in ways I can't put into words. You've given me more than any man has a right to expect in fifteen lifetimes. That's what. . . ."

"Sam!" Her eyes flooded with tears; her hands were clasped in front of her in an attitude of prayer. He covered the distance between them in three strides and pulled her to her feet and crushed his arms about her.

"Oh, my God, Sam. Oh, my God."

He held her, containing her terror, caressing her hair, kissing her tear-stained cheek softly, repeatedly. When the sobbing sub-sided, he said, "Now, I want you to listen carefully."

"Is it . . . someone else?"

He couldn't help himself. He choked with helpless laughter and she stiffened in his arms. He held her closer and whispered in her ear. "There isn't, never was, never will be, *someone else.* Boy, you're all woman, Mrs. Hanlon; I'll give you that. I offer to bare my soul and—bingo—it has to be a secret love life. Is that the *only* sin in the world?"

She breathed hotly on his chest.

"That's *not* what you're trying to tell me?"

"No, goddamnit, it isn't!"

She raised her face to his and her smile won total victory over tears, swollen eyes, and smudged makeup.

"Then it doesn't matter." She buried her face on his chest again. A wave of idiot laughter started up from his diaphragm and exploded in his chest, but he imprisoned it there. My wife doesn't understand me!

"Well, I'm sorry to disappoint you. I don't have a mistress to my name. But there's something else . . ."

She snuggled closer. "It doesn't matter. I don't care. You don't have to tell me anything. Period."

He pushed her away and sat her on the couch. He walked back to the gun case then turned and half-sat on its protruding ledge. "I'm not the guy you married, baby. I'm not . . ."

She opened her mouth, but he waved her into silence.

"I came here, to Teague's Landing, because I was sent here. I was under orders and I'm still under orders. Everything I've done since we first met—the Center, my business interests, my contacts, even our social life here—was phony. I've been. . . ."

"You're going to tell me you work for the Government, right?"

He stopped, shocked.

"What d'you know about that?"

She was relaxed, happy, reassured. "Did you really believe you could marry someone who loves you as much as I do and keep her out of reach?" She nodded as if in answer to her own question. "Yes . . . you would. Little boy playing big boy's games. You have the little boy's philosophy, too. Girls wouldn't *understand*. Poor little Carrie. Innocent child, married the man without knowing a thing about him. Believed in him. Loved him. And he done her wrong."

She eyed him softly, transmitting love, mother to child. "You don't have to tell me. There were enough clues at the beginning. Remember Boston? Those men you sent to bring me home? The trips you *had* to make. And I found your revolver, too."

"So why the hell didn't you say something?"

"You mean be as open and honest as you?" She was still smiling and it was genuine. No malice.

152

He shook his head slowly, bewildered but relieved. "Oh boy, you must have thought I was a real prize . . ."

"Ssssshhh." She put her fingertip to her lips.

He crossed the room, sat beside her, and pulled her head onto his shoulder. Her hair smelled of jasmine.

"All right, for the record," he said quietly. "You and Bobs are apart from all this. Get that straight. The rest . . . I'm not proud of the rest. I was in OSS during the war. I did fieldwork for the CIA afterward in Europe. I got hurt. My shoulder. . . ."

She raised her head. "It's all right though, isn't it?"

"Sure. It's okay. But it got me out of the mainstream and I was assigned here. Surveillance. A known Russian group—deep-cover spies—were planted in 1963. Here, at the Landing. My job was to watch them. I needed a cover. You weren't part of it, by the way. You were a bonus."

"And these spies . . . ?"

He drew in a sharp breath and spat out the names:

"Carradine, Shawn, Fish, and Cater."

He felt her muscles contracting under his arm. Then she relaxed.

"Were they . . . killed? Were those accidents just . . ."

"I don't know, baby. I honestly don't know."

"But it wasn't . . . you."

The thought took his breath away. "No! It *wasn't* me!"

She nodded, her hair sliding like silk across his shoulder. "That's all that matters." She sat bolt upright. "I've just thought—what about Helen and Grace? And what about Margo and Daniel? Oh, Sam, they don't know, any of them. Do they? Do they have to be told? I mean it's bad enough they're alone. Where are they? D'you think we could . . . ?"

He slid his hand under the fall of her hair and massaged her slim neck. "I think you should just act naturally, whatever happens, baby. If you hear from any of them, be yourself. But don't go looking for trouble."

"Because that's your job. Are you going after Frank?" She

ran a hand down his cheek. "God, Sam, I can't grasp it, I *can't*. Is that really his name?" She shuddered. "It's creepy. I can't think of him except as Frank. Are you sure he's . . .?"

She stopped and a new realization transfused her face. "Why did you let him go? If Fr—, if he's a spy, why did you . . .?"

Hanlon got up and paced across to the gun case. "I don't know why. He was my responsibility. I ducked it. I can't explain. I'll pay for it. Unless . . ."

"Unless you go find him."

"Unless I go find him."

"When?"

"Tomorrow. Eight forty-five from Boston."

The stairs creaked and Bobby called, "Mom. Hey, mom!"

Carrie's face froze. She shook her head warningly. "In here, darling."

Bobby came through into the room in his pajamas and stopped. Like a young animal sensing danger, he flicked his head left and right, registered his mother's tear-stained face and the graven seriousness of his father. His natural tact took over quickly.

"Say, does anyone remember seeing Danny? I couldn't find him all day."

40.

The call came at one in the morning. The voice was low and urgent. "Remember the town with the blonde," instructed the caller. "Now take this down."

Hanlon grabbed for a pencil and switched on the bedside light.

"UONABBOJOO," said the voice. "That's all."

The line went dead. Hanlon stared at the letters. The town with the blonde. No, not the long-legged, big-busted variety, but short, stocky, and with a grip like a monkey wrench. Stefan.

For three unforgettable weeks he had played host to Hanlon and Alan Farrar when they moved from Italy into the Balkans. The town had been Ljubljana in Yugoslavia. He wrote it down

L J U B L J A N A

Under it, he wrote the numbers from one to nine: L being 1, J being 2, and so on.

UONABBOJOO

or, to put it another way,

3089440200 using the four O's as zeros.

He switched off the light before it woke Carrie, slipped out of bed, and pulled on a sweater and jeans. He tucked the scribbled note into a hip pocket and ran out of the house. The nearest pay phone was in the square. He dialed the number. If he was right in his guess, it was another phone booth. Alan Farrar came on before it rang a second time.

"Sam? I'll be quick. Sorry about the histrionics."

"For chrissakes, Alan, you don't have to do this," Hanlon protested. "You've done enough."

"Shit," said Farrar. "Even kids get Action Man to play with. These days I get nothing. Put it down to the male menopause. Now, listen. This evening I got the buzz from a guy along the corridor that your file is going to be moved."

"Moved?"

"From 'operational' to 'surveillance,' Sam. You know what that means."

"What?"

"You've been turned over, Sam. The other side of the fence. It's *you* they'll be watching now, Sam. They're laying your head on the block. It could get nasty from here on in."

"I know," Hanlon said mechanically.

"Good. Now get back to bed and think about it, Sam. You've got a couple of days at best before they move in. Anything else I can do, call me, but not too direct, huh?"

"Thanks, Al."

"Forget it. But not what I've said. Take care. Ciao, Sam."

"Ciao."

155

That was all he needed. If he'd had any doubts about getting the Boston flight in the morning, they had just been put to rest.

41.

The map said Ceuta was about an hour and three-quarters west at a steady speed of 50 kph. Frank Carradine checked the speedometer of the Simca; the needle was steady on forty-three.

Margo and Danny. Where were they? God forgive him if they were at this moment arriving at the villa. . . . He jammed his foot on the brake pedal and, from behind, an Opel sedan blared its anger and swerved to avoid a collision. Behind the Opel a string of vehicles eagerly joined in the horn symphony. Carradine withdrew his foot and stamped hard on the accelerator. The Simca coughed and spluttered and slowly picked up speed again.

No, it was no good. He couldn't go back. Face it, he didn't dare go back. That night . . . those men . . . the blood—there had to be a logical explanation. Who would harm a woman and child? And for what possible motive? He checked the column of cars behind him in the rear-view mirror, then looked back to the road as their headlights dazzled him. No, these people weren't interested in women and children. They were probably on his tail right now. Back there, behind a pair of quartz-halogen yellow lights.

An hour ago he'd driven off the road in Marbella and parked behind a vast palatial hotel to watch for suspiciously loitering cars, but there were far too many, all loitering and all suspicious in his eyes. He'd bought a drink at the bar by the underground pool and watched every face, but that just wasted time and confused him.

When he hit the road again a tail of traffic built up in his wake in minutes. As he drove through the almost unbroken string of tourist villa developments, he knew he dare not stop again. It was dark when he reached the wide road that snaked around the bay to the east of Gibraltar, and he could see the lights of cars bounding across the slabsides of the Rock.

Algeciras was a madhouse. Traffic converged on badly lit, suicidally signposted intersections, and Carradine crossed two sets of red lights before his eyes adjusted to the miniature Spanish traffic lights and their poor placement positions. No one seemed to care. Drivers swore at him automatically whether he drove within the law or not. He cringed close to the curb.

As he took a sharp right out of the town, a British Airways jet thundered up into the night from the Rock's airstrip, its three lights winking wickedly as it turned north for London's Heathrow.

At nine forty-five he reached Ceuta, his unshakable tail of traffic hooting him on as he crawled, terrified, through the narrow, broken streets of drunken, shabby little houses. The city thinned and finally disappeared, and one kilometer farther on he nearly mounted a triangular traffic island. Behind him horns brayed impatiently, and he swung right. Water gleamed left and right and ships' lights twinkled through the night mist.

He hit the toll road at last and the big motorway signs told him Jerez was just thirty kilometers away. He still had his convoy. At ten-thirty, the Simca bounced over the potholes of the town's mean southern approach road, and he was engulfed by life, light and noise. The street outside the Hotel Los Cisnes was jammed with shoppers and through them weaved Japanese motorcycles in whining, snarling squadrons. He took a chance and turned right at an intersection and right again and ended up in the blessed peace of a tiny square with a central garden. He parked the Simca outside a bar, removed his suitcase, and set off in search of the hotel.

As he walked away, the Opel glided into the square and stopped. Frank Carradine was too tired to think of looking back.

He was received at the reception desk with open hostility. Latecomers, the clerk's manner suggested, could not by any measure be respectable. Five hundred pesetas convinced him of his error. In his room overlooking the courtyard, Carradine unpacked, changed into a dark suit, and bought a drink at the bar. The faces meant nothing to him, but the number of American accents worried him till he remembered the American base at Rota, then he relaxed. Jerez was an obvious water hole for base personnel on furlough and, besides, at this time of year United States tourist traffic was high.

The restaurant was full but the maître suggested he come back in an hour. He wandered across the lounge and through the open glass doors into the courtyard. For an instant, he forgot everything. The hotel was three stories high, the second housing the spacious rear terraces of the luxury suites. Above him and to his right, the flower-filled balconies rose clifflike to the dimmed stars. To the left was a long white wall, broken halfway by steps that led to a flower-decked arbor. Built into the wall was a crude white arch where a claustrophobic little tunnel ran down to a bar and the square in which he'd parked the Simca.

In front of him, rising like a genie from the paving stones, a giant magnolia, heavy with virgin white blossoms, reached for the velvet sky. Around it, their blooms burning like demon's eyes in the floodlighting, hibiscus grew. And over it all, quelling the scents of cooked food, sunburned brick, and the all-pervasive tang of sherry, floated the paradise musk of night-scented jasmine.

Carradine raised his nose to the air and followed the perfume beyond the magnolia, under the trailing hibiscus, to the far end of the courtyard. He stopped.

Under an arched wall lay an ornamental pool, perhaps six feet wide and ten yards long. At its center sat a swan, head imperiously high, eyes fixed on nothing. Carradine tiptoed slowly to the left of the pool. The bird ignored him.

He watched it hypnotically. The bird's wing feathers had

158

been clipped, and from time to time the graceful head turned to pluck at this lost freedom. It moved neither forward nor backward but held its position at dead center in the pool, soulless and deflowered. Carradine experienced a horror so great that he shivered involuntarily. What kind of human being could do that?

He became aware, quite suddenly, that he was no longer alone. Directly across the pool, a middle-aged man in a dinner jacket and black tie was also watching the swan. Their eyes met. The man ducked his head in Germanic greeting.

Frank Carradine's body would not move. He tried to throw off his terror with a word, a gesture in response, but nothing came. He couldn't take his eyes from the man's face. It was burned dark by the sun: handsome, aquiline. The hair was silver gray and swept off his forehead in a piratical swirl that belied his age.

The handsome face leaned forward, down, eyes on the imprisoned swan, and a hole appeared in the center of the bronzed forehead and grew ragged. A millisecond earlier, Carradine's nerves had leaped at the thunk of steel on wood as the bullet struck the bole of the magnolia tree and deflected.

The silver-haired man appeared to straighten, the expression of sympathy on his face still intact. Then life ebbed from every muscle and fiber of his body at once and he pitched forward into the pool.

The swan hissed with displeasure and backpaddled to the far end of its prison. Around the man's head the water clouded darkly.

A gust of laughter rose from the restaurant at the far end of the courtyard, and from somewhere a gypsy guitar strummed the prelude to a flamenco, but there was no movement under the floodlit trees. Carradine backed away. No, the man might be alive. He must make sure. It . . .

His back touched the high white wall. The arch. The tunnel to the square. He ran.

159

42.

Boston. London. Malaga.

Hanlon took the indirect flight and arrived in early evening to find the town sulking under a heavy rainstorm. The sky was the color of old pewter and the wind tasted of rock salt. Sheet lightning flashed an improvised *son et lumière* in green and white as he drove the hired Fiat down the coast road to Fuengirola. He made good time. The storm had driven traffic from the roads, and he reached the resort in a little over an hour. He approached the villa from the beach below. Wet sand oozed into his shoes and his eyes stung with the spray scratched by the wind from the tops of breaking waves. He bit off great lungfuls of air and swallowed deep. There were compensations in everything.

In spite of the persistent small voice that told him he was making a fool of himself, he felt good. Even the nagging pain in his shoulder seemed to be trying to remind him of things past, better forgotten. He ignored it, sucked in more air, and let his mind weave and bounce off the ropes as he prepared for the next round. It would have made sense to go directly to Jerez, but he had to know why Carradine had quit the villa.

He would have felt happier with the .38 in his armpit, but bringing a gun through the security checks at the airport would have been risky. Before leaving, he had taken from the desk in his den a small leather money pouch with a cord drawstring. It was still full of the heavy lead shot and three silver dollars (for luck) he had last used twenty-five years before. It now hung from a snapcatch on his belt, in his trouser pocket. It bulged firmly, reassuringly, against his thigh.

He kept off the regular path from the beach and was moving

through a small grove of orange trees when he saw the car. An old Volvo. Driver and one passenger. It halted in front of the villa gates and the occupants got out. The two men went in, came out with their arms full, returned again. They worked with quiet efficiency, packing the trunk and the inside of the car.

He moved closer, stooping low, dismissing emotion, keeping his mind detached. He wiped the rain from his palms, poised, then made the dash from the trees to the back of the villa. The men were struggling with a small portable refrigerator which they were trying to wedge into the trunk.

Hanlon leaned against the wall of the house and released the snapcatch at his waist. He eased the pouch from his pocket, wound the cord around his fist, and cupped the weight in his palm.

What was left of one of the shutters swung back quietly, and he slipped over the window sill into a bedroom. He could hear the voice of one of them. *"Una vez más,"* it said. Footsteps in the hallway. He pressed himself to the wall behind the door and unwound the cord until the pouch swung a foot from his fist. As the footsteps reached the door, Hanlon whirled the pouch in the air.

The man went down without a sound, his knuckles hitting the floor vertically as he jackknifed forward. There was a sound like cracking ice as his mouth hit a broken tile. Hanlon dragged him into a corner and turned his head to one side so that he wouldn't suffocate in his own blood.

He waited.

He needed a prisoner he could interrogate. He had to find out who had paid them to turn the villa over and why.

It wouldn't be that easy. The behavior of men in tight corners was dictated by the state of their nerves and their bowels. Quick to act, slow to think. But capitulation, whichever way you sliced it, was infinitely preferable to being crippled. Before he could swing the pouch again, the second man was in the room, knife outstretched. He held it pointing down, a fighter's grip, and made a move crabwise in front of Hanlon's body, gauging distance.

Hanlon half-turned to the wall, pressing his body against it in a curve of fear, legs bent in submission.

"Don't kill me!" he shouted.

The knifeman moved in. "*No puedo de jarte vivir, amigo,*" he breathed.

Hanlon bent his left leg high until his knee almost touched his chin, crouching even lower as the knife rose.

"Aaaaaaagh!" He screamed at the top of his voice. Hands braced against the wall, his body uncurled like a spring. His foot swung at piston speed, high and textbook straight, and took the knifeman squarely in the rib cage.

He slapped whitewash fastidiously from his hands and grimaced at the mess as the man pirouetted in agony in the middle of the room. Both arms cradled his broken chest, his eyes bulged with shock, and his mouth ballooned like a feeding fish. Then with a grating cough he sat down heavily on the floor.

"Right," said Hanlon in English. "Having got that settled we can do one of two things. Understand?"

The man moaned in anguish.

"Good. One, *Uno.* You can tell me what I want to know, in which case I'll call a doctor as soon as I've gone. Or *dos,* two, you don't and I call the undertaker. Undertaker?"

He pushed an exploratory foot under the sitting man's rib cage and won a scream of agony.

43.

Albert Manzoni.

Hanlon propped the injured Spaniard against a wall and

wiped his face. "Bite on this when it hurts," he said, folding the cloth into a pad. "The doctor will be here as soon as I get into town."

Albert Manzoni!

The knifeman had had enough suffering. No money in the world bought that much loyalty. He had been hired to wreck the place and no one had told him why. The money had been good, and he was told the contents of the villa could be regarded as a small bonus. All he was required to do was to frighten the expected visitor away. It had been his own idea to slaughter a goat, butcher it, and splash its blood around the floor and walls. The man they were told to expect was a Señor Karradin.

The señor who made it happen was Albert Manzoni.

Now that was really nostalgic.

Albert Manzoni was the Company's man in the south of Spain when Truman was still in the White House. Fat and failed, absurdly incompetent, he had been rooted in the least active area on Langley's map and allowed to vegetate. This mission must have been the first recognition the Company had made of his existence in twenty years. A measure of their desperation. How Manzoni had penetrated Intelligence no one claimed to know, but rumor had it that he came from a long line of Mafiosi who had done a deal with Domestic Operations. Strings had been pulled and Albert found himself working for the CIA. The story was apocryphal, but Hanlon was prepared to believe every word of it.

It was going to be a pleasure to meet Fat Albert again.

44.

There were forty-seven steps up to the offices of the Royola Shipping and Packaging Company behind a gate that burst its lock with suspicious ease. It was midnight and even at street level Hanlon could hear the whine of music from the top floor and a girl's high-pitched giggle.

He took the steps two at a time. If he guessed right, Manzoni would have been given only the barest information, enough to forge one link in a long chain, no more. If he guessed wrong, Fat Albert would be on the other side of that door with enough hardware to decimate a platoon.

He hammered on the door with his fist. "Manzoni! You in there? It's me, Hanlon."

The music stopped abruptly. The girl's giggle subsided.

"Albert Manzoni. For chrissakes, stop playing James Bond and open the door. I'm bushed."

Silence.

"Have it your way, slob. You'll enjoy the Alaska Station." Hanlon retreated three steps down and the door was flung open. A girl peered into the night, clutching a man's dressing gown around her shoulders.

"Mister? You there?" He brushed past her and walked into the room. Fat Albert peered around the bedroom door.

"What a lousy trick," Hanlon grinned, "even for you. Sending a girl out like that. What did you hope I'd do? Empty my gun into her?"

"Sam," Fat Albert advanced with open arms. "Sam Hanlon. I was just checking the street out back through the window here. Can't be too careful . . ."

"Cut it out, Albert. If you catch a cold you get somebody else to cough. I know it, you know it . . . maybe now she knows it."

The girl slumped irritably into a chair and sipped at a brandy balloon of gin.

Hanlon sniffed. "What's she on, grass?"

"A little," shrugged Fat Albert. "These days, what can you do? One has to move with the times."

"I suppose you know why I'm here."

164

"The villa business, huh? Sure. Well, everything's under control here."

"Does she speak English?" He turned to the girl. "Hey, bitch, you stink, know that? Like a whore. You sleep with your father, I bet."

The girl stared into space.

Manzoni put down his drink and sucked in his breath in a show of outrage. "See here, Hanlon, don't think you're goddamn God around here. You're in my territory. I don't . . ."

"Shut up, Albert, you give me stomach cramps. Now then, let's just keep it formal. Tell me about it."

He prodded Manzoni in the chest, took the joint from his lips, and flicked it at the wall where it exploded in a shower of sparks.

"Okay?"

"Of course, Sam, if you're here on business, I'll do everything in my power . . ."

"You have no power, Albert. Zilch. At the moment it all belongs to me. I have the power, for instance, to have you busted out of here quicker'n you can blink. If my report goes back to Langley on what happened at the villa, how you *lost* Carradine, how—like always—you didn't do the job yourself . . . well, Albert, you'll be lucky if they let you clear out the johns in Manila after this. Unless they decide they can live without you."

Fat Albert shuddered and swallowed a mouthful of Scotch. He had five chins. They fought for air as he lowered them onto his chest. "Hanlon, like I say, I'll do anything. The villa—well, I thought you wouldn't want to. . . .

"I would, Albert. Like treading on a fly." The girl wiggled her fingers in a comic wave.

"They didn't tell me it was important, Sam. I just thought it was some dumb trick to scare this guy off. I didn't know . . ."

"Did you know who Carradine was . . . is?" Casually.

165

"No. He was just a guy. What's he done to get you over here?"

"Don't get involved, Albert. Just help yourself out of the pit. Where is Carradine now?"

"Jerez, last I heard."

"What do you mean, heard?" Albert was having trouble focusing. "Christ, Manzoni, you really do want to get busted, don't you?"

"It's true, I swear it." He broke away, picked up a notebook from beside the telephone, and riffled the pages.

"Yeah, Jerez. Hotel Los Cisnes."

Hanlon felt suddenly tired. The sweet stench of grass seemed to have impregnated the walls of the room itself. He had had enough of playing Bogart to Manzoni's Sydney Greenstreet.

One more time. Play it again, Sam. "So you get a phone call, telling you exactly where the man you lost is now staying and you do nothing about it. I'd get the girl out of here, Albert. She might faint at the sight of blood."

"Back off, Hanlon! On my mother's life, it's true! I got the phone call saying he was there. That was all I had to do. I passed it on to Control." He slumped down beside the girl.

"From whom? Who called you, Albert?"

Manzoni was glazing over. He tried to wet his lips, but his tongue was dry.

"Gunter," he said.

Hanlon stared down at him. His disbelief was genuine.

"Hit me if you like, Hanlon. It won't change anything. It *was* Gunter. I know it sounds crazy, but that's the way it is. I swear." He snatched the joint from the girl's lips and drew deeply on it.

Hanlon turned away. Boris Gunter was a KGB field officer in Spain. Top man. A veteran. If he was on talking terms with Albert, the hunt for Carradine was now a combined operation. Orders like that could only come right from the top on both sides.

166

45.

From: Aleksander Rostov, First Secretary of the Central Committee

To: Marshal Vasili Bunin, First Deputy Chairman of the Council of Ministers of the USSR

Instructions have been given to the Special Investigations Department for the suspension and detention of Stefan Andreyev, KGB Chairman, pending his arraignment on charges of gross dereliction of duty. Other charges may follow. It is with a sad heart that I authorize this course of action. Andreyev had impressed me in the past with what I took to be a genuine commitment to détente. That impression, I am now forced to accept, was false. Department S has been given the task of preparing evidence, and I agree with you that Dmitri Orlov is a fitting choice for the office of acting Chairman of the KGB in the interim.

From: Stefan Andreyev, KGB Chairman

To: Aleksander Rostov, First Secretary of the Central Committee

So it has come to this, Comrade! I am sick at heart to learn that you will not see me and that you have ordered my suspension and detention. I, who have supported you in your great plans, who have worked for your greatest and most controversial venture: détente. I am too distressed to state fully what I feel in my heart. But you must know that there are elements in our country who seek to jeopardize our plans, who see peace abroad as a threat to their saber-rattling at home. It is that very opposition that I know to be behind this travesty of justice. They have plotted and planned to convince you of my perfidy so that they can take power from me. Yes, I was head of the First Directorate those many years ago when the KING-FISH cell was seeded. Yes, it *was* under my control. So were many others, long forgotten. But no, I did not activate them, Comrade. No, no, no! Their awakening could not have occurred without the greatest effort on the part of those who seek my destruction. One man who could help me has disappeared. A cipher clerk—Anatoli Repin by name—is the only man who would know the activation code and the group at which it was aimed. He retired five years ago, and my search for him in Kiev has been unsuccessful. He alone could explain this. I beg you, give me time at least to find this man and let him tell his story. I know the soldiers are coming for me, and I will go with them. Only you can save us both, Comrade.

From: Dmitri Orlov, Acting KGB Chairman
To: Director, Fifth Directorate, Kiev Station

SUBJECT: ANATOLI REPIN, CIPHER CLERK.

REPORT RECEIVED. IMPERATIVE TOTAL SECU-RITY MAINTAINED. SUBJECT REPIN TO BE KEPT UNDER DETENTION AT ALL TIMES. NO HARM MUST COME TO HIM. I WILL NEED HIS WRIT-TEN CONFESSION WITHIN TWENTY-FOUR HOURS ALONG THE LINES I FORMULATED.

46.

Bobby Hanlon was becoming aware of two immaculate truths. First, he was being excluded from something by Carrie and that probably meant it was pretty bad news. Sam had taken off for Boston that morning before six o'clock and he'd missed his swim. Now Carrie was trying to play it cool and making a lousy job of it. Last night they'd traded glances when he asked them about Dan, and they'd been especially careful to be with him and involve him. But they wouldn't *give*.

The second thing was he was missing Dan. Now that was plain damn stupid because he'd spent years thinking how great it would be to have no one to look after, no one to please, but himself. Dan was someone a guy tripped over, pulled out of trouble, not someone you missed.

Till now.

There was something very weird going on, that was for sure. The way Jack Shawn had got himself killed. And old Marv Fish. And Doug Cater, though that was easier to understand because everyone knew about him and his fits, poor guy. And then the way the women just up and disappeared. Then the doc. Then Dan and his mom.

Now Sam, No, Sam was different. Sure.

The phone rang and Bobby dodged like lightning into the hallway. Carrie was out, but if this was Sam. . . .

"Hey, is that you Bob?" Dan!

"What do you think you're doing, crumb! Where are you? Sam's been trying to. . . ."

"Shut up a minute, will you? I haven't got much time. I just wanted to make sure you know things are okay. Okay?"

"Hey. Wait a minute yourself. Where's your mom?"

"She's . . . she's okay. She's here."

"Where's here?"

"It doesn't matter where's here. She's okay and me, too. I didn't want you to . . . well, you know, worry."

"Worry!" Bobby fumed. "Everyone's standing on his ear back here worrying. Where are you?"

Daniel was silent. Then his voice came through clear and cold. "It's got something to do with my dad going away. I dunno—it's all mixed up, kinda. My mom isn't the explaining kind."

"But where are you going? To your dad?"

"She won't say. I can't explain things over the phone, Bob. If I hear anything, I'll let you know if I can."

"What do I say if my mom asks?"

Daniel's voice rose an octave. "You don't say anything: I got to have your promise on that. Okay?"

"Why?"

Silence again. Then, slowly, reluctantly, "Because I promised her I wouldn't call anyone. Specially you."

"But . . ."

"*Please*, Bob." Daniel's voice was shaking. "I can't . . . she can make things bad for me. Just don't say anything."

"Okay. I promise. But just tell me one thing . . ."

"Sorry. I can't. I have to go now."

The line went dead.

47.

Hanlon had not slept since his catnap on the plane sixteen hours ago, but he didn't feel tired. He was in overdrive. The clerk at the Hotel Los Cisnes admitted reluctantly that there was indeed a Mr. Roberts registered at the hotel. His clothes, his suitcase, were still in his room, but the police had not yet found him. Police? Yes. There had been a murder at the hotel the night Mr. Roberts checked in. Hanlon left quickly.

The damn fool! He had told him unequivocally that if Fuengirola got too hot or if the situation changed, Jerez was to be the point of consolidation. Its American population in July was high. A pursuer would find it hazardous to plan a controlled fatality in a town as thick with people as this one. But if he found he had to fall back there, he was to stay cool, keep his head down, and avoid trouble at all costs. Trouble!

What else had he told him? If for any reason he couldn't use the Hotel Los Cisnes, Carradine was to sleep in the rented car or check into a small hotel. One that offered a wide choice of escape routes.

Failing that, he was to station himself for five minutes only, twice a day, in the public gardens by the parking lot overlooking the Gonzalez Byass bodega in the center of town. At two o'clock in the afternoon, when all sensible citizens were taking siesta, and two o'clock in the morning, ditto.

Hanlon checked his watch. One forty-five. If he hurried— if Carradine was still alive—he might catch him.

The pavements were deserted as Hanlon strode quickly through the narrow cobblestone streets. The heat of the afternoon sun was unbearable. Sweat ran freely all over his body, reducing his already limp cotton suit to a rag. His shirt was plastered to his chest and a scarlet rash enflamed his neck and throat where his tie had been. He turned into an alley and saw, through an archway at the end of it, the parking lot floating in the heat haze. He stopped a yard short of the arch. The lot was deserted except for an old peon in a discolored white coat who lay on the bench of his ticket hut. His crackling snores drifted clear across the square.

Above the lot, a flight of wide stone steps led up to the gardens and a long sun-bleached wall, where climbing plants grew in a riot of scarlet and gold. On a bench under the wall sat Frank Carradine. He could have been asleep. He could have been dead. Hanlon circled around and came up on him from behind. He had to shake him roughly to bring him to life.

Carradine yawned wide and rubbed sleep from his eyes. "Sam . . . I can't tell you . . ." The yawn engulfed him again. "I didn't know what to do. The hotel . . ."

"On your feet, Frank. We're wasting time. Forget the hotel. You can't go back there. Nor can I. First off, we find a pension and I make a couple of calls. Then I'm getting you out of here fast. No arguments!"

"No arguments." Carradine grabbed Hanlon's arm and heaved himself upright. "Not a word."

Hanlon led him back the way he'd come. In one of the side streets he had noted a flaked sign—Good Beds and the Best of All Cuisine—hanging outside a gloomy courtyard. He found it again and spilled crisp new peseta notes all over the wakened doña's sweating palms. She forgave him the untimely arrival to the extent of not asking why they had no luggage.

Carradine fell onto one of the lumpy twin beds in the curtained room and closed his eyes. Hanlon opened his briefcase and tore the wrapping paper from a bottle of Johhny Walker. He splashed the Scotch into bathroom glasses and pushed one at Carradine. They drank in silence, greedily and without thought for the effect. Carradine emptied his glass and held it out for more. Hanlon tipped in two fingers and stopped.

"That's your ration. I need you sober and functional. Now tell me what happened."

It took Carradine a half-hour to tell his story. He was a stickler for detail and his pursuit of it often led him so far from the point that he lost his train of thought entirely. Hanlon stuck with him, nudging, backtracking, probing. At the end of it he had confirmed his suspicions: Langley *had* made a deal with Moscow.

He said, "How d'you feel?"

"Bushed," yawned Carradine. He stretched luxuriously on the bed. "I could sleep for a week. That's if I can stop my body from shaking. God, Sam, I'm too old for this. I've never been so shit scared."

"Good," Hanlon said sourly. "Stay scared. That gives me some kind of guarantee that you'll do what I tell you this time. And there's something else. I want you to know something, Frank—I want you to know now, before we take this thing any further."

Carradine did his best to focus his attention, but it was a

futile attempt. Exhaustion had drained the curiosity out of him and the Scotch had pushed him over the threshold into the no man's land that precedes sleep.

"Anything you say, Sam. Anything."

"Listen!"

Carradine nodded, eyes hooded, almost shut. "Sure. Anything you say."

Hanlon felt an acute sense of the ridiculous. This was lunacy. He ploughed on.

"I am an officer of the Central Intelligence Agency, Frank. You understand what I'm saying? From the moment you stepped into the town limits back home I've had you under twenty-four-hour-a-day surveillance. You haven't cleaned your teeth without my knowing about it. You haven't eaten a meal, taken a shower, talked to a patient, made a phone call, cleared your throat—anything. For fifteen years, Frank. I've been right there inside your *head*. So all I want now is to hear you tell it, okay?"

Carradine shook his head violently, marveling that he was awake. "I never . . . Jesus, Sam, I wouldn't have known in a million years. I. . . ."

Hanlon grabbed him by the shoulders and hauled him into a sitting position. Carradine's head drooped helplessly.

"I said I want to hear you say it, Frank. Tell me."

Carradine struggled helplessly against the blanket of sleep. "All right, Sam. Anything. If I'd known. . . . You wouldn't believe. . . . Scared out of my . . . skull . . . day and night. Margo. . . . Dan. . . . Sick with it. . . . Why didn't you . . . ?"

Hanlon shook him savagely. Carradine's head snapped back onto his shoulders and forward again.

"Please, Sam . . . I hear you. Don't care any more. Just get me out of this, Sam. . . . Anything you want." His head sagged drunkenly to one side. Hanlon dropped him onto the pillow. His mouth gaped and the first shuddering sobs of sleep filled the little room.

Hanlon refreshed his drink. He sat perched on the edge of a washstand and examined his prize. Well, that was it. That was Kingfish—sewn up, sealed, and bonded. He'd said it all—all he needed to say to confirm everything Langley had waited for. Without fear, without regret, without a sense of failure.

Either Frank Carradine was a fool or he was beaten. The only other possibility, of course, was that he was buying time.

48.

Hanlon came to in a sweat. His fists were bunched and his knuckles bled where he'd struck the steel headboard in some torturous nightmare scuffle. He squinted in the darkness toward the other bed. Carradine's breath rumbled deep in his chest as he slept.

The dirt-stained window of the room overlooked the court-yard. Hanlon twitched the curtain to one side. It was dark. A single uncertain electric bulb flickered from a wall bracket on one side of the courtyard, and at a table beneath it the doña sat gossiping with three women and a man, *copetas* full.

Hanlon lowered himself into a hard chair and tipped it back against the wall. Carrie had put her finger on it. Why had he let Carradine go? Because friendship ran thicker than patriotism? Crap! Because a man is innocent till proved guilty? Because even a spy has the right to due process? Forget it! Carradine had no rights. Kingfish had no rights. Langley was the power and the glory. It molded Hanlon in its own image.

That was nearer the truth. He'd slipped the chains on Carradine because Langley had cut him out of the game; because the machine had considered its corporate navel, reached a corporate verdict, and appointed an executioner. Frank Carradine would have become just another name in Merrit Leitch's accident file.

Carradine groaned in his sleep.

Fine. So he was a great humanitarian. He was now also on Langley's blacklist. He had smuggled Carradine out from under their noses, and they would collect that little debt with pleasure. And yet they'd allowed him to follow when it would have been the easiest thing in the world to pick him up at the airport in Boston or have him arrested at the stopover in London. Right? Right! Conclusion: they were happy to let him run. Why? How deep did a national crisis have to run these days to make Langley reconsider its priorities? Carradine was a priority; killing him—and the others—had been important enough to persuade Langley to double-cross a resident agent, break the link with his case officer, and call in a hatchet man. That called for one hell of a lot of executive clout. Blood-letting was not a pastime the Agency could afford to indulge in any more, not with Senate investigating committees leering over its shoulder and every two-bit newspaperman in the country thirsting for the next big break since Watergate.

He eased the chair into an upright position, reached for the Johnny Walker, and gulped from the bottle. Speculative conscience was no match for raw Scotch. The liquor flooded his system with comforting heat and cleared his brain of obstructions. There was something Allen Dulles said once. What was it . . . ?

"Policy must be based on the best estimate of the facts which can be put together. That estimate, in turn, should be given by some agency which has no axes to grind and which itself is not wedded to any particular policy."

Made sense.

He tilted the bottle again and the golden liquid bathed him with its beneficent balm.

Okay. Alec Lamb was a measure of Langley's capacity to grind axes. So was Merrit Leitch. And Fat Albert. Langley had put out a contract on Carradine; they'd even marked the card for the KGB's fieldmen. They had tunnel vision. They were wedded to a kill policy at any cost.

175

All right. The only thing left was to prove his point. Neck first.

He took one more slug from the bottle, set it down, and tiptoed to Carradine's bed. He would be out for hours. Hanlon unlocked the door and let himself into the corridor.

The doña was not easily persuaded to leave her company, but a thousand-peseta note salved her irritation. It took fifteen minutes to put the call through to Teague's Landing and another thousand pesetas to persuade the old woman to rejoin her friends.

"Sam?"

"No questions, baby," he told her quickly. "Just listen."

Carrie choked. "Are you all right? You . . ."

"Listen, baby. Listen."

"Don't talk. Sam, did you hear me? They've been here. I think they've done something to the phone. It's . . ."

Lamb again! Well, he knew it had to happen. They'd have run a tap on the house phone an hour after he took the plane.

"I know," he said. "Don't worry about it. When I put the phone down, I want you to call Alec Lamb. You'll find him in my address book in the bureau under Canning Technology. There are three numbers. Try them all. If he's done something to the phone, maybe you won't have to bother anyway."

"Sam, I'm half out of my mind . . ." She was crying. He hardened himself against an impulse to comfort her. No time.

"Listen to me, baby. Tell Alec Lamb this: I have Frank Carradine. I . . ."

"Oh God, Sam. . . ."

"*Listen.* He's all right. I'm all right. Alec knows where we are. Tell him I can't stay here. Tell him Gunter—got that? Gunter—is right behind me. I'm getting Carradine out of Spain."

Carrie controlled her weeping, but not too well.

"What can I do, Sam? Is there . . . ?"

He closed his eyes and bit on his grazed knuckle. Then a thought electrified him. "Yeah, baby. There's one thing. Have you heard from Helen?"

"No. Not since . . ."

"What about Grace? Or Joan Cater?"

"No. Not a word from anyone. I, well . . . I think Bobby might have had a call from Daniel. He hasn't told me anything but . . ."

Hanlon froze.

"Is Bobby there?"

"Yes, but . . ."

"Get him. Bring him to the phone. Now."

"All right." He heard her call out. An answering shout from Bobby. Then. . . .

"Hey, that you dad?"

Hanlon grinned. If Lamb still had blood in his veins he would get a jump in heart-rate from that eager young voice on the phone bug.

"Hi, son. I've got to keep this short, okay. Your mom says you've heard from Dan. True?"

Pause. Then, uncertainly. "I said I wouldn't tell you, dad. But I guess if you already know. . . ."

"What did he say, Bob? It's okay. You'll be doing him a favor. He could be in big trouble."

"He just said he was okay and his mom'd give him hell if she found out he called me."

"Where was he calling from?"

"I dunno. He wouldn't tell me."

Damn! There had to be something in that call. Lamb would have to work it out.

"Was it long distance, son? Did the call come through an operator?"

"No. I picked up the phone and he came right on."

Local. Maybe.

"Okay, son. Put your mom back on."

177

Carrie had had time to steel herself. She sounded remote. "Does that tell you anything?"

"No. But it might give Lamb something. Tell him to run through the tape on this call, baby."

"Do I have to do anything else?"

"No. Lamb'll take care of everything. But he'd better do one more thing. Tell him to re-run the Kingfish tapes from trigger-day and check out the women's calls. All of them."

"Kingfish?"

"Don't ask questions, baby. He'll know." He stopped. He had to finish this quickly now. He said mechanically, "I love you. Remember that." He hung up.

He went back upstairs and took another belt from the bottle of Scotch.

There was no going back now. He'd set himself up—Carradine, too—and Alec Lamb would take every advantage of it because he was a good pro who played it straight. There was a vague chance that Hanlon's call would assuage his guilt in the Company's eyes, but the possibility was far from bankable. Nevertheless, they'd do what he asked for no other reason than that they couldn't afford not to.

Hanlon took a swig from the bottle again. Strictly according to Allen Dulles, he'd given himself the right to determine policy. He had the best estimate of the facts. But was he an agency with no axes to grind?

49.

"Margo?"

"Who is this?"

"Helen."

"Ah!"

178

"I thought you were going to be there two days ago. You said . . ."

"There were complications. I couldn't let Daniel stay at the Landing. He's unsettled enough as it is. I can't afford to have him going to pieces now."

"Aren't you worried? For God's sake, Margo . . ."

"I have too many things to think about for self-pity, Helen. So do you. Are you alone?"

"Of course, I'm alone. I don't dare set foot outside this place. Look, Margo, you've got to tell me. You swore to me they were accidents. Jack and Marv and Doug. Well, I think you're lying. So does Grace."

"You've seen her?"

"No. She called. I'm worried about her. We both knew how she felt about Marv Fish. I told you from the beginning the way it was shaping up and you let it go on."

"What's wrong with her? Is she emotional?"

"Emotional? She's *hysterical!* You must have known she would be. She's not like . . . the rest of us. She can't get what happened out of her mind. She can't sleep. If she takes it into her head to . . ."

"Don't be ridiculous. She'll do as she's told. I *am* her doctor, you know."

"My sister's keeper!"

"Spare me the dramatic irony. You're safe as long as you keep out of sight. You know that. So is Grace."

"You'd better try telling her that yourself. She won't take it from me."

"I will."

"*And* Joan."

"I've talked to Joan. She's perfectly all right. She'll be driving over to join Grace tomorrow. I'd rather have them together than apart. And Helen?"

"Yes?"

"I hope I can count on you to stay cool. No swooning fits."

179

"Don't try to psychoanalyze me, Margo. You're wasting your time. I'm sorry about Jack, but you know how it was with him and me."

"I just wanted to be sure, dear, that's all. You're right, I *did* lie to you about the accidents. They weren't. They couldn't be. I just didn't want to alarm anyone unduly."

"My God, Margo . . ."

"Yes?"

Pause.

"Nothing."

"Good. You're being very sensible. Now don't call me again. When the time comes, I make contact. I want you to stay where you are. Don't go out."

"Don't worry, I *won't*."

"Then I'll call you in a couple of days. And make sure your car's working properly. You'll need it. Goodbye."

50.

Manzoni had been following the Fiat for ten minutes, and Hanlon was praying he would have enough sense to keep clear. Just stand back and take notes like a good boy, Albert. You run a lousy tail.

"Is someone following us?" Carradine half-twisted in his seat.

"Yes. But he's probably harmless."

"The police?" Carradine swallowed hard. He was never far from panic.

"Something like that." Hanlon swung the car into the airport parking lot. He switched off the engine and watched Manzoni's Opel hug the wire fence and turn into a space near the fire sheds. He turned to Carradine.

"Look, Frank. I won't pretend all our problems are over, but if we clear this hurdle, the rest is downhill. So do exactly as I say and we'll get our hides out of here in one piece." He grinned. "Sorry about the cloak-and-dagger bit, but you know what I mean."

"Sam, it's up to you. You're the boss. If you can get us out . . . ," Carradine shrugged, ". . . of whatever we're in."

They walked across to the airport terminal building, keeping the pace slow and natural. Carradine's face gave nothing away and that fact concentrated Hanlon's attention again. Even now, when he must know he was in the last stages of a game he was bound to lose, Carradine was still miraculously complaisant. He would bear watching.

"Remember we're just a couple of guys on our way home after a holiday. So act normal."

"I am normal, Sam," said Carradine, his voice even.

They checked in at the ticket counter, showed their passports, then moved on and ordered warm beer at the bar. Carradine swung the Pils bottle reflectively between two fingers, tracing a pattern with its base on the bar top.

"Sam, when this is all over . . . what happens to you? Me? Do you think anything will ever be the same? Is there anything left?"

Hanlon stretched his aching back, swiveled on his stool, and ran an eye over the other travelers in the bar.

"For me? Well, maybe. Things'll settle down. Maybe we'll up stakes. Carrie likes Boston. Bobby likes New York."

Where the hell was Manzoni? The last thing they needed now was a blundering clown ruining the act at a time like this. The chances were Langley had briefed him on Hanlon's status, and he was just fool enough to try to put his house in order before they discovered he had fouled it up. An incompetent, everyday Fat Albert was bad enough, but dealing with a clown like Manzoni when he was *really* trying could be disastrous: a chilling combination of farce and tragedy.

". . . part of the question?" Carradine was saying. Hanlon shook himself. "The question?"

"The second part, Sam. What happens to me?"

Hanlon finished his drink and motioned Carradine to do the same.

"I didn't answer it because I can't, Frank. Only you know that. God knows, you knew it had to come." He swung down from the stool and led the way out into the sun. They had a good fifteen minutes to kill and he didn't want any more word play. He took the stairs to the observation platform with Carradine at his shoulder. Three aircraft; including theirs, baked in the remorseless sun, their shapes dancing in the heat haze. A catwalk led from the platform to a larger area with a shop and a cigarette booth. The shop was closed and the man in the booth dozed behind his spread of papers. "Saving his strength for the siesta," said Hanlon dryly. Two cleaners clattered down from the observation platform, their tin buckets rattling against the railings.

At the bottom of the steps one of them glanced back in the direction of Hanlon and Carradine and slipped a chain across the entrance.

"This way." Hanlon took Carradine by the arm and urged him along the deserted catwalk past the cigarette booth. "Just keep walking and don't stop for anyone," he said. And stopped abruptly. Manzoni stepped out from behind the booth. He wore an open-necked black shirt, and a gold charm in the shape of a dragon glinted out from the bush of black hair on his chest. He reeked of cologne and his fingers flashed with rings as he stretched out a hand to grip Hanlon's elbow. In the other he held a Luger waist-high. It was pointing at Carradine's stomach.

"Nothing funny, Hanlon. No smart talk. No wheeler-dealing. Just do as I say. Turn around. You, too, Carradine."

"Do as he says, Frank," said Hanlon.

"Frank!" Fat Albert poured disgust into it, and a shower of

fine spittle settled on the back of Hanlon's neck. "Okay, *Frank*, keep very cool. Now walk."

They obeyed. Halfway across the catwalk, Hanlon stopped and turned deliberately.

"You know this is a waste of time, Albert. Gunter's set you up. There never *was* a deal. The KGB wants Carradine for its own reasons. The second you wrap us up, Gunter will be down on you like the cavalry." He shrugged. Albert's eyes bulged with anger.

"I said no bullshit, Hanlon. I meant it." He waved the Luger briskly and a trickle of spittle ran from the corner of his mouth.

As slowly as he dared, Hanlon began to move again. He slipped a pack of cigarettes from his pocket in one innocent move and shook one into his mouth, keeping his body between Carradine and the wary Manzoni.

"I said none of that, you mother fucker! What you got there?" Manzoni moved closer to Hanlon, who stopped again and held his arms wide, an unlit cigarette dangling from his lips. "You're out of training, Albert," he said pleasantly. "It's just a cigarette."

Manzoni lunged out to knock it from his mouth. Hanlon angled the butane lighter and flipped the wheel. A foot-long flame roared through space and rapiered into Manzoni's face. Manzoni bellowed with pain. Hanlon moved in closer, the flame licking the fat man's head. The bellow bubbled into a scream. His arms flailed and the Luger clattered on the marble of the catwalk.

"Get the gun!" yelled Hanlon. He swept Manzoni's flailing hands away from the lighter, forcing it into his face until the hot metal touched his skin. Albert screamed and staggered back, clutching at the air until the railings pressed against the backs of his legs.

The lighter guttered and died, and Hanlon slammed his open palm under Manzoni's chins. With a grunt he toppled backward and down in one lightning somersault.

"God in heaven!" Carradine grasped the rail. The lifeless mound of Fat Albert Manzoni lay spread-eagled in the back of a parked garbage truck, face down.

51.

Somehow, Carradine kept his composure on the flight from Seville to Madrid, but it was a white-knuckled, lip-biting holding-on as if he were holding his breath. The appearance at his shoulder of a stewardess or the innocent passing of a fellow passenger was enough to send his nerves leaping. Hanlon shoved him into a cubicle in the men's room when they reached Madrid and ordered him to stay here until he returned.

It took a half-hour to locate the kind of party he was looking for and another twenty minutes to persuade them to let him and his colleague join them on their charter flight back to Boston. The secretary of the New England Veteran All-Star Golfing Society argued that his only defense, were the American authorities to question him, would be that Hanlon had paid the full transatlantic fare, not the preferential charter fare. Hanlon parted with the bribe more than happily. His lack of luggage was considered an advantage, but the secretary pointed out that he would be forced to deny their transaction if anything went wrong.

Hanlon went back to the men's room and released Carradine from purdah. They stripped off jackets and ties and washed. It wasn't easy. There was no soap in any of the dispensers and the hot air driers were broken.

Carradine wiped his hand on his shirt. "What happens now?" He didn't seem to care whether the answer to that was good or bad.

Hanlon stared into the mirror, found his eyes, and held their reflection. "What d'you care, Frank?"

"Don't play games, Sam. I'm too tired."

"Well, hang in there, Frank, because you're within fifty minutes of Immigration. An hour after that. Zoom, zoom, zoom."

"Where?"

"Where d'you want to be?"

Carradine let out a racking sigh. "Home. I don't care what the hell they do when I get back there, just so long as. . . ."

"Just so long as they let you in, right? Fine. Do as I tell you, Frank—*exactly* as I tell you—and they'll let you in."

"Are we . . . ?"

"We're members of the New England Veteran All-Stars Golfing Society and we're chartering home with a song in the air. We've had a couple of weeks drinking our way around the greens of sodden Spain, we're happy as pigs, and if we're lucky, someone's going to find our clubs and send 'em home to us. But what the hell, it was fun losing 'em. Okay?"

"You really believe people are going to accept that crap?"

"If you keep your head down, Frank, and everything goes smoothly, no one's even gonna bother to ask. Customs and Immigration don't look on charter parties as people. They're figures. A percentage of the quota. Ten percent of all home-ward-bound charters get turned over by Customs and about eight percent by Immigration. Not because they're obvious suspects. Because that's sufficient to keep an officer's intervention quota up for the whole day. You get it?"

"Suppose we're part of the quota?"

"So we're part of the quota. No one's going to expect you and me to walk back into the U.S. of A. having sprinted out of it two minutes before with the pack at our heels."

"I wish I could believe it."

"Believe it, Frank. Believe it all the way. Convince yourself and you'll convince everyone else."

In the airy transit lounge, Hanlon led Carradine to a seat in a corner. His agreement with the secretary of the All-Stars was that they would keep their distance until the very last call for the flight. He'd also agreed to wait the full fifty minutes in transit rather than walk through to the departure lounge. He closed his eyes and sought sleep, but it writhed away each time he thought he had it beaten. He sensed that Carradine was having the same problem and with unreasoning ill temper hoped he was having it worse. Christ, the way this was working out. . . .

Think of something else. Carrie and Bobby . . . Teague's Landing . . . a blue-white summer day with the sun hammering the sea flat and the wind coming off the land deodorized with pine. . . . The kids up on the Ridge, flickering mirrors at the sunbathers spread-eagled on the dunes below. . . . Grace and Joan . . . and Jack and Marv and Doug . . . Frank. . . .

Margo and Daniel!

Hanlon opened his eyes, focused, and stared grimly into space. "Frank?"

"Yeah?"

"I've got to ask you something. Just don't get the wrong idea, okay?"

"Shoot." Carradine's voice was hollow. It seemed to have been that way since he watched Fat Albert's plunge from the catwalk at Seville Airport.

"Margo," Hanlon said, feeling for an opening. "You and Margo."

"What about me and Margo?" Disinterested.

"You marry in church, Frank?"

"What is this, 'Truth or Consequences'?"

"No, I was just wondering. . . ."

"About me and Margo."

"Yes."

Sigh. "Yeah, we married in church. White wedding, all the trimmings. Marv Fish was my best man."

"And then along came Danny."

"What's that supposed to mean?"

"Nothing."

Carradine squirmed around on the seat beside him and stared him in the face. "If you've got something to say, Sam, why not come straight out with it."

Hanlon nodded slowly as if to himself. "You and Margo got married in March 1959, Frank. Danny wasn't born till October 1966." He clenched his teeth in anticipation of the explosion.

It came.

"What goddamned business is that of yours!" Carradine swung up and out and glared angrily, his mouth twisted in anger, the whites of his eyes yellow with sleeplessness.

"None," Hanlon said soothingly. He touched Carradine's arm gently. "Frank, I'm sorry."

"You bet your ass."

"I'm sorry," Hanlon repeated mechanically. He looked his man in the face and went for the big one. "You told me a few days ago that you and Margo lost a child in 1959. Did you marry her because she thought she was pregnant? All right. Hit me if you want, but I need to know. Would you have married her otherwise?"

For a moment he thought Carradine was going to smash him in the face, and he clenched his fists in preparation, but the outstretched hand merely gripped his wrist and the face paled and the liquid yellow eyes fixed on Hanlon for a full half-minute. Then Carradine slumped back in his seat.

"Why ask that, Sam?" he croaked helplessly. "Why ask a question like that when you already know the answer?"

52.

From: Dmitri Orlov, Acting KGB Chairman

To: Aleksander Rostov, First Secretary of the Central Committee

SECRET.

Former cipher clerk Anatoli Repin was arrested in Kiev early today and has freely admitted his involvement in the awakening of the KINGFISH cell. His written statement (attached) states that on the first day of this month he was contacted personally by Stefan Andreyev and instructed to furnish him with all the details of the original 1958 seeding. Repin told Andreyev everything: the code of awakening and how to code the target. The original Helsinki station intermediary has been actively monitoring the group on the orders of a person as yet unknown to us. Repin felt he was in no position to refuse Andreyev's orders. He disappeared, he says, because Comrade Andreyev told him his life was in danger. The most disturbing fact to emerge is that the coded instruction was a *mokrie dela*, a "wet affair." In the parlance of the Executive Action Department a "wet affair" denotes an assassination order. The target is coded as the word "shall." Clearly further information has been transmitted through Helsinki detailing where and how the strike will take place. We have no way at present of alerting the Chinese of the possibility that their leader is facing an assassination attempt, but that may not be necessary. The agent Carradine has been arrested in Spain by a CIA operative with the assistance of our own agent. Marshal Bunin informs me that Stefan Andreyev, KGB Chairman, is under guard at Lubyanka, having refused the offer of room detention at 2 Dzerzhinsky Square.

From: Finance Department, KGB
For Personal delivery to Director, Administration Directorate

INTERNAL ONLY.
SECRET. NO COPIES, NO FILE.
FOR YOUR EYES ONLY.

This is to confirm the expenditure involved (see attached requisition) for the purchase of a dacha and Moskovich car. They are to be credited under BUILDING RESTORATION/KIEV. As such they must be entered into records. The property and possessions have been purchased on behalf of this agency for use by subject ANATOLI REPIN as ordered by Acting Chairman Orlov. DESTROY THIS FORM ON RECEIPT.

Keyline Red-Moscow/Washington
From: the First Secretary to the President
For the President's eyes only.

Urgent. Urgent. Urgent. Information now available confirms planned assassination of Chinese leader by Kingfish cell. Urge efforts to secure all known surviving members of Kingfish. Greatly concerned. Consider it vital, if necessary, to postpone summit meeting. It would be unwise to inform the Chinese of current situation.
Your reactions, please.

PART THREE **REALITY**

53.

"Another brandy, sir?"

Hanlon shook his head and winked at the stewardess. She was a pint-sized version of Faye Dunaway and in the past hour and a half he'd invested her with a dozen changes of underwear, from the allover one-piece to all-but-nothing monokinis. It was a way of passing the time.

Carradine accepted the stewardess's brandy with graceless alacrity and slung it down to join the rest. He was far from drunk and not especially despondent, but he was obviously preparing himself for a descent into hell.

Hanlon stole a glance at him from the corner of his eye. Carradine stared straight ahead, eyes frosted over, features relaxed, hands in his lap. Come the next visit from the stewardess with the next slug of brandy, he would grin dutifully then return to his Buddhist attitude of contemplation. And sometime Hanlon would have to tell him what was lying in wait for him at the other end.

"You want to sleep?"

Carradine turned to him, eyes wide, wakeful. "No thanks."

"You must be wishing me to Hell."

Carradine's eyes fluttered nervously. "Why, Sam?"

Hanlon waved a hand at the serried rows of All-Stars around them.

Tight-lipped half-grin. "This? We're out of it, aren't we?"

"What about the rest of it?" Hanlon persisted. "The guy at Jerez. Manzoni?"

Carradine rubbed a hand across his jaw, grating the heavy

growth of beard that discolored his jowls. He leaned closer, his voice low. "You haven't done anything about . . . Manzoni?"

Hanlon shook his head wearily.

"Are you going to?"

"Are you?"

This time Carradine couldn't trust himself to reply. His chin sank onto his chest. After a moment or two he said, "I surprise myself a little more every day. A week ago I could no more have turned my back on a dying man. . . ." He stopped.

Hanlon closed his eyes. "A week ago you were someone else. Then I told you to run. Remember? Why did you?"

Carradine waved an arm in the aisle and the stewardess caught the signal and set another brandy on the folding shelf in front of him. He brought the glass to his lips, sipped experimentally, then put it down and studied it compulsively.

"How many people can I be, Sam? How many's allowed? That's good comforting American logic: yesterday I was someone else and tomorrow's person isn't mixed yet."

Hanlon shrugged. "I didn't say that."

"Didn't you? I apologize. Well, I admit I'd like an arrangement that gave me so much latitude. Why did I run? I ran. . . ." He pinched the bridge of his nose between finger and thumb. "I ran, Sam, because I was afraid." He squinted owlishly. "Afraid of what, you ask?" He stopped himself and he stretched his lips over his teeth. "No, you don't have to ask, do you, Sam? I was forgetting. You're another person, too. Well, I can only deal with one Sam Hanlon at a time. I like the old one best."

"There's no change," Hanlon retorted gruffly.

"No change," echoed Carradine. "Yes. Well, I'm the original changeling, Sam. But I suppose you know all about that."

"About what?"

"All right. We'll play it your way. In 1956 I escaped from Hungary. Me and my father. The Russians broke up our group after the uprising and chased us as far as Paris. From there we made it to London. For a time we lived with our hearts in our mouths. Then, one night, this Russian knocks at the door. Says he's from the news agency, Novosti. Says he has news of my mother, my three sisters, and my wife and two sons."

Hanlon's head whipped around instinctively.

"Your wife and sons!"

"That shocks you, does it, Sam? That's very American, too. Yes. I had to leave them behind. There were a lot of cases like mine. However . . . he wanted help, as he put it. My father pleaded with me to do what the man told me, but he didn't have to beg. I was a coward, Sam. Most people are cowards in that situation. I agreed to do as I was told, to obey without question, to tell no one. In the fine, safe English democracy of Walthamstow I bartered my soul for the lives of my family."

"What did they make you do?"

Carradine opened the fingers of both hands, fanwise.

"How would I know? Journeys were booked in my name—sometimes by air, sometimes across the English Channel by steamer—and I was given a passport with another name and luggage to take and luggage to bring back. Nobody explained. Nobody offered any excuses. But I'm not so big a coward I can't work things out in my head. Berlin, Stockholm, Danzig, Cairo, Rome. I stay two or three days, never leaving my hotel, and then back to London. What would you guess I was doing?"

Hanlon growled. "What then?"

"Then?" Too brightly. "Then, my father, who was a much greater coward than I was, because he loved my mother and sisters and my wife and sons more than I did, my father waited for me to leave on one trip then called my Russian friend and threatened to go to the English police. He told me this when I came home. I cursed him. I swore he was the murderer of his own children. And then I let him sweat it out. In the morning, I went to his room. He'd hanged himself from a light fixture."

Carradine slumped deeper into his seat and raised the glass to his lips. He put it down again without drinking.

"Suicide. Nothing excites the interest of the English more than suicide. There were policemen and social workers and Immigration and local authority snoopers. The Russian stayed away. Suddenly, I'm a coward without support. *Moral* support. It brought everything to a head. I left the apartment, stayed in a Salvation Army hostel near the docks for a few days, and finally stowed away on a Dutch freighter bound for New York."

He made a face. "It wasn't as dramatic as it sounds. Eight days later I was on the streets of New Jersey. Two weeks later, a group of Hungarians in exile found me. There was no difficulty finding papers. Hungarians learn the mechanics of survival very quickly. Then I met Margo. For a woman she was remarkably efficient. She taught me the language, cared for me. She found people who could provide me with an identity, passport, credentials, a good American medical background. I owe her everything."

Hanlon gave himself a minute to let it sink in, then he said, "You said you and Jack Shawn, Doug Cater, and Marv Fish had something in common."

"We had our escapes in common. Shawn ran from Czechoslovakia, Fish from Poland, Cater from East Germany."

"And you're telling me you all miraculously came together in Teague's Landing? Four exiles with the same kind of background?"

"If that's a miracle, yes."

Hanlon shifted uneasily in his seat. "Did you ever discuss it, the four of you?"

"What was there to discuss?"

"All right. What made you *personally* come to the Landing?"

Carradine raised a tired smile. "Margo heard the practice was up for sale. Old Doctor Warren had just died. Besides, Margo thought she was pregnant, remember, and we weren't married yet. It would have embarrassed both of us to stay in New York."

"Warren's practice was a damn good one. It must have cost a fortune."

Carradine face clouded. "Margo was always a good manager. Much better with money than me. She raised a loan on the basis that we'd both be in practice."

"What about the others? Who made the decisions in their case?"

Carradine sighed. "Women always make these decisions, Sam. Helen Shawn is sharp as a cutthroat, and Grace Fish is tougher than you'd give her credit for. Joan Cater may be neurotic, but she pushed Doug harder than he could push himself, poor bastard. Why?"

Why? Hanlon reached across his companion and lifted his brandy glass. He took the contents in one gulp.

"I asked you before," he began slowly, "whether you would have married Margo even if she weren't pregnant. That was the key; the first time I saw anything in this monkey puzzle that made sense. Up to that moment, what you *seemed* to be, the four of you, fitted perfectly."

"Fitted with what?" Carradine stirred.

"With what we were led to believe." Hanlon paused.

"In 1963, we—my organization—were given the names of four foreign radicals living in Teague's Landing. Four surnames —Carradine, Fish, Shawn, and Cater. Our information was that they formed a Russian sleeper cell. I was moved in to the Landing to back up that information. You made it easy for me. All four of you gravitated to one another, became friends. And when the time came, three of you died . . ."

"Because of me. Because the Russians caught up with me and thought . . ."

"You're wrong. Nobody's interested in you. They never were."

"So what in God's name does it mean?"

Hanlon tipped the brandy glass and drained the last droplets trapped in the well at its center.

He said softly, "It means, Frank, that four queens outbid four kings."

54.

The Assistant Director's office at Langley had about it rather less of the atmosphere of electric urgency than when Alec Lamb last sat there. The candle had burned at both ends and only its smoke was left to suggest there had been fire.

The AD had worked through the night with George Strauss. Both of them had been called to the White House for an hour at four in the morning, a few minutes after the duty officer woke the President to take the hotline Telex flash from the Kremlin. The order to convene an emergency meeting of the Intelligence Resources Advisory Committee went out shortly afterward. It was in session by five o'clock with representatives from the State Department, Defense, the Office of Management and Budget, and the CIA sitting under the chairmanship of the Director himself. IRAC's week-to-week role is to prepare the financing of the intelligence community and monitor its efficiency, but it was called in this case because of the wide-ranging powers of its individual members.

"Don't give me a sermon on protocol," the President had told the AD tersely. "Get those guys around a table and give me some options. It took us three years to get China to come to the table. I intend to keep it that way. I don't care who's playing the percentages. Just keep them out of my hair any way you have to."

The AD and George Strauss had been called to advise the Committee and were later briefed on general targets. Lamb received his call at Teague's Landing at six-thirty and the helicopter dropped down in the grounds on the Coach House at seven-fifteen.

When he arrived at Langley, the AD was midway through a desk-top brunch of ham and eggs and coffee. His manner was conciliatory, his smoothness and polish gone. Somewhere along the line, Lamb figured, he'd taken a swift hard kick in the pants from a fast-moving collective boot.

The Kremlin, said the AD, had come through on the Kingfish mission. Man to man—from the private suite of the Soviet First Secretary to the Oval Office. The hit was to be made three days from now; the target was the Chinese Prime Minister.

Strauss looked grayer than ever, subdued, resigned. But he could still play the devil's advocate.

"The President won't take this lying down," he growled. "So we've got ourselves one helluva problem. The way I see it, this could be just another ploy out of Moscow to louse up the summit. Okay, it's a maybe, but I have to say it: the whole thing stinks of smart-ass KGB chess-playing to me. But the President doesn't see it that way, and I can't begin to prove it. Deadlock. So, what you and I have to do, Alec, is sew this bastard Carradine into a shroud before he can make a hit. What d'you say?"

Lamb reached for a cigarette to give his hands something to do. This was the moment to spill his theory about the taped conversations he'd listened to in Hanlon's office. About the trigger call. But it was still only theory. It had to be checked out. It was meaningless unless he could backtrack on every one of those fourteen seemingly innocent callers and run them through the meat grinder. If they *were* innocent, if Hanlon had been merely reaching in the dark—or worse, tossing him a red herring—then it would waste more time than they had. Later, when the men reported in, he'd talk to Strauss and mount a sweeper operation to pick up the Kingfish women. A couple of hours, no more. But this was the wrong time. . . .

"What about Leitch?"

Strauss ran his fingers through his mop of unruly gray curls, a characteristic sign of rising temper.

"Don't give me the article of faith bit, Alec," he said tautly. "I can't use it. Leitch had his orders. No one's sorrier than me it had to be this way. I think the chances are Hanlon thinks he's doing the right thing. Well, that's too bad. We have priorities. His hide isn't one of 'em."

"Have you figured what happens to the priorities if Hanlon's right?"

"I figure what I can see and hear, not what I can speculate on. Moscow gave us names—names we already had. Names we acted on. What do you want me to do, admit we executed innocent men?"

"If you're right about this being KGB chess-playing, yes. I'd say we have to be prepared to accept the fact that they were innocent men."

Strauss stared at him as if attempting to pierce his brain.

"Have you got anything to substantiate that?"

"Nothing you'd call evidence."

"Then work at it till you have. Meanwhile, we go ahead as planned. I'll feel more inclined to listen when I get confirmation that Carradine and Hanlon are out of circulation."

Lamb snapped his lighter to the cigarette. "What happens if they foul it up?"

George Strauss looked at the AD and they both nodded simultaneously. "We all go look for a good undertaker, Alec," Strauss said. "You included."

55.

They were the last to leave the plane. Hanlon had hidden a large brandy under his seat a half-hour before landing and he gave it to Carradine as the All-Stars thrashed their way toward the exits. It lasted three jolts and maybe fifteen seconds, but its effects were immediate and material. Carradine stretched languorously and waited with infinite patience for the plane to clear. He allowed himself to be led from the plane and stood quietly to one side as the All-Stars located their bags and clubs.

Hanlon judged his timing perfectly. Neither he nor Carradine were fingered as they passed through Customs, and Immigration spared their passport pictures no more than the required minimum scowl.

They were in the concourse and moving with deliberate nonchalance when the hairs on Hanlon's neck pricked up. He turned, but there was no one who appeared less of an obvious traveler than he and Carradine. He urged his companion toward the entrance.

He spotted them at once. In a way he hadn't expected anything else. Okay, so he could con himself and half-convince Carradine that it was all going to be fine, but in the final analysis he knew they would be there. George Strauss and Company were not dealers in chance. If Hanlon went out that way, he comes in that way. He could hear Strauss saying it. He could also hear Strauss on the subject of surveillance. He wouldn't have been pleased. Good undercover men choose one of two categories: the obvious—postmen, porters, waiters, cab drivers—stable categories they called them at Camp Peary; or the incidental—casual travelers, shoppers, drunks, loiterers. The second category was by far the most hazardous to get right and was therefore used only in a crisis. This one had all the signs of a last-minute dash.

There were two of them. One at the door, one near the parking lot entrance. Both had that mid-sixties look common to mature fieldmen: dark suits, straight trousers, polished laced shoes, narrow-brimmed soft hats, short dark raincoats. The guy on the door wore a black glove on his left hand. His right was bare. A lousy giveaway. Conclusion: he wore his automatic under the left arm and had orders to shoot if necessary. A gloved hand slowed the responses in a fast dip to the holster.

The other wore a muff of newspapers over his right hand and wrist. Amateur!

Hanlon drew Carradine into the wall. "There're two friends up ahead, Frank, see? Watch the guy by the door. We're going to walk right up to him and say hello, okay?"

Carradine flinched. The memory of his confrontation with Albert Manzoni at Seville was still alive and simmering. "Will they . . . ?"

"They won't cause trouble if they can avoid it," Hanlon said soothingly. "Just let me do the talking. Let's go."

The man at the main door saw them as they came around a group of pecking women and children and squared his shoulders instinctively. Hanlon grinned approvingly. Shoulders back, shoulders forward, the little nudge that squared the holster into a perfect draw position in the armpit. The man opened his feet, steadying himself. Out of the corner of his eye, Hanlon saw his compatriot closing in on an interception course.

Ten feet from the door, Hanlon raised a welcoming hand and headed straight for the officer. "Hi, Dave. Sorry we're late. Got held up on the other side."

The agent froze. His colleague actually stopped.

Hanlon grabbed the ungloved hand and shook it. "You know Frank. Frank, remember me telling you about Dave?"

A porter with a trolley emerged hopefully from a bunch of travelers. Hanlon waved him away peremptorily. He dug a hand under the tensed triceps of the unhappy "Dave" and said softly, "I have to talk to George Strauss now. No trouble." Then loudly, "Dave, I have a couple of calls to make. Let's get ourselves some coffee."

Dave's features were set in concrete. Any rebuke he intended making died in his larynx the moment he tried to give it air. Hanlon swung him around and headed him toward the coffee shop. He found a table, guided the man to it, and shoved Carradine to the counter. "Coffee all around, Frank. Sandwiches, too. Ham, cheese—whatever they've got."

The second agent appeared in the arched door of the coffee shop, observed and retreated, presumably to a phone. How many more of them were there?

Hanlon stitched a smile across his face and said conversationally, "You're not communicating, son. I said I want to talk to George Strauss. You know what that means?"

The impassive face flickered experimentally. "Don't ramrod me, Hanlon. You'll do as I say. We'll get up from this table and walk quietly to the. . . ."

Hanlon threw back his head and roared with delight. His hand rose and fell good-naturedly on the agent's shoulder and finally came to rest—hard. "One telephone call or two very nasty incidents, son," he said, still grinning. "If you think I'm going to let you pick me up without a hassle, you're mistaken." He patted the young man on the shoulder several times. "You're also"—he opened his big hand on his lap, below the level of the table—"unarmed." The agent's .38 lay across his palm. "Now call your friend over and have him put through a call to Langley." He snatched a corner from the menu propped in the middle of the table. "This is the code number. Recognize it?"

The young man bent his head to study it. He was about thirty years old. Peacetime soldier, thought Hanlon absently. Civil Service mind. Computer instincts. The young man nodded. "So?"

"Do it. That's all."

The agent used a long stare to X-ray his own uncertainty, then he turned in his seat. His companion reappeared as if by magic, stood for a moment in the door, then walked over.

"You okay?" he asked suspiciously.

The young man gave him the scrap of paper. "Call it," he ordered brusquely. He nodded at Hanlon's lap. The newcomer angled his head and Hanlon obligingly opened his hand to reveal the .38. The second man scowled.

Ten minutes later, the airport loudspeaker system clicked on.

"Will Mr. Teague and his party come to reception, please. Mr. Teague and party. There is a phone call for him. Thank you."

The second agent was waiting by a soundproof booth. He slid to one side and Hanlon took the receiver. George Strauss said, "What in hell's name are you playing at, Hanlon?"

"Apple in the barrel, George, and it's getting a bit tiresome. I want you to call off your gorillas and give me safe passage, George. Me and Carradine."

"Why should I?"

"Because your skin's intact and you want to keep it that way."

"And you can guarantee that?"

"I came back, didn't I?"

"That could mean you're just goddamned stupid, Sam."

"But you don't think so."

"I don't?"

Hanlon blew contempt silently down the line.

"Did you have the tapes re-run like I suggested to Alec?"

"What suggestion, Sam?"

"Please, George. We don't have that much time. I called my wife from Spain and Alec had the phone bugged, right?"

"So he did. Yeah, I remember."

"Well?"

"Well, what?"

Hanlon seethed. "Did Alec re-run the tapes?"

"Uh-huh."

"And they told you what?"

Strauss sighed hard. "We checked 'em. You were right. We should've double-checked this end before."

"Who?"

"Shawn."

"How'd we miss it before, for God's sake?"

"Simple. What d'you know about Helen Shawn?"

Hanlon looked quickly over one shoulder at Carradine. He bent his mouth closer to the instrument. "What are you asking me?"

"You register a place in New York called La Belle Alsacienne?"

"Sure. Helen's dressmakers. Kinda boutique place. Lamb checked it out way back."

"They called the house once, twice a month. Discussed clothes they were making for her. You know the kinda stuff."

"Number codes?"

"Of a kind," said George Strauss sadly. "The Shawn family also ran a phone tap. On their own phone. Automatic answering machine. The way we see it, Helen Shawn was the dummy in the middle. This boutique place is a cell—a communications cell that linked Helsinki and Teague's Landing. The boutique picks up instructions, relays 'em to Helen Shawn in the form of some junk about dresses and such. Jack Shawn runs a tap on his own phone to decode in his own time. You buy it?"

"Do you?"

George Strauss chuckled. It was a brittle, dusty sound.

"You're the expert, Sam. You tell me."

Hanlon bit his lip. "Have you found Helen Shawn?"

"Nope."

"What about the others?"

"We're looking."

An icecap settled on Hanlon's brain and slid down his spine to his feet. "How much time d'you figure you've got, George?"

"Time?"

"Oh, come on, George! Give us both a break."

Silence. Then, grudgingly. "Three days. Less."

Hanlon gnawed away at his lip. Strauss waited, then called impatiently down the line. "Well? Well?"

"Okay. Listen to me, George. Just listen." His voice acquired a new urgency. "A father is out walking his child. There's an accident. A car kills the father and knocks down the kid. He's rushed to hospital. A surgeon goes to the bedside, looks down at the boy and says, 'It's my son.' "

"Are you goddamned crazy or something?" roared Strauss.

"*Listen.* Just tell me what it means to you."

"It tells me you're cracking up and if I. . . ."

"George! What does it tell you?"

"Okay, okay. It tells me the surgeon is lying. We know the kid's father died in the accident, already."

"Who said the surgeon was a man, George?"

The sound of George Strauss's breathing was all Hanlon heard for a full minute. He went on, "We all assume the same thing, George, that the surgeon has to be a man. That's male superiority for you. Take any situation where a *role* is a dominating feature and we predetermine it as *male*."

George Strauss exhaled slowly. "The surgeon's a woman."

"Right," Hanlon hissed down the line. "What does that tell you?"

"What d'you want, Hanlon?" Strauss interrupted gruffly.

"I want to get Carradine out of reach and keep him there till you've cleared up this mess."

"Where?"

"Tully Masterson's place at White Falls River."

"Take a train," said George Strauss. "Beat it."

George Strauss set the receiver down with massive care as if it were primed to explode. He sat watching it for several minutes, then, shaking himself from a dream, he pushed out of the chair and crossed to the map that covered one wall of his office. It was a Mercator projection of the world and too old by far to be of use. It was an adornment, as the AD's Copernicus globe was an adornment, but one that could be called to account if the need was great enough.

Strauss stuck one stubby finger on Spain and ran his hand across the Atlantic. He stood on tiptoe to stare more closely at the New England area, but he knew it was pointless. Not that he actually needed to *see* anything. From Olympus, all men were of one size, man-sized and therefore irrelevant. Hanlon was less than a fly crawling across this map, and Carradine was too small to see and, therefore, if necessary, too small to be.

In sixty hours, two men were due to arrive in New York from two other irrelevant parts of this map, and it was planned that one would die. That was a truth. It had to be because three men were now dead in pursuit of that immutable certainty. Strauss blew breath from slack lips and planted a hand on his chest where the passage of sixty cigarettes in fourteen hours had left a surface stickier than a tarred road boiled by the sun.

Trust me, George. That was Hanlon for you. Trust me, George. Let me walk through walls, George, because I'm good and true and you can trust me. I ran away and stole your victim, but now I'm back because you got it all screwed up, George. Just leave it to Hanlon and don't interfere.

Talk to the AD? No, no need. He knew what he would say. And Alec Lamb, too. Sixty hours is no time at all and in no time at all a man might die. Unless two other men died first. In isolation, he believed Hanlon's story, but that wasn't enough.

He slouched back to the desk, sat down, and picked up the phone. His secretary got the number and presented him with Merrit Leitch, bright-eyed and bushy-tailed as ever, and as full of respect as a Mafia *consiglière*.

He told Leitch where they would be and what he had to do with them. Leitch made no interruption and at the end asked only one question.

"If you have to," George Strauss said heavily. "But I'd prefer to have him alive."

He waited a whole minute, hand on the receiver, so that it shouldn't run away. Then he called Alec Lamb and told him the story of the boy who went walking with his father. Alec Lamb must have heard the story before because he just waited to be told what to think about it.

"What are you doing about these women?" Strauss asked innocently.

"We'll get to them. Don't worry."

"But I do worry, Alec. I worry a lot. So does the President. I suggest you throw every man you've got into this thing. I want you to tell me in the next forty-eight hours that these good ladies are safe and sound, Alec. Do I make myself clear?"

"Yes, sir." Formal. "You had news of Hanlon and Carradine yet?"

George examined his Mercator projection from afar. "No, Alec," he said without a flicker of conscience. "When the AD's good and ready, I'm sure he'll tell me."

56.

From the bed, Grace Fish could see the final curve of the driveway where it looped around the kidney-shaped pool and met the pink-and-white mock-marble flagstones.

In the past hour, only two cars had appeared around that bend, neither of them the one she was waiting for. She checked her watch. Four-thirty. In Teague's Landing, the boats would be coming in, bumping to their moorings along the quays, the crowds already gathered to select fish for supper straight from the hold. Marv had loved to stroll through Old Harbor to the docks in early evening, drinking in the bouquet of the sea, great lungfuls of salted air. Together, leaning over the white-painted rails, they would watch the boats approach, deliberately avoiding a race to be first at the dock, until they fell into line abreast and sidled in to their moorings, the brine momentarily swamped with the smell of diesel.

Without moving her eyes from the window, Grace reached to the bedside table, found a cigarette, and lit it.

Teague's Landing. Life would be going on as usual. Evening barbecues were being planned and, down at the Yacht Club, they would be preparing for a long light night—a run along the coast past the overhanging bay windows of the Marlin Club out on Mackie's Point where Jimmy Page was this minute flicking lint from his white tuxedo and applying another layer of cream to his hair before doing battle behind the bar.

Grace drew hard on the cigarette. Well, they certainly had

plenty to talk about back there now. Jimmy Page would be dealing to a full house at the Marlin Club as the hunt began for those vital snippets of information that would give the blue-rinse brigade a head start next morning.

"Grace, you there? It's me."

She swung her feet to the ground and opened the door.

"No one's arrived," said Joan Cater. She had been drinking a bottle of tequila in her room and her speech was ludicrously precise.

"What difference does it make?" Grace retorted waspishly. "You expect someone to wave a magic wand and make it all better?"

Joan didn't reply. She sidled across the room to the dressing table where a bottle of whisky stood untouched. Grace watched her. "There's a glass in the bathroom," she said.

Joan poured three fingers of Scotch and dumped herself into a chair. She said, "I'm not worried. If anything needs to be done, it will be done."

Grace was at the window, still watching the drive. "What exactly is that supposed to mean? Do we stay here for the rest of our lives, geting food parcels every week. Or do we start all over again. Change our names and become librarians in Schenectady!"

"If you're making a point, baby, make it," Joan yawned from the chair. "We all have our problems."

Grace closed her eyes and willed calm to her shaking body. She said stiffly, "Don't you see, Joan? Don't you see it's different for me? I failed in every way. I fell in love with Marv. Failure One. Failure Two, I killed him. Yes, if it hadn't been for me, he'd still be alive."

"What do you think they'll do?" Joan asked coolly.

"Who are they? I don't know any more. I guess I don't care very much, either. Maybe it *is* best if we just disappear. Get out and find some meaning before it's too late." She shook her head dismissively.

"Won't work, baby," said Joan. She poured another.

"I know that," said Grace, her eyes on the driveway. "Don't you think I know that?"

"Whatever happens, you can't go on like this, you know that," said Joan. She lit a cigarette. "You can't go on letting it eat you up like a cancer."

She sucked in smoke, tasting the nicotine, then angled her head and stared at Grace, her eyes blinking away the smoke curling from her lips.

"One day, you knew something like th . . ." She caught Grace's look and cut herself off in midsentence. "All right, none of us guessed. But it's happened, baby, it's happened. Marv is dead, Jack is dead, Doug is dead. Poor little Doug. God, even I didn't wish that on him. Not even me!" Her lower lip trembled and she sat up and groped for her glass, averting her eyes from Grace as she deposited the cigarette into the half-full glass like a specimen into a killing jar. "Christ, you know something? I think I'm crying."

"It's the smoke," said Grace, coldly. "Smoking can be very emotional." She went back to the window to watch the motel manager idling on a broom by the reception office.

Joan Cater dabbed her eyes with a crumpled tissue, "You never liked me, Grace. I know it and there's no point denying it. I don't blame you. Twenty years have done a lot of things to all of us. Made us hard. Made us different people. Have you ever thought about that, baby? Being someone different?"

Grace Fish continued to stare through the window, waiting for the car. Her tight-fitting satin shirt accentuated her figure and her hair was down over her shoulders. She glanced at Joan Cater, then back to the window, biting her lip.

"I need someone, baby," persisted Joan Cater. She got up from the chair and began to pace the room. She stopped at last beside Grace, lightly touched her shoulder, turned her away from the window.

"Baby, I'm scared. Real scared." Her breathing was rapid, urgent; her mouth was loose, showing the teeth.

"Baby."

"I wish you wouldn't call me that," Grace snapped.

"Why do you hate me?" Joan Cater's eyes oozed tears. She rocked tormentedly on her feet. "I'm frightened. You should help me. You should. Don't you remember?" She rested her head on Grace's shoulder, her voice breaking.

"I loved Marv," said Grace flatly, turning back to the window, ignoring the clutching hands. "It wasn't what I wanted. I didn't plan for it. I didn't intend to let it go on. I played it as I was told to play it. But I couldn't help loving him. It was the only life I knew and it tried to live itself, despite everything." She had forgotten Joan Cater.

She whispered, "Marv, Marv," as if the name could conjure life, as if she were discovering its texture for the first time. Softly, keening, "Marvin."

"I know," Joan Cater's arm encircled Grace's waist, "Doug. My Doug, too." Her left hand fell across Grace's right shoulder. It slid carelessly down over the thin satin and came to rest. The tears still ran on her cheeks, but her face wore an expression of intense expectancy.

"You're younger than me, baby," she moaned softly. "Stronger, fitter. You're beautiful. I won't let anything happen to you. To us." She brushed back the long hair from Grace's face and her fingers toyed with it. "You're beautiful, baby," she crooned. Her hand began its slide into the thin slit of material that plunged to the breasts.

Grace broke away. "That car," she said abruptly. "That's the one." She strode to the door and stood waiting.

"Good Christ," swore Joan Cater. She wrapped her arms around herself, rocking as if numb with cold. Grace said from the door "I don't hate you, Joan. Not hate. It's just that we're two different animals, you and I. Trained in the same arena, brought up in the same cage. But different." The knock at the door broke her train of thought. She grasped the handle and pulled it open.

211

The shock was still in Joan Cater's face as she stared at the figure framed in the doorway. Her mind was still alive with Grace's body, redundant adrenalin, and the pain of rejection. She saw an outstretched hand, a kid glove, saw Grace falling, and didn't understand. Said, "What kept you?" to the doorway but suddenly it became the wall and the window and the ceiling as she spun, her eyes catching Grace's face, wondering at the sudden splash of crimson drawn across it. And then she was down, breathing thickly. Heard the door slam.

Died.

57.

The train clanked off up the valley, trailing its tail of four flattop cars and their gaily painted cargo of tractors. It disappeared around a bluff and they were alone. A shaft of uncertain sunlight bled from a blue-black cloudbank, splashing one gray house on a distant hillside with bronze fire. Along the valley, a scattering of small frame houses, too widely scattered to be a community, crouched in the scarred landscape, secretive and withdrawn.

Carradine shuddered involuntarily and tugged his lightweight jacket around him.

A lone porter spared them a laconic glance, noted the absence of luggage, and offered a monosyllabic greeting that called for no response. From the shelter of the station entrance he followed them with his eyes until the main street carried them out of sight.

White Falls River had been a hamlet when Hanlon first stepped off a train there, but its character had changed beyond recognition. Civilization had come to White Falls in the form of parking meters, a motel, and a couple of diners. Carradine eyed the diners with silent desperation as Hanlon led him past their windows. In the square, a '69 Plymouth squatted at the curb with a Taxi card taped to the front window. Carradine automatically moved toward it, but there was no driver in sight and Hanlon didn't even bother to turn his head.

They hadn't exchanged a word since they left the train, and Carradine was reluctant to be the first to break the silence. He had been wracked for hours with nightmare variations on the theme of Daniel's state of mind and Margo's hostility. The two were by now interlocked. He could only guess at Margo's reasons for not following him to Spain, but it was not an exercise that required supernatural inspiration. Throughout their life together, Margo had always been the initiator. Margo had made the propositions, enunciated her reasons, made the decisions, carried them through. He had been required only to acquiesce. He hadn't thought of that when, on impulse, he bought the tickets to Malaga and told Carrie, in his innocence, to instruct Margo in what to do. Ten seconds of mature consideration would have told him that Margo would do what she had always done—her own thing in her own time.

Where was she? What had she told Daniel about him?

Hanlon took him by the elbow and powered him off the road into a screen of dense bushes. A bus swept around the curve ahead of them throwing up a storm of dead leaves and dust in its wake.

Hanlon dragged him back to the road again, checked his bearings, then scrambled up the steep bank to the pine wood that climbed to the skyline.

Hanlon forged on ahead, shouldering a path through the densely planted saplings, body bent, head down as though determined to push himself to the limit of endurance. Carradine trailed after him, panting hard. After a half-hour, Hanlon stopped, but not for his own comfort. He leaned into a young tree and watched Carradine collapse on the carpet of pine needles. When the older man's breathing had regulated itself, he set off again without a word.

They reached the plateau a little after five o'clock. One and a half hours of total physical commitment had reduced Carradine to a quaking mess. He had removed his jacket and his shirt clung to his sweating back. His hair hung in his eyes, his sticklike arms fell helplessly at his sides, and his face and throat were streaked with needlepoint gashes where branches had whipped and scourged him. He fell forward on all fours and clung to the coarse grass.

A cold wind moaned over the naked, treeless plateau, but from time to time raised its voice in passionate gusts of ill temper as if challenging their right to its terrain. To their right, the plain rose to low foothills and, beyond that, to a crest. In the far distance lay a low mountain range. It was a primeval landscape, unreal, a haunting ground for battle-butchered ghosts and lost causes.

Hanlon roused himself. He pointed to a flat-bottomed cleft between two hummocked hills far to the left. "That's where we need to be. When you're ready."

Carradine nodded, swallowing air to refuel his aching lungs. "Minute. Just give me . . . a minute."

"That's about all we can spare," Hanlon growled. He was feeling curiously pleased with himself and unreasonably scornful of Carradine's shortcomings. A man should look after his body, especially a doctor. His own had withstood the assault and was electrified. If they ran into trouble up here. . . .

"I guess . . ." Carradine levered himself to his knees, then to his feet. "I guess there are worse places on earth, but I'm damned if I ever saw one."

"Be grateful for it, Frank. You'll get used to it. And remember. The ground can be pretty mucky up here in places, even in summer, so stick to the paths and don't wander."

"Don't worry." Carradine swung his jacket on. His teeth were chattering as the wind sliced through his shirt and turned his sweating body ice-water cold. "I wouldn't move a step in this place I didn't have to."

Hanlon studied him with ill-concealed impatience. "I thought you'd hunted up here. Last year, wasn't it?"

"We came to Vermont, sure. I brought Danny. We hunted with crossbows. But it wasn't this kind of country." He stared around him. Behind them, the pine mantle plunged down to the gray snaking road. The town was a barely visible exclamation point in the sweep of the valley. "How do we get to where we're going?"

Hanlon grunted. "The bus service is kinda thin up here. We take the path and head for those two hills. The road runs just below them and the cabin's about a half-mile along the road. About an hour, I'd guess."

Carradine shook his head despondently. "I've got blisters on my heels bigger than oranges, Sam. I'm warning you. But I'll do my best."

Hanlon led the way again, keeping his pace to a funeral crawl.

"Do people actually come up here, for God's sake? Voluntarily?" Carradine called after him.

"Skiers in winter. Place is thick with 'em. Practically every house in town takes in paying guests. You get hunters, too, in season. Plenty of deer, although this time of year they'll be up in the mountains for the summer grazing. If we're unlucky, we might run into a bunch of hitchhikers or lunatics on orientation exercises—you know, map-reading, that kinda stuff. Otherwise, there's just the birds, sheep, wildcats, and foxes." He flashed a comforting grin over his shoulder. "And you and me."

The road was deserted and remained so during the ten minutes they clung to it. Hanlon sighted the cabin in its protective pocket of shelving ground and quickened his pace. Carradine groaned in his wake. The blister on his heel had burst a mile back and the agony was acute. He was a full two hundred yards behind when Hanlon reached the stone-walled little house. He waited. Carradine shuffled up and sank to the ground, his back to the unpolished oak door.

"Look, Sam, this is stupid. I'm not going to be able to move a foot come nightfall. Why don't you just find some kind of transportation and pull us out of here? Let's go back, huh? Get it over with. All this . . . it's just putting off the inevitable."

Hanlon held his temper in check with difficulty. "You know what the inevitable is, do you, Frank? Got it all worked out?"

You know what I mean." Apologetically.

"Do I? Maybe I haven't got it across to you. Your life's worth less than a Forty-second Street whore's gift certificate. You're home but, take it from me, you're far from free. If Langley believed me when I told them I could work this out alone. . . ."

Carradine's head came up with a jerk. He said, almost disbelievingly, "You didn't tell them we were coming up here, for God's sake!"

Hanlon's cool exploded. "How the hell d'you think we got back into the country, dummy! Why do you think Langley called off the two guys in Boston?"

"And what happens if they didn't believe you?"

Hanlon waved a hand in disgust. "They'll believe what they want to believe, and right now they want to believe you're out of the way and under wraps."

"Why? What am I supposed to have done? I ran because I was scared out of my skull. You know that."

Hanlon pulled him roughly to his feet and put his shoulder to the door. It didn't budge. He walked around the cabin, examining the windows, Carradine at his heels.

"How long do we have to stay here?" Carradine ventured.

"Three days, maybe. I don't know. They'll be in touch."

He selected a rock, broke a windowpane, reached in and swung open the casement. He levered himself inside, walked through, and opened the front door.

"Welcome," he said, his anger gone, "to your holiday hideaway."

There was no food in the cabin, but sleep was the only provision they needed and the beds were comfortable in spite of the dampness of the stored blankets. They were too tired even to light a fire. They slept a full sixteen hours and woke hungry.

Carradine rose first. Hanlon found him crouched in front of the stone fireplace, a blanket clutched around him, blowing on spitting logs to kindle a flame. Outside, the sun was bright but the air was straight from the refrigerator; a brisk wind raced headlong across the plateau and hurled itself at the door. It screamed in the chimney and the logs writhed with flame and began to burn. Carradine straightened triumphantly.

Hanlon began a routine inspection of drawers and cupboards.

"Don't tell me, the cupboard's bare," shivered Carradine.

"Very."

Alongside the fireplace was an inset cabinet door. Carradine tugged at it experimentally. It didn't budge. "What's in here?" he asked. Hanlon grabbed the poker and forced its blackened point into the space below the handle. It sprang open to reveal a deep recess. In one corner stood four old twelve-bore shotguns, barrels and breeches oiled and wrapped in cotton. Six boxes of cartridges, too.

"Hey," Carradine turned with a grin to Hanlon. "How about that? What d'you say we grab one apiece and go find breakfast?"

Hanlon shook his head. He closed the cabinet door and shoved it firmly into place. "I'll get the chow," he said. "But in White Falls River." He laid a hand on Carradine's arm. "We can't afford to attract attention, Frank. So I hit the road and you hold the fort." He pulled on his jacket and turned at the door. "And no heroics, okay? If anyone comes knocking, there ain't no one here but us termites. Right?"

Carradine dropped casually onto the bed.

"Is that understood?" Hanlon snapped.

For a moment he thought Carradine was about to rebel. Then his teeth clamped down hard on his top lip and he nodded slowly. "Whatever you say, Sam. You're the boss."

He kept his fingers crossed until he found the old bicycle in the lean-to behind the cabin. It had been Tully Masterson's one concession to technology and only then because it had a certain masochistic attraction. Tully's sojourns were directed at three targets: to cleanse his mind of Langley (and, since his retirement, of Madison Avenue); to punish his desk-lazy body, to purify the spirit. To these ends, he foreswore electricity and running water, preferring oil lamps and spring water, and he insisted on leaving his car at home and surviving on minimal stores and anything he could hunt, fish, or trap. Hanlon had roughed it with Tully a half-dozen times and had come to admire the old guy's grit and determination.

He exhausted himself blowing air into the bike's flat tires with a wheezing handpump, then mounted up and bumped down the rutted track to the road.

It would take perhaps a half-hour to reach town but probably three times as long to make the long uphill haul back. He paused one foot on the grass, and checked the landscape. It was wildly empty. Behind the cabin, the two low hills reared over the roofline, clipped grass at their feet, swathed bracken at their waists, outcroppings of metallic gray rock at their summits. Tully would sit for hours with a pair of field glasses watching every movement across those slopes. He was the very image of a naturalist, fascinated by the behavior of birds, but part sadist, too, because he had sown fox traps all over those hillsides and never failed to be excited when a creature fell victim to a pair of steel jaws.

The downhill trip was faster than Hanlon had anticipated. At the first store in town, he filled a plastic bag with boxes of dried soup, some flour, sugar, bread, and dried milk, some canned fruit, and a carton of cigarettes; he checked the local newspaper on the display rack, then turned for home. The wind was in his face, the road rose up to challenge him every inch of the way, and, halfway up the mountain, dizziness swept over him forcing him to sit by the roadside to regain his balance.

He had been away for nearly three hours when he pulled the

bike off the road a hundred yards east of the cabin. He had been standing on the pedals, his head low over the handlebars, fighting the wind, seeing nothing but the pulsating pink patterns behind his own eyes and the glint of sweat trails on his nose.

He had traveled ten yards when he realized he was riding in a tire track. A fresh tire track. The bike swerved violently and dumped him into a drainage channel.

He left it where it fell and scrambled on his hands and knees along the ditch toward the house. The car tracks left the road in a tight swerving turn and disappeared behind the cabin. Judging by the churned-up mud and the deeply gouged tracks, the driver had counted on high speed to win him a degree of surprise.

Hanlon made a slight detour to come up on the cabin on its blind side. He edged around to the front and darted a glance through the window.

Carradine was still sitting on the bed, a blanket around his shoulders. He was staring at the floor, hands supporting his chin, as though he hadn't moved since Hanlon left. Hanlon changed his position and found a better angle. He peered closer.

The working end of the Magnum automatic appeared head-on to his nose on the other side of the glass. It stared at him, suspending his breathing and the sound of his heart in his head; then a face fell into line behind it. Merrit Leitch slipped off the window catch, threw the casement wide, and beckoned him in. Hanlon hauled himself over the window sill and Leitch backed away, grinning widely.

"Well, how nice," he drawled. "Be my guest. Be my *second* guest."

The blanket had fallen from Carradine's shoulders and he looked thinner and older and tragically vulnerable. The bridge of his nose was beginning to distort in a pool of angry bruising and his cheeks were mottled.

Leitch found a position where he was satisfied he commanded the destinies of both of them. "Well," he beamed hospitably, "this is just dandy. But I guess we can't waste time, you agree?"

He looked from one to the other and nodded his head sagely.

"So you thought you'd just walk right on in like nothing's happened, huh? You know, I have to hand it to you, Mr. Hanlon. That's *real* machismo. Stupid, of course, but real hairy. Pity is, you thought everyone else was going to fall into line and watch attentively while you skated figure eights around the Company." He shook his head sadly and bounced the Magnum lightly in his fist.

"So." Briskly. "Let's talk business, shall we?"

Hanlon ignored him. He strolled across the room, across the field of fire, and dropped on one knee in front of Frank Carradine. He said, "You all right?"

Carradine winked painfully and attempted a grin. His upper lip was split in three places and when it rose over his teeth, blood was visible on his tongue.

"What did he do, hit you with the floor?"

Carradine winked again. There were tears in his eyes, whether of pain or self-pity Hanlon could only guess. He was a little shocked when his automatic reaction was to believe it was self-pity.

"Don't worry, Mr. Hanlon. He'll survive. For now." He waved the automatic expansively. "But you know how field conditions can alter cases. Comrade Carradine's been playing games and I don't have time to play games. I invited him to talk. He declined. I couldn't accept that. Now why don't you explain to him how much more painful it gets as it goes on?"

Hanlon got to his feet and turned slowly. He clenched his hands at hip height and walked deliberately into the black eye of the Magnum.

Leitch's face remained impassive. He said gently, "I think I'll have to shoot you, anyway, Mr. Hanlon. All you're doing is making it easier."

Hanlon froze.

"Thank you." Leitch ducked his head in a little bow of gratitude. "Now walk to the bed and sit down beside him. I want him to talk and fast, Mr. Hanlon. There isn't time to take him anywhere official, no time for inquests, inquisitions, trials, lawyers, and civil rights. I want names. I want to know Kingfish inside out. Who they are, what their orders are, and who's left. Who's left, Carradine?"

"What d'you mean, Kingfish?" Carradine began.

Without any show of speed or sudden movement, Leitch was over him, the Magnum raised above his head, the barrel flattened for the pistol whip.

"Leave him!" Hanlon half-rose from the bed.

"You, too!" Leitch swung on him. His arm flashed down with lightning speed and the cold metal smashed into Hanlon's face. He felt his cheekbone distort as skin and muscle dragged down one eye, incising the flesh. Then he struck back. His left foot snapped up into Leitch's genitals; his right arm swung high and chopped down on the bent neck. Leitch crumpled at their feet and lay still. They were both shocked at the speed of it. Carradine stared disbelievingly at the sprawling figure. He half-bent to reach for the throat pulse point.

"Forget it," Hanlon said roughly. "He's alive. You can't kill that kind of bacteria." He touched Leitch with the toe of his shoe. "Take his gun. We'll use his car, right?"

Wrong.

The keys were in the ignition and the Ford Mustang was wheel-locked for a fast getaway but that was where their luck ran out. As Hanlon swung open the door, the black-and-orange dog hurled itself across the driver's seat but throttled back on the chain that was locked to the steering column.

"Shoot it! Shoot the bastard!" Hanlon shouted. He threw himself to one side, giving Carradine a clear field. In quick succession, there was a click and a muffled oath. Hanlon swung around. The Magnum was barrel-deep in mud and Carradine was on his knees scrabbling for it, his face upturned to the snarling Doberman.

Hanlon pushed him out of the way and reached for the automatic, but as he did so, there was a splintering crash from inside the cabin. Hanlon leaped to his feet, grabbed Carradine by the arm, and lugged him away from the car.

He yelled back at the open doorway. "Stay where you are, Leitch, or I'll blow your head off." He looked back longingly at the Magnum in its bed of mud.

Had Leitch been in command of himself he might have chosen the better part of valor, but the rabbit punch had left his head singing and his reactions were feeding on pure reflex. He lunged into the doorway with one of Tully Masterson's twelve-bores in his hands, the cotton still intact on the barrel and breech, and a half-opened box of cartridges spilling its contents over the ground.

Hanlon yanked Carradine to the left in a whirling movement that nearly made him lose his balance. "Run, for chrissakes. Run!" he yelled. He leaped through a gap in the stone wall that Tully had built for no good reason along one side of the track and loped off toward the nearer of the two hills. He looked back. Carradine was pounding after him, his face creased with pain. Leitch was still in the doorway, shaking fingers, trying desperately to slot cartridges into the breech. The dog stopped barking and began to howl. Leitch roared at it petulantly and stumbled to the car.

Carradine whoofed with pain ten yards behind him and Hanlon stopped. "My heel. God, my heel, Sam!" Carradine blundered past him, half-dragging his right leg. He had had time only to slip into his shoes and the blistered right foot was bleeding freely. Carradine splashed on ahead through a series of green-slimed puddles. "Make for the hill!" Hanlon shouted after him.

Leitch had finally loaded his twelve-bore and was engaged in the trickier exercise of unlocking the Doberman's chain from the steering column and attaching it to his wristband. Hanlon raced on in Carradine's wake, overtook him, and angled his run across the face of the rising ground. The idea had hit him out of a black cloud of sheer panic, but it tasted good. Leitch came blundering through the gap in the wall, the Doberman rasping on its leather neckband as it hauled its master bodily after the quarry.

Hanlon reached back for the laboring Carradine, got a hand under his elbow, and dragged him on a crablike run straight up the angle of the hill. "Sam, I can't. . . ." Carradine tried to complete the sentence, but he hadn't the breath and Hanlon's grip on his arm didn't relax for a moment. They reached the shelf halfway up the hill and Hanlon backed into the belt of bracken.

What had Tully said? "What's the point of laying them if you can't see them?" he'd said.

See them from the house, he'd meant. Farther around, then, much farther around. Hanlon looked at Carradine. He was doubled over, hands on his knees, the breath sobbing in his throat. Leitch was beating a ragged path right into the angle of the hill, the Doberman straining ahead on its chain, the twelve-bore broken over the crook of his arm.

"Come on!"

Hanlon dragged Carradine behind him again, this time ploughing through the thick bracken, working around to the back of the cabin which now huddled like a matchbox toy below. The change of direction brought a yelp of warning from the dog and Leitch raised his head quickly. The dog changed course to take the shortest distance possible and Carradine burst out, "No good . . . , Sam. It's. . . ."

Hanlon saw it a good twenty yards off. A flash in the grass as the sun fingered its steel jaws and curved springs. One of Tully's fox traps. Right where he could watch it in comfort from the back stoop.

Hanlon stopped and Carradine cannoned into him. Hanlon pointed up the hill. "Get going, Frank. Hard as you can. Top of the hill. In those rocks."

"But . . ."

"Do it!"

Carradine lumbered upward, using his hands to clutch at grasses and bracken to help him on his way. The dog yelped again excitedly and Leitch hauled back on its chain when he saw Carradine's clumsy climb.

He snapped the twelve-bore shut quickly and leveled it from the hip. He shouted, "Carradine! Hear me? I could kill you now."

Carradine stopped and fell on all fours, expecting the blast. Hanlon turned and ran to his right. "Keep going, Frank!" he shouted over his shoulder. "Run, man!"

Leitch swung the shotgun after Hanlon's weaving figure. "Don't make me kill you, Hanlon," he bellowed. "It'd be too easy."

Ten feet, five, there!

Hanlon swung around and faced down the hill. "You want me, Leitch? You come and get me. Just the two of us, eh?"

Leitch swung the shotgun but the Doberman howled and writhed at the end of its chain, its taste and smell tugging it toward the quarry up there on the hill. Leitch stood confused for a moment, then stabbed the release button on his wristband. The Doberman sprang away and bounded in great hungry leaps across the slope toward Hanlon.

As if freed from a chain himself, Carradine threw everything he had at the hill, scrabbling hand and foot to put distance between himself and the dog. Hanlon heard him shouting, urging himself on or swearing at Leitch maybe, but he took no notice. The dog was covering the distance between Leitch and himself at incredible speed, and he knew that if it was to work, he would have to offer himself as an unmoving target and hold his position right up to the moment of the dog's leap for the throat.

He snatched a look down to the grass, planted his feet on either side of those grinning steel jaws, and leaned forward so that his trunk overhung the trap. The dog's final spring would be automatic, part of the primitive computer print-out that would launch it from a point nine or ten feet from the victim.

Leitch was shouting something at the dog but the order, whatever it was, went unheard. The Doberman slowed slightly, bounced on spring-heeled feet, like a high-jump athlete, then raced in for the kill. Hanlon's nerves shrieked for release but he held his position, his fists tight over his crotch, his chin flat on his chest to close the gate on the throat. Twenty, fifteen, twelve. . . . The Doberman's feet came together in two parallel triangles, took the sinking weight of that muscled body, then straightened and propelled the animal in one last lunging leap.

Hanlon threw himself to his right, but he was still not fast enough. The reaching paws touched his left shoulder fleetingly and deflected the dog downward. Instantly, the paws conjoined in midair, forming the parallel triangles again, to take the force of its fall. As Hanlon hit the ground the trap thudded home on muscle and tendon and bone and the Doberman exploded with a yelp of such agony that the hills seemed to ring with it. Leitch came to a full stop, his mouth open in wonder. Hanlon bounced to his feet and ran up the hill toward the rocks. When he'd gained twenty feet he looked down.

Leitch reached the trap and threw the shotgun into the bracken. The Doberman was wailing in low, bubbling ululations, its back legs pinioned in the serrated trap, its weight pulling it at right angles to the line of the jaws. Leitch went down on his knees and got a grip and heaved. Hanlon stopped, observing man and dog in cold isolation, observing their mutual horror, their mutual pain. Then he began to slide back down the hill, half-jumping in his haste. When he reached the spot, Leitch looked up without emotion and said, "If you could get a grip on one side of the trap. . . ."

It was pointless and they both knew it and after a minute, with the Doberman's eyes rolling whitely, inches from his own, Hanlon got to his feet. He picked up the twelve-bore and broke it. He slipped one of the cartridges into his hand and closed it with a snap. He handed the shotgun to Leitch.

"All right?"

Leitch took it and his knuckles curled tightly around the stock and barrel. He glanced at Hanlon and for a second the tip of his tongue danced out from dry lips and licked them. He stared for a few seconds more at the dog, as though mentally willing it to understand, to believe, to accept the inevitability of it. Then, in a flash of concerted movement, he shouldered the butt, aimed, and fired. He lowered the shotgun and stood over the pulped head and the still-twitching back.

Hanlon held out a hand and Leitch let him take the shotgun. Carradine was slithering down the hillside toward them. Hanlon waved him to silence as he came up.

Leitch's eyes were glued to the last contortions of the dog's nervous system. He stared till the body was still. Then he straightened, looked at Hanlon and down the hill to the cabin.

"I told him to stop. You heard me. Told him to come to heel. First time he ever disobeyed me."

He trudged off down the hill without another word.

58.

"Bobby!"

The voice was low but insistent, breaking the rapt concentration with which Bobby Hanlon was flicking pebbles into a tin can at a range of twelve feet. He turned his head and Margo Carradine beckoned him from the window of her car. He ran across to her.

"Mrs. Carradine! We thought . . . Mom said you'd gone away. Danny!"

Daniel Carradine leaned forward from the back seat, smiling with relief.

"We did. For a little while," said Margo Carradine. "But

226

things are sorting themselves out now. Don't you worry your head about it." She lowered her voice and Bobby had to bend forward to hear her. "Fact is, Bobby, I've got to drive into New York. See someone. I thought you'd like to come along."

"How about it?" said Danny. "We stay . . ." Margo waved him into silence.

Bobby looked hesitantly back at the house. "Sounds great. But, y'know, mom is on her own right now . . ."

"I saw her in town," said Margo brightly. "She's all for it. Gives her a chance to straighten things out while the men are away." Daniel opened the rear door.

"Well . . ." said Bobby doubtfully. "If she said so . . ."

"Oh, it doesn't matter," said Margo. She began to wind up the window. "Just thought you might want to come. Danny'll be all right on his own. Maybe some other time."

Bobby put his hand to the glass. "No, Mrs. Carradine. I'd love to come. Honest. Great!"

He looked down at his denim jacket and sneakers. "I'm not what you'd call exactly dressed for the city, but it'll have to do." He slid in alongside Danny, who punched him lightly on the shoulder. "Maybe we can take in a movie, Bob."

Bobby moved his bunched fist slowly toward Daniel's face and they both giggled secretively. Margo swung the car around and headed for the Main Ridge Freeway.

"What's all the whispering about?" asked Margo, watching them in the rear-view mirror.

"Just a movie, mom," said Daniel. They laughed soundlessly, hands to mouths.

"*What* movie?"

"Oh, just one we read about. It was in the papers," said Bobby moving to Daniel's aid. "A horror movie. We like 'em on TV. You know, 'The Mummy's Tomb,' that kind of thing. This one's on in New York. 'The Texas Chainsaw Massacre,' it's called. Creepy."

"Zzzz," droned Daniel, slicing Bobby in sections with a flattened hand.

"Bloodthirsty little devils," laughed Margo. The laugh was brittle and a shiver ran through her as she turned on to the freeway.

59.

A little over three hours later, Margo Carradine crossed the Tri-borough Bridge into Manhattan. The boys had pestered her to tune the radio to the monotonous whinings of a Country and Western station and, as she drove in to the East Side, Tompall Glaser offered his breakin' heart to an uncaring world. As she turned on to Second Avenue, the boys were on their knees in the back seat, faces riveted to the rear window, their chattering so loud that she snapped at them in her anxiety and told them to sit down and be quiet.

She was not a practiced driver and shrewd enough to realize that she was also a nervous one. At one point, trapped diagonally across two traffic lanes, she fumed silently as a cab driver edged in beside the Plymouth and volunteered his opinion of her wheelmanship in less than civil terms.

At last, with her nerves shredding, she pulled to the curb outside the Forty-second Street entrance to Grand Central Station, switched off the engine with a sigh of relief, then delved into her handbag. She swung around in her seat to face Bobby and Daniel.

"I've got to make a call. Just check something out. You kids wait here."

"Sure," said Bobby. "No sweat, Mrs. Carradine. Can you turn up the radio?"

Out of the car, freed from the boys, she felt cooler, more confident. First the call. Then Bobby and Daniel. She entered the main concourse and stationed herself where she would have a clear view of a line of telephone booths. She scanned the crowds. Agitated rivulets of humanity flowed around a news-stand, broke in waves against the ticket windows, and washed back in confusion as gates slammed against tides of hollow-eyed travelers. Whistles blew, buzzers buzzed, the public-address system boomed, and voices shouted recognition, exasperation, despair, delight.

Margo ignored the masses, raised herself on the tips of her toes, and listened to a mental recording of the voice of Grigory Loginov. In 1956 he had been seconded to the Illegals Directorate, Directorate S, from the Higher Intelligence School 101 outside Moscow; he had brought with him a fabric of experience that had not been bettered in more than twenty years. His lectures became textbooks; his theories were exploited and found to be watertight under the strictest field conditions.

One of his fundamental principles was enshrined in Target Approach—"Sweeping" as his students called it: the art of establishing the existence of hostile surveillance in a critical zone of operations.

"Look for those who wander aimlessly within a small area. People going innocently about their business seldom loiter, no matter what their intention. Look for those who study station wall maps, who read newspapers, who browse at bookstalls. People with time to kill are easily bored and display their boredom. Look for those who study wrist watches with a pensive air, as if awaiting an arrival. There are many clocks at stations. It is a displacement activity. Look for those who whistle, who smile at children, who stroke dogs. Look for those who pretend disinterest in the people about them.

"Look for women who wait. If they are not obviously prostitutes, be careful. Even women spies do not expect to encounter women counterspies."

Two long-haired young men were seated near the telephones, deep in communion with hot dogs and Coke. Nearby a railway official was talking to a newspaper vendor. The official

229

looked appreciatively at a passing pair of high heels, and the vendor spat and made a remark that made them both laugh.

The long-hairs munched happily. They looked clean—too clean in a surveillance sense—and that could mean they were either middle-class hippies or agents who were not too high on street lore. Margo decided to take a chance. She slipped into one of the booths and dialed a number.

A woman's voice: "Russian Embassy. Good afternoon, can I help you?"

"I wish to speak to the Trade Counsellor," said Margo. Almost absently she ran her fingers over the receiver for any telltale wires or microtransmitters, although the chances that every phone in Grand Central was bugged were ludicrous. Twenty years. Loginov's Law. She was getting into her stride.

"Hello. I am afraid the Trade Counsellor is engaged at present."

"Then I will speak to Markelov," said Margo curtly. The line clicked and she went cold, but the girl was only making the connection.

"Andrei Markelov, Assistant Trade Counsellor." The voice was flat, as metallic as an answering machine. It gave away absolutely nothing but its owner's sex. Andrei Markelov had not become a colonel in the KGB at the age of thirty-five for his capacity to project warmth.

"Mr. Markelov," said Margo, "I wish to register a complaint. A very strong complaint. I have bought a Russian car. A Moskovitch . . ."

"Just one minute, madam."

Markelov would be calling the switchboard operator on another line, ordering her to switch the call to the private exchange. Her call would almost certainly be recorded.

"Markelov speaking," he said after a while. "You may talk now."

"Eight-O-Four-Six-Two-Three. Kingfish," said Margo. "I'm vulnerable. I need help quickly. I'm talking from a booth at

Grand Central Terminal and I may be under observation. Can you assist?"

"Take a cab to Pennsylvania Station. A car will be at the main entrance," Markelov said mechanically. "It will have diplomatic cover but that doesn't necessarily guarantee safe passage. You must lose your surveillance. If you fail to do so, do not approach the car. If it is necessary, use the station as a diversion. And remember, do exactly as you are told by the driver of the car. Good luck."

The phone went dead. Margo replaced the receiver. Her hand was shaking. Loginov would not have liked that. She took a deep breath and glanced around her. The long-haired couple had gone, the detritus of their meal still littering the bench. It took all of her self-possession not to run back to the car.

"Are you all right, Mrs. Carradine?" asked Bobby. "You look kinda worried."

"I am worried, Bobby, I'm worried and annoyed." She slid into the driver's seat and her wedding ring rapped a tattoo of agitation on the rim of the steering wheel.

"What's up, mom?" Daniel leaned over the back of the seat. "Your friend didn't turn up?"

"No, he's not there." She paused for effect. Then, "It's no good, there's only one answer. I'll have to go and pick him up."

"Where?"

"He's not far from New Haven. That's the first stop out of Penn Station on the Boston line. Really, this is too much!" Softer, shifting in her seat to observe the boys. "I'm sorry. Really I am. Still, it doesn't matter. I've got an idea. Right. Now you and Bobby go to . . ." She rummaged in her handbag and produced a piece of folded notepaper. "Here, it's a small hotel. They know me. There's the address and I've drawn you a little map. We'll get you a cab. It's not far. If you go there and wait for me I'll be, what?" She looked at her watch. "No more than two hours, say three in case of delays. I'll meet you there. We might still have time to take in your horror movie."

231

Daniel took the paper and studied it. Bobby looked over his shoulder. "Sure, Mrs. Carradine," he said. "Piece of cake. Leave it to us."

To his amazement, Margo Carradine stretched across the seat and kissed him on the cheek.

"You're good boys, both of you. Now," she took a small green case from the passenger seat and pushed open the door. "Out you go. We'll leave the car here."

Bobby looked doubtfully along the sidewalk. It was not a parking zone, and he knew it would be a matter of minutes rather than hours before the car was towed off by the cops, hoisted or stripped of its hubcaps. He raised a hand to tug at Margo's sleeve, but she took Daniel by the arm and turned away. The two of them crossed to the wall of the station and Bobby sensed that Margo wanted Daniel to herself for a moment. He stuck his hands in the back pockets of his jeans and walked a few paces away to give them privacy. Her funeral if she had no car when she got back.

Margo pulled Daniel around in front of her and bent her face to his. She pushed a rolled ten-dollar bill into his hand. "Now listen to me carefully. I want you to remember exactly . . . *exactly* . . . what I say."

"Mom?" Daniel shrunk back a step. She took off her gloves and gripped his arm firmly, her right hand resting on his forehead. He knew what she was about to do and he hated it, but there was no way of stopping her, not here, not without causing a scene. She touched the center of his forehead and with one long slim finger traced a silken path down, down along the line of his nose to the tip. And again. And again. Her eyes held his, unwavering, unblinking, drawing him into their dark brown depths, and her soft finger touched his forehead and ran its course, and again and again and again.

As he felt his mind sigh away into submission, he remembered the other times, lots of times over the years, when her finger had soothed away his fears and his anxieties and his fits of brimming anger; when the brown eyes took away his pain and the probing voice touched the nerves that held his identity.

"Are you listening to me, darling? Are you listening to me?" He nodded his head because that was all he could do. "You'll go to the hotel. You'll stay there tonight. Do you understand that? You'll stay there with Bobby tonight. Tomorrow morning, I shall telephone you. I will tell you then what you have to do. Now, I want you to remember a number. All right? The number is six-two-one-two-six. Now you say it."

"Six-two-one-two-six."

"Very good, my darling. Tomorrow, I'll tell you what it means."

Her face hardened—a deliberate tightening of the features against reflex. Then it softened. A brief smile illuminated the deep brown eyes and drew a reflection from his own. She bent quickly and kissed him and her lips clung to his young cheek.

She stood back, distancing herself. "Back to Bobby, now. Go straight to the hotel and . . ." she held out the green suitcase. "Take this with you. You'll need it tonight." She puckered her lips in a secret kiss and called Bobby over.

"We've made another plan, dear," she told him brightly. "I may not be able to get back as soon as I had hoped, so you two can stay at the hotel tonight and we'll go shopping when I get back tomorrow. And we'll take in that movie, too."

Bobby blurted, "But I can't. Mom doesn't know I'm staying out overnight. . . ."

"It's all right. Don't worry. I'm going to call your mother now."

"But. . . ."

Margo pulled on her gloves with finality. "I really must dash now. Daniel knows where to go, Bobby. The hotel's on West Sixty-sixth Street. Now, let's get you a cab."

She hailed a taxi out of the mainstream and Daniel got in without a word. Bobby stood helplessly hovering between cab and curb, then followed his friend. Margo watched the cab pull

233

away, Bobby talking heatedly into Daniel's ear, waving his arms. Then she spotted another cruising Yellow Cab, flagged it down, and got in.

Through the rear window she saw the Ford sedan tweak up to the curb in front of the station. The two young men she had seen by the phone booths, in denim jackets and jeans, raced across the sidewalk and dived into the open rear door, their long hair flying.

She handed the cabbie a five-dollar bill with a curt "Keep the change" one hundred yards from the entrance to Penn Station. She was on the sidewalk before the pursuing car could pull out of a traffic snarl-up, and ran into the station. She bought a ticket for Boston, moved toward the gate, and slipped into the crowd.

The train was pulling out as the young men skidded to a halt, panting. One stayed. The other ran to the nearest phone.

60.

In moments of supreme detachment, far from the wailing walls of the Company, George Strauss secretly indulged his professional's hatred of the Assistant Director as Christians might once have kindled contempt for the lions. The ingredients of his hatred were of much the same coinage. Envy of an inferior being politically ennobled beyond his merit. Anger at a mindless power that functioned only when goaded. Frustration when the first reaction to cold logic was a baring of fangs. The amateur always displayed emotion, never judgment. In a crisis, his first thought was for his vulnerability.

George Strauss had to work hard to stifle those feelings now. He stood alone in the office of the TWA security chief at Kennedy Airport, phone in hand, one fist bunched around the cord as if to choke the life out of it.

234

The Assistant Director said at last, "You know what they're going to ask me, George. How in God's name we let this Carradine woman board a train from which she couldn't possibly escape and . . ." He trailed off as the impact of his own message sank in. "How'd she do it, for chrissakes?"

Strauss replied coldly, "Maybe she didn't get on the train at all."

"And no one thought of that! No one stayed around long enough to check it out?"

Strauss closed his eyes. He knew it was coming—the true amateur's ultimate weapon: the theory of what-might-have-been-if. "They did what I would have done. They got help along the line to New Haven and held the train there. It was the obvious thing to do. The right thing."

"And they let her get away." The AD squeezed it out with the agony of a rattler shedding its skin. He lapsed into silence again. In a four-minute call at least two minutes had been given over to his weighty silences.

Strauss prompted, "The Hanlon flight's due to arrive in ten minutes. I need to be there."

"Sure. Okay, George. I know that. It's just that . . ."

Strauss tried again. "We're out looking for the Carradine woman. There isn't a local or federal officer between Boston and New York who doesn't have her description. It's Priority A-1. We'll pick her up if she moves an inch . . ."

"And suppose she doesn't? Suppose she's locked in tight?"

"Sometime, somehow, she has to move," Strauss grated, his temper rising. "According to Helen Shawn . . ."

"Hah!" The AD clutched at the straw eagerly. "Isn't she what you'd call 'the obvious'? How do you know she isn't a plant? Maybe that's her job. If you . . ."

"Bullshit!" Strauss had the telephone cord twisted around his fingers, biting deep into his soft pink flesh. "Alec Lamb questioned her himself. She's close to being mental-ward material."

235

"Except *she* came to *us*." Triumphantly. "One minute to midnight on the Doomsday Clock and she gives herself up. Think about it, George. Forget your goddamned Company guide to rules of standard behavior and look at it in *principle*."

Strauss sat himself on the corner of the desk and stared malevolently at the draped flag in the corner. Two years and eight months from now he would step down from Operational to Advisory. In any other walk of life it would be called retirement, but the CIA blessed its senior officers with a "preparatory" two-year breathing space. Strauss's rank guaranteed him the right to produce his memoirs—on government time and at full pay. Every mission, every blinding success and ignominious failure, would be relived on paper and added to the Agency's massive, perpetual secret history. Dick Helms had initiated the idea in 1967 as a means of releasing the pent-up frustrations of outgoing veteran officers without embarrassing the Family. He would need at least a chapter to deal with Discrimination in Political Appointments to High Grades.

"The Principle," he said, suddenly tired, "is simple: Can Kingfish still do the job? The way we see it, Margo Carradine is the instrument. This is the final phase. She was ordered to cancel out the rest of her group; she got Grace Fish and Joan Cater. Helen Shawn knew she was next on the list the moment she found the other two women dead. That's why she decided to give herself up. Kingfish has got itself perfect security now, if she can make the hit. Well, we can sure as hellfire sabotage that."

"How?" The AD smelled salvation.

"We cancel the Chinese Prime Minister's flight. Postpone his arrival. Change it, I don't give a damn what you do as long as we keep him out of reach till we've got the Carradine woman pinned to a board."

The AD's deflation was audible. "If that's the sum total of your advice, George, you're wasting your breath." Petty, waspish; a Bofors gun firing bottle corks. "Maybe you weren't listen-

236

ing the last fifty times I said it. Okay, I say again: the summit is *on*. Period. There will be no changes, no postponements. That comes directly from the Oval Office. And remember this: Moscow is standing on its head to cooperate in this. They're revealing assets, Point One. They're sanctioning our disposal of their assets, Point Two. And Point Three, if we can't keep the Chinese Prime Minister alive on American soil *with the KGB working with us*. . . ." He stopped—"Well, George, who d'*you* think they'll blame?"

Not you, you bastard, thought Strauss. He said, "Then you're stuck with me."

"Are we sure there's no possibility of another group? Another . . ."

Strauss glanced at his watch. Hanlon's plane was scheduled to land in four minutes. "As of this morning D.O.D. has four hundred and twenty-seven known or suspected Russian agents, informers, sympathizers, and collaborators on ice. They'll be held till after the arrival of the two leaders. No, there's no other group. It's Kingfish all right. Margo Carradine. One woman."

"It doesn't sound like much, does it?" the AD said slowly. "Not for the biggest goddamned manhunting machine on earth."

"That's right," Strauss agreed equably. "It doesn't *sound* like much at all. *Varium et mutabile semper Femina.*"

"I didn't get that."

Strauss grinned to himself. No, he wouldn't get that. "Latin," he said. "Virgil. 'A fickle thing and changeful is woman always.' "

"You better believe it," the AD retorted.

"I do," said George Strauss with feeling.

61.

The Navy chopper fluttered down to the long grass and George Strauss led Hanlon and Carradine in a Groucho Marx run under its rotors to the sandy track where the two Boston D.O.D. operatives lounged jacketless on the hood of the Chevy hatch-back. They turned and watched the helicopter rise from the flat-flowing grass, angle itself briefly, then turn toward the sea.

They had exchanged no more than a dozen words since the cross-examination in the TWA security office shortly after Han-lon and Carradine stepped off the plane. There was nothing to talk about. Spain, Fat Albert, White Falls River, and Merritt Leitch were pencil entries in the case incident file. Like the budget on-costs for surveillance in Spain and the official report compiled for the Guardia Civil on Manzoni's death, they were academic footnotes unlikely to appear in the final submission to the President.

Carradine, thought Strauss, appeared to have shrunk. His gray hair was white, his complexion yellow, his bony arms and hands brittle looking. A mental breakdown was probably wait-ing just around the corner and that, in the end, might be the best thing that could happen to him. He was a man who had to be born again if he was to survive. He needed a recitation of his wife's double-dealing double-life like Custer needed more Indians. Carradine had left the talking to Hanlon and, there, it seemed to Strauss, a benign providence had wrought her earthy miracle. Hanlon had found an energy source and re-charged the flame.

He'd hunted and been hunted, tasted blood, felt the years falling away. Strauss had seen it before, tasted something of the same vintage himself. It was heady. It left a hangover that was part physical exhaustion, part spiritual remorse.

The car sped onto the Main Ridge Freeway and down past the station into town. Hanlon raised a half-hearted objection when they missed the turn to his house but fell quiet when Strauss laid a paternal hand on his arm. The two D.O.D. men took their positions at the security door to the penthouse, and Hanlon poured three Johnny Walkers on the rocks. His next thought was for the electronics, and one glance told him everything had been disturbed. Strauss sensed the question in his mind. "TSD was over," he said. "I thought they should edit the Kingfish tapes here."

Hanlon made a face. The Technical Services Division had installed all his electronics, geared the telescopes, and planted the bugs in the first place. "So what now? What are we doing here? What are *you* doing here?"

Strauss lowered himself gingerly into one of the deep leather chairs on the raised central deck. "The AD has this preoccupation for double indemnities. He wanted you and Carradine under wraps and a long way from the action. Know what they say—no place like home."

"I want to see my wife."

"I know. Sorry, Sam. It'll have to wait."

"Why?"

Strauss won more time by taking a series of thoughtful sips of his Scotch. He set the glass on the floor beside him. "She's under sedation, Sam. You couldn't talk to her till morning, anyway."

Hanlon was over him in a half-dozen strides. "What the hell're you trying to say?"

Strauss eyed the bunched fists warily. "She's okay. I didn't want to tell you till Alec got here. I'm not up-to-date on this."

"Tell me!"

Strauss nodded at Frank Carradine. "Carradine's wife. She picked your son off the street." He saw Hanlon flex his body like a vaulting-pole on impact. "Wait a minute! They could be okay. The woman gave us the run around in New York. The stake-out team followed her and she lost 'em. She sent the boys off in a cab. We'll find them, don't worry."

Frank Carradine's head came up with a jerk. "Boys? You mean Daniel is . . ."

"If anything happens to Bobby, so help me . . ."

Strauss shouted, "Shut up! Both of you! The boys were with her—both of 'em—when she left Teague's Landing. That much

239

we know. They weren't around when she picked up a Boston train at Penn Station."

"You *think!*" Hanlon whirled on his heels and strode to the far window. "She's using them, right?"

"Margo wouldn't harm . . ." Carradine began impulsively.

Strauss ignored him. "We've had no ransom demand, if that's what you mean. For crying out loud, Sam, cool it. For all we know she just dumped the kids somewhere. She couldn't move with them. They were only useful while she was in a bargaining position. That's finished. What she has to do now she can only do herself. Carradine's right. She has no reason to harm them."

"What do you mean *what she has to do?*" Frank Carradine's arms and hands poked from his short-sleeved shirt like broomstraws.

"I can't tell you that," Strauss returned flatly.

Hanlon turned from the window, one hand squeezing the palm of the other. "You expect us to stand around while you theorize about this?"

"Well, what else d'you suggest I do?" Strauss flared back. "Go ahead, tell me. What would *you* do? You want to search New York on your hands and knees?" His face softened. "Sorry. My temper could use some sleep. We stay here because that's the way Langley wants it. And this makes as good a base as any. Lamb is due in a few minutes. New York and Boston will pass all messages through here. So will the Company. Anything anyone sees or hears reaches this phone," he slapped Hanlon's red instrument, "before it goes anywhere else. Now, will you sit down?"

Hanlon threw himself into a chair alongside Carradine. Carrie unconscious, out of her mind with worry. Bobby—no, even Margo wouldn't kill Bobby.

"How do we know the boys are still alive?" Carradine uttered the one question Hanlon dared not ask.

Strauss fixed his eyes on the misty outline of Jonathan's Rock and the gray sky above it. "We know they were alive yesterday afternoon. That's the best I have. But you should know your wife best, Carradine. Do you think she could do it?"

Carradine's parchment face drained to an even paler shade. He sat with the glass of whisky in his lap, clutched in both hands, untouched. His eyes, bloodshot and ringed with red ridges of sleeplessness and fatigue, brimmed with tears. "Do you believe . . . ?" he began.

Strauss continued to stare fixedly into the untainted world beyond the window. "I had to tell Sam's wife this morning that the boys had been taken by Margo. She. . . . We had to sedate her. I guess maybe she believes. . . ." He waved his hand in tired dismissal of the obvious.

Hanlon swore softly. "You'd better make sure you get to her first, George. If I'm around when she. . . ."

The light on the red telephone blipped urgently. Strauss ripped the receiver from its rest. "Yup!" He listened for the space of twenty seconds, then snapped, "Right!" and put it down. He looked at Hanlon grimly. "No sign of the woman."

"And the boys?" Hanlon could hardly breathe.

"We're working on it. It's a big town."

Carradine gave out a low hissing sound. His eyes rolled upward to display bloodshot whites. His head lolled, tongue protruding from one corner of his mouth. His hands unclasped and the glass slopped Scotch and ice hunks onto his lap.

62.

From: Aleksander Rostov, First Secretary of the Central Committee

To: Dmitri Orlov, Acting KGB Chairman

I arrive in New York tomorrow morning and am informed

through our embassy in Washington that diplomatic relations between our countries have in no way been affected by the unfortunate events of the past few weeks. Much of this can be directly attributable to your actions. Whatever the outcome of the pending investigation into the activities of Stefan Andreyev, on my return we will discuss a number of matters concerning your position. Your revelation that the man Carradine has been detained and the cell eliminated calls for my personal congratulations at your delicate handling of this, and Comrade Marshal Bunin echoes my thought.

From: Dmitri Orlov, Acting KGB Chairman
To: Aleksander Rostov, First Secretary of the Central Committee

My truly humble gratitude for your kind words. I have instructed the Foreign Minister to stress to his American counterpart that the utmost security is essential from arrival to departure, particularly in the case of the Chinese leader. We have done all we can, but still I will be restless until your safe return. By the time you receive this message you will, no doubt, have heard, through Marshal Bunin, of the unfortunate suicide of Stefan Andreyev in Lubyanka. He hanged himself with his belt from a window catch and was dead when the guards found him. I have, of course, ordered an immediate investigation but feel there is little of consequence to be gained by it.

From: Dmitri Orlov, Acting KGB Chairman
To: Marshal Vasili Bunin, Deputy First Secretary and Acting Chairman of the Council of Ministers of the USSR

Attached is a copy of my last note to the First Secretary. As you suggested, I have included in it my disquiet and attached responsibility for any incident to the Americans. We must now wait and see. I know you are familiar with Shakespeare's *Hamlet*. We may take counsel from these lines:

> Let Hercules himself do what he may,
> The cat will mew, and dog will have his day.

63.

The plaque would have been discreet had the brass been clean. Wakemore Building, it revealed in soot-black Roman lettering. It was a gallant attempt at respectability that fell disastrously short of the truth. There was no doorman, no striped awning, nothing to suggest that this bland plaster shell housed a hotel. Bobby checked the pencil-drawn map Margo had given them. There was no mistake. Wakemore Building, West Sixty-sixth Street it said. He reluctantly allowed Daniel to pay off the cab driver.

From the sidewalk, the Wakemore Building climbed eight ugly floors, its windows thick with rain-washed scum. The only hint of pretentiousness in its makeup was a pair of double-glass entrance doors. The boys pushed through them unwillingly.

"Where's the footmen?" hissed Bobby, grinning. Daniel punched him to silence with his free hand. Just inside the door, a wide wallplate listed a half-dozen names—Colnard-West Publications, D. G. Weingott Gems, Inncort Researches. Bobby stopped to read them, but Daniel dragged him forward to the small semicircular desk at the far end of the black-and-white tiled floor. A stout woman, black hair slatted with gray, was on her feet behind it, eyeing them over gold-framed half-glasses.

"Carradine," Daniel announced briskly. "My mother said you know her and we're to stay the night." He jerked a thumb at Bobby. "My friend, Robert Hanlon. Robert James Hanlon, if you want to write it down."

The woman's eyes narrowed. She gave no indication that she wanted to write anything down, but she turned and bent and produced a blue Moroccan-bound ledger and opened it and crooned over a page. "Hmmm. Carradine, Carradine, Carra . . . got you. Dr. Margaret Carradine. Booked and . . . yes, of course."

She bunched her face into an expression of hideous good humor, a favorite grandmother toying with the credulity of her grandson. "I mustn't make fun of you, must I, Daniel Carradine? Your mother called just a while ago from the station to say you were on your way. Now you're going to wait till she comes by tomorrow, is that so?"

Daniel nodded. He was looking at a blue/green Tretchikoff of a weeping woman hanging behind the desk.

"That's what she said," the old woman agreed stupidly. "Now I've got grandsons of my own, so I know you won't have much fun stuck up in your room waiting for her and I want you to promise you'll both be on your best behavior. Promise?"

They nodded dumbly. The elevator pinged and the doors ground wide. A lean man in a creased linen suit with soiled elbows struggled out with three cardboard boxes piled in his arms. He spared them a cursory, unpleasant examination, winked at the woman, and went out into the street. The woman caught Bobby's unspoken question and buried it quickly.

"Here now, you two," she said, "I'll take you up myself." She took a key from below the desk and raised the hinged flap. Her voluminous black dress reached almost to her ankles and she wore flat leather slip-ons.

"I've had a TV put in specially," she told them in the elevator. "There's a Bogart movie on and 'Kojak', but you ought to go to bed early, your mom says, Daniel; so don't you let me down, now."

The elevator stopped at the fourth floor and she led them down a corridor of pebbled glass doors. Some bore aging signwriting on them; others had small cards pinned over the locks. The room next to theirs had Inncort Researches painted on it in gold script outlined in black.

"There!" She swung open the door and handed Daniel the key. "Room Forty-seven. See? Television and everything." She flashed a portcullis of huge imperfect dentures. "Any little thing you want, you just ring down and ask me, Mrs. Kantzler." She dropped her voice to a conspiratorial whisper. "Later on, I'll get you some sandwiches and ice cream."

She turned to leave. "Be good now," she giggled.

They stood unmoving for a few seconds and Bobby broke the silence. "Be good now," he mimicked. Daniel flashed a brief smile and placed his suitcase gently on a chair.

"I don't know about you," said Bobby, taking a flying dive onto one of the twin beds, "but I've never seen a hotel like this before in my life. Boy, what a dump! And did you see that guy who came down in the elevator?"

He stood up on the bed and fell into a James Cagney swagger, thumbs in his belt. "You get insomnia in this place, you guys, and we put you to sleep the hard way. D'you get what I mean? What I mean?"

Daniel sat on the side of his bed. "We're supposed to behave ourselves," he said passively. "So behave yourself."

"Say, what's the matter with you, big boy?" cracked Bobby, still the quintessential Cagney. "See here, you bum. When I say behave, I mean behave but good. Get it? Got it? Good!" He tired of the play-acting and bounced down squarely in the middle of the bed. "Aw . . . come on, Dan, loosen up. Relax. What d'you say we cruise around? Grab a doughnut? Take in a movie?"

"You heard what the old lady said," Daniel retorted stubbornly. "She said wait, so we wait. It wouldn't be fair to her. She promised. . . ." He stopped.

"I know. She promised your mom. Great! Oh, that's really great."

"She might get fired if we disappear," tried Daniel.

"Who said anything about disappearing? Just a look around. Like we're in the Big Apple. Let's have ourselves a bite."

"No!" Explosive. Daniel shrank visibly. "Do as I say, Bob. I don't want to argue. Just do it. Okay?"

Bobby shrugged helplessly. "You and your mom." He flopped back on the bed. "All right, have it your way."

245

"I'm sorry."

"Don't be."

"It's just that . . ."

"Sure."

"I'm asking you to understand."

"So, okay—I understand."

"No, you don't." Daniel's eyes blazed. "You don't understand. You call yourself my friend, but when it comes right down to it you back out. Fine—if you want to go—go. Walk out and that's it. Finished. I don't want to know." He turned away, his chest heaving with the effort, his cheeks crimson.

Bobby held out his hands in supplication. "Look, Dan, you know me. I didn't mean to. . . ." But the storm had died.

Daniel shuffled awkwardly and ran his gaze over the room. "You're right about one thing," he said lamely.

"Yeah?"

"It's a dump."

They watched a procession of comic cartoons and B-rated movies on the TV. The sandwiches were delivered around eight-thirty, a pile four stories high that lasted through five killings and what might have been a rape scene before the TV censor got to it. Bobby said little. Daniel's outburst had been so out of character, so intense, he had no intention of encouraging a repeat. Nevertheless, it was identifiable. It reminded him of Margo Carradine. The way she talked to people. The same viciousness. The same instant hatred as though she knew people would be too embarrassed to hit back. What had she said to Dan back at Grand Central? Why the sudden change of plans?

On screen two cars were playing tag in an underground parking lot, weaving between concrete pillars, wheels screaming, bullets ricocheting. They crashed and cops and crooks alike were thrown bodily through crunching glass and burning gas.

"That picture," said Daniel quietly.

"Uh?" grunted Bobby warily.

"The one down there in the lobby."

"Yeah."

"It reminded me of someone."

"Mmm?"

"My father. I saw him cry once. It reminded me of that."

The screen exploded in Technicolor flame.

Bobby rolled onto the bed and began to peel off his sweat shirt. "I'm for bed," he said. "I'm tired."

64.

"What we're witnessing today," intoned Walter Cronkite in steely close-up, "is not just an exercise in academic bridge-building. If it were, none of us would have the right to expect more than formal declarations and obsequious communiqués. Well, we do expect more. As the President himself told us in a special program from the White House last night, and I quote: 'We have set the scene. We have sworn our allegiance to a common cause of human dignity, freedom, and peaceful co-existence. We will sit down as equals. We will talk as men. History will turn on the decisions we take, and damn us if we fail.' "

Hanlon yawned widely and bit deep into the ham on rye. Still no news of Bobby and Daniel; not a sign of Margo, although the telephone had rung ceaselessly throughout the night. Strauss had let him talk to Carrie, briefly—minutes—and her tears had flooded him and they'd wept together. They wouldn't let her come to him. Earlier this morning one of the Company's accredited psychiatrists had arrived, needled Frank Carradine with Sodium Pentathol or something similar, and taken him off in an ambulance. They hadn't said where he was going and Strauss refused to discuss it.

247

". . . . so let's go over now to Kennedy Airport," Cronkite said smoothly.

Alec Lamb had arrived just after midnight, went into a huddle with Strauss for fifteen minutes, and left again. He had returned at eight-thirty with sandwiches and coffee and switched on the television set for the arrival of the Russian and Chinese leaders.

The commentator at the airport was filling in time till the countdown.

"State security," he drawled, "is the modern folklore and no more so than at this kind of summit level. Here, today, the degree of protection afforded these three men is unparalleled in history. But then, so is this meeting. The State Department is naturally reticent about just how many security and police officers are on duty, but one informed source told me before we came on the air that it involves a minimum of eight thousand personnel. Two thousand of those men and women are here at Kennedy. Two thousand more are posted between here and the river. Another four thousand are covering the route from the Triborough Bridge across town through the Sixty-sixth Street Transverse to China's Mission to the U.N. at 155 West Sixty-sixth Street, where the three leaders will meet informally for an hour. In the past twenty-four hours, the NYPD, assisted by the security agencies, have checked out every conceivable vantage point. Our own crime staff estimates that as many as three hundred suspects living or working in the city have been detained for questioning."

The screen was filled with a shot of low-lying cloudbanks; then the camera zoomed in on the speck of a silhouette.

"And here," the commentator said excitedly, "is the Chinese Prime Minister's plane. In the tower here, controllers will already have the Russian leader's supersonic Concordski on scan, too. Again, the preparations for the reception of these two aircraft are unprecedented. All traffic in and out of Kennedy is to be suspended for one half-hour. The cost to the airport authorities will be millions of dollars—not that anyone's counting the cost of today's spectacular dollar for dollar."

Strauss sat down behind the desk and watched the Chinese plane land. Cameras followed it every inch of the way but, as it reached the terminal, the screen switched again to the clouded sky and a powerful lens found and held the droop-snout outline of the Russian SST.

"Right on time," shouted the commentator. "To the second."

The phone rang and Strauss closed his free ear with one finger. He banged the instrument down. Hanlon had not taken his eyes from him. Strauss shook his head.

". . . . a VIP suite fit for kings—or, at least, for the three most powerful men alive. The Chinese Prime Minister will await the arrival of his Soviet colleague in the transit area—this is at his own request—so they can meet the President together. At every stage of the way, protocol will be observed microscopically. Only when these men sit down to talk have they agreed to dispense with the niceties of the diplomatic scene. There will be no artificial obstacles to free exchange. It's man-to-man, no holds barred."

The camera in the VIP lounge sailed over a sea of faces and found the President, his wife, and his daughter. Behind the child, propped up against light wooden frames, were two enormous floral sprays. Two Secret Servicemen guarded each bouquet. At any other time, Hanlon might have found it amusing.

The lounge fell silent. From a door at the far end a short frail man in a simple gray uniform appeared. He stopped and waved to someone behind him. The Russian leader, his quiff of silver hair glinting in the television lights, moved forward to join him. They stood motionless for a moment, as if paralyzed by the scene that met their gaze; then the little Chinese took his companion by the hand, and like reluctant children at a prize-giving, they followed the red carpet down the steps, across the open room, toward the dais. They were still twenty yards away when the President strode forward, arms wide, the familiar grin cleaving his face. One by one he embraced them. The camera picked up the President's wife. She was laughing excitedly through tears of tension.

The speeches were short, predictable, but tinged with an unusual humility. It was, opined the commentator, not the moment for overconfidence. Then the Secret Servicemen formed a Roman shield around the three men and they walked offscreen.

On the apron at the main entrance, the guard of honor snapped to attention, and the three men dutifully patroled its ranks to strains of a military band. They returned to a point where the security guard waited, shook hands warmly, and joked through their interpreters. They shook hands again and the guard divided itself into three and surrounded each of the men.

"And now, their cars and escort," said the commentator. "Each man will have a Praetorian guard of twelve motorcycle outriders—six in front, six in the rear. Each of them will also be covered by Secret Service cars—two in front and two behind each leader's car. Absolutely no chances are to be taken with *this* procession. Police, federal, and army marksmen have been placed at critical points along the route into the city—at street level, on rooftops, in command positions in apartment buildings and private homes. Anyone who attempts to fire a gun at these three men will die in a hail of bullets that will make the D-Day landing look like . . ."

Hanlon reached for another sandwich. George Strauss gulped down a blast of hot black coffee. Alec Lamb came up the stairs from below, raised a hand in greeting to Strauss, lit a cigarette, and sat down to watch the screen.

The first group slid away from the TWA terminal building. Six outriders, two open cars bristling with Secret Servicemen, the closed car of the Chinese Prime Minister, two more Secret Service cars, then another six outriders. Three minutes later, the President's car and escort moved away. Another three minutes and the Russian Premier followed. The television screen blinked to a helicopter camera high over the route. Two of the processional groups were visible, worming their way along the black ribbon of road like streptococci. George Strauss watched the first, the Chinese Prime Minister's group, and his hands closed one around the other and tightened.

"Thank Christ for that," he breathed.

"Amen," said Alec Lamb.

65.

The hammering at the door was loud enough to drown the fusillade of bullets stitching its way across the breakfast TV screen from the gun of Kid Craig and his partner, Matt. Bobby rolled across the bed, but Daniel had leaped from his chair and beaten him to it. It was the old lady from the lobby.

"Everything all right, you two?"

"Yes, thank you," said Daniel.

"You're Daniel?" The old woman swung her finger back and forth between the two boys.

"That's me."

"Then the call's for you. On the phone at the desk downstairs. Will you take it there, the caller says."

"Who is it?" Bobby broke in.

"It's for Daniel," the old woman said severely. "You just watch your TV, young man."

Bobby grinned. "Sure would have been boring without it."

"Boring? Boring? Everything's so boring these days for you youngsters. Now when I was young, we had no . . ." She changed her mind and with a flap of her hand shuffled to the door.

"This way, Mr. Daniel, if you please."

The lobby phone was housed in an old-fashioned wooden box recessed into the wall behind the desk. It smelled strongly of lavender polish.

"Hello?"

"Daniel? Daniel, it's good to hear you. How are you?"

"Fine, mom, fine. When are you coming? I did what you said. We waited, but Bobby is getting fed up and you know . . ."

"Yes, I know, darling. Something has come up. I can't tell you now, not over the phone like this. Now, do you remember what I told you yesterday?"

"Mom?"

TODAY IS THE FIRST DAY OF THE REST OF YOUR LIFE read a card stuck into one corner of the mirror.

TOMORROW NEVER COMES read the scrawled addenda.

NOR DOES MARY POPPINS ran a line in green ink scrawled across them both.

"Listen, Daniel. Listen very carefully and don't be frightened. Are you there?"

"Yes."

"It's about your father, Daniel. He's in terrible trouble and now I'm in trouble, too. We haven't done anything wrong; there are men after us, and they are bad. They want to hurt us." She paused. "Do you remember the times we talked in my room, Danny. Our talks. The things I've taught you?"

"I remember. I'm not frightened, mom."

"There's nothing to be frightened of, darling. But I've only got you to help me now and if you don't I'll never be able to . . ."

"Able to what, mom? You know I'll do anything. Please."

"Be strong for me, darling. Promise to be strong, will you?"

"I promise. If anyone's hurt you. . . ."

"No. No one's hurt me. Not yet. But they might. And that's why you have to remember what we talked about. Our secret talks, Danny. You and me."

A draft played on the back of Daniel's neck. He swung

around and the old lady flashed her perfect smile. "Everything all right?"

"Go away!"

"Wha . . ."

"Go away, I said. This is a private phone call!" Daniel's face was puckered with tension. His eyes narrowed to slits. He slammed the door shut on the woman and leaned back on it.

"Danny, what's happening?" Margo's voice was calm, almost crooning as she reestablished contact.

"Nothing, mom. Just some old woman who keeps butting in."

"Don't listen to anyone but me now. Do you hear me?"

"Nobody," said Daniel obediently.

"Good. Very good. Now, are you alone? Can you talk? Can anyone hear what I'm saying to you?"

"No, not now. She's gone. The old woman."

"Fine. Just fine. Now, don't you bother your head with her. Don't bother your head with anything, Danny, except what I'm going to say. Just listen to what I have to say."

"I'm listening, mom."

The boy stood with the receiver to his ear, unmoving, unblinking as Margo talked. The old woman waited outside the booth for a few minutes, but as the call went on she shrugged and went back to her desk and buried her nose in a newspaper.

At the "ping" of the replaced receiver she turned her head and raised her eyes over the half-rims of her glasses. She watched the boy leave the booth and cross to the elevator.

"Mr. Daniel," she said softly but firmly. "I think a word of apology might be in order, don't you?"

The boy turned as if the sound of her voice were a light breeze rousing him to wakefulness. He stared at her, at the reception desk. Then, as if convinced he had not heard correctly, he shook his head and marched slowly up the stairs.

66.

Bobby was standing at the open door of the room. When he saw Daniel, he blurted, "I'm cheesed, man. Even if your mom comes now it'll be time for starting back and we'll have seen nothing and done nothing." He stood aside as Daniel walked past him into the room.

"Well?"

Daniel pulled the traveling case from the chair and placed it on the bed. "Well, what, Bob?"

"Are we going to do something or aren't we?"

"What do you want to do, Bob?" Daniel pulled up another chair and sat on it. His hands slipped the catches of the case.

"I want out, Danny boy. Your wandering around like a zombie doesn't help much either. Like talking to myself. Some day out! Oh boy!" He wandered back into the room but left the door open as a mark of his determination. "What's got into you, Dan? You sick or something?"

"No."

"Then what? You've hardly said a word since we got here, except to jump down my throat." He looked quizzically at his friend. "What did your mom have to say? It *was* your mom, wasn't it?"

"No," said Daniel patiently. "It was somebody who wanted to talk to her. I took a message. Business, I guess."

"Long message?"

"Long message," said Daniel flatly.

"And he knew the number and that she'd be here?"

"Seems so."

"Pretty clever, seeing nobody else did."

Daniel shrugged. He ran his hand protectively over the smooth lid of the green case and checked his watch.

"Great! Just great!" Bobby kicked the side of the bed and

swung around petulantly. "What kind of a dummy d'you think I am? Why'd you ask me to come in the first place? If I'd. . . ."

The room phone squawked shrilly, almost under his hand and he jumped. Daniel tore the instrument off its cradle, listened passively, then handed the instrument to Bobby. "She wants you," he said tonelessly.

The voice of the fat weirdo in the lobby purred, "Mr. Robert Hanlon?"

"Yes."

A cackle that set his ear buzzing. "Sorry, young man, but I've been very, very remiss. You didn't complete the register, did you?" Before he could reply, she cackled again. "My goodness me, you'll have every cop on the West Side on my doorstep if you don't get down here."

He started to argue but she cut in again. "No use. No use at all you arguing the rights and wrongs, Mr. Robert Hanlon. Down, please. Right away." She almost sang the lines. He tried to say something and she broke into an idiotic pipping sound. "Tup-tup-tup-tup-tup-tup-tup!"

Her last words were, "Quickly now!" Then she rang off.

Bobby said sullenly. "Look, I'm abandoning ship. Okay?"

"You wouldn't know the trains or anything," Daniel said evenly.

"I'll phone Carrie, wise guy."

Daniel eyed the telephone. "What'd *she* want?"

"Me. I didn't sign the stupid register." He swayed indecisively from foot to foot. He was still smarting from the lie. The phone call to Dan must have been from his mother. Why tell lies about it? In all the years, he'd never known Dan quite like this. Moody sometimes, sure. Out of reach in a kind of lost-sheep way when his mother had got to him. But it was never this bad. There was a distance between them right here in this room that he couldn't bridge, couldn't knit together with a joke or a playful punch in the ribs. In the past it had never been difficult to locate her influence—indirectly, when

255

Dan emerged in one of his sleep-walking what-time-is-it states, or directly, when she would interrupt their games with the impact of an ice-cold shower.

Bobby hovered over the phone on the table between the two beds. "You'll be okay here on your own, waiting for your mom?"

Daniel avoided eye contact but nodded firmly.

"I'll just call Carrie then," Bobby said and reached for the phone.

Daniel shouted, "No!" There was venom in the word. Fear, too. "Downstairs!" He pinched his lips tightly shut, regretting the outburst, then stumbled on, more reasonably, "I mean, you have to go down to the lobby to sign the register, right? You might as well. . . ."

Bobby replaced the receiver as if it were a meringue. "All right, Dan," he said softly. "Anything you say."

Daniel closed the door after him and went quickly to the green case on the bed. He opened it and his heart jumped. It was swathed in polyethylene, but he knew exactly what it was and marveled. He stripped away the packaging and took out the components and reverently laid them side by side on the bed. The stock was carved from one piece of beautifully polished walnut. The runners were of aluminum and the rear and fore sights were matt black. The prod was cast in a special spring alloy, its tips recurved for added cast. With spring alloy, the weapon could be kept loaded for a long time without straining the prod or affecting the cast. Its pulling strength would be at least 115 pounds, but the absence of material mass in the limb design of the prod meant it had an efficiency far greater than weapons of a higher draw weight.

God, mom, it's beautiful.

Yes, here were the special spring clips fitted so that the crossbow could be pointed vertically up or down without letting the bolt fall out. It was built to carry a heavy payload. He lifted a long, slim box from the suitcase. The telescopic sight was matt black, too, and about eight inches long. He assembled the components, caressing them in his hands, feeling the tactile power of each part. "This is the finest I can give you, darling," she'd said. "If you love me, if you love your father, use it. Use it. Make it fly, darling."

He got up and tested it at his shoulder. He took the goat's-foot lever and drew the string its full twelve inches. He aimed, traversing the room, picking off targets in his mind's eye. He put it down on the bed and drew out the bolts. They were single shafts of fine light steel. For a moment he held one before his eyes, seeing it in flight, then he went back to the case and withdrew the black oilskin package she'd told him would be there.

"Think clearly and remember the number. Repeat it to me, darling. Tell me the number."

Six-two-one-two-six.

He unrolled the oilskin and looked down at what was in his hands. It was gray and tacky like modeling clay, except someone had molded it into a shape like the business end of an Indian club.

"You must understand, darling, because you must make it work. You must understand," she'd said. Listen to her. Listen to her.

The top third, where it came almost to a point, was hollow and into its head had been fitted a percussion cap detonator. It looked almost decorative. A one-pound hollow charge of C4. On impact the blast would discharge itself forward, driving a six-inch hole even through armor plating. At the base of it, a channel had been forged to take the bolt. He slipped it in gently until the two were a rigid whole. He placed it in the prod and engaged the retaining clips.

"When I call you on the room telephone, be ready," she'd said. Be ready. "Six-two-one-two-six. Concentrate on the one in the middle. The target is the one in the middle."

Daniel looked at his watch and thought of Bobby.

First off, Bobby had to listen to a speech from the old lady who was mad at something Danny had said. Then he had to sign the grubby register. Then he had to wait while a man in the phone booth worked through a list of taxi firms, and called a half-dozen, apparently in vain. Finally, the man banged the phone onto its cradle and stomped back to the elevator.

"Won't get a cab around here for the next half-hour," said the old lady philosophically.

"Couldn't he just go out and flag one down?" asked Bobby.

"Waste of time, son, till the motorcade's gone by. Reckon you couldn't cross West Sixty-sixth Street right now if you were the King of Siam." She checked the lobby clock and nodded agreement with herself.

Bobby slipped into the booth and made his call. No reply from the house. He tried again. No one was answering. Maybe Carrie had gone over to Helen Shawn's. No, Helen had gone. Perhaps one of the others. Joan Cater? No, why worry her. He thought of calling the Center and talking to Sam but decided against it. Sam would consider him an idiot for getting all tied up in Margo's apronstrings like that.

He replaced the phone and began to rehearse his lines for Danny. Since he couldn't find anyone anywhere, it was best he stay with Dan. Wait till your mom gets back, sonny, so she can play sheepdog instead of me. Don't let him get off too lightly, right?

The woman came from behind the desk and placed an arm on his shoulder, drawing him toward the street. She said, "Your friend Mr. Daniel just got another call. From his mom. I put it through. We ought to let them talk private. You going to come see the people go by?"

Bobby grinned, a reflex his father had urged on him when dealing with intractable schoolteachers, old people, and idiots. This one had to be old *and* kooky. "No, thank you," he said politely. "I've gotta get back up there."

"Oh, come watch the parade, son," she said. She came back

into the lobby and reached out a clawlike hand. It locked with surprising strength over Bobby's wrist.

"Hey! Just what is this?" He tried to pull away. The old lady smiled but retained her grip.

"You come with me and watch the parade. It'll only be a minute."

Bobby shook his arm vigorously. "I don't like parades. And you're hurting my arm. Will you let it go or . . . please."

As he spoke, she propelled him to the reception desk, raised the hinged counter top, and pushed him through. Bobby was beginning to feel not only inadequate but quite foolish. One crazy simple-minded old broad, pushing him around like a kid. What was he supposed to do, kick her in the shins? Knock her down? Now that would look great, wouldn't it? Young Thug Mugs Old Lady in Hotel Lobby. Bobby tried another approach.

"Okay, then. I'll watch the parade if you want. Just so long as you let go my arm, okay? There's no need to push me around."

She beamed at him fondly. The small cramped world of reception was piled high with newspapers and magazines and balls of wool and scraps of knitting. A large black cat peered dully at Bobby from a nest of mixed wool and yawned before burrowing back into the heap of abandoned purl and plain.

The old woman flicked the switch of a portable television set on a shelf behind her. The screen brightened.

"We won't see much of that parade outside," she said, half to herself. "Always see it better on TV. More real on TV, I always think."

That was too much. With a downward lunge of his arm, Bobby broke the woman's grip on his wrist, ducked under the hinged flap, and backed out into the lobby, muttering nonsensical apologies. The old woman seemed to be searching for something in the knitting basket, so he took her inattention as a gift of the gods and bounded up the stairs. She turned, too late, the aerosol can of Mace poised in one hand. She clicked her tongue in her teeth and replaced the can.

"I'm getting too old, Sebastian," she said to the cat. "Too old and too soft."

She plugged a line into the telephone switchboard and dialed a number. A voice replied at once.

She said, "I kept him down here as long as I could. He just went back up there. You want me to make sure he doesn't . . . ?"

The reply was clearly ungracious. She paled and drew in her breath. "I'm sorry. I did what I. . . ." The line went dead.

Sebastian purred softly in his sleep.

Bobby took his time climbing to the fourth floor. He was grinning to himself. What a crazy old lunatic. Watching on television the parade that was running in front of her own front door. More real on TV!

What was he going to tell Dan now? If Margo had called Dan, he would have to come up with a better excuse for staying than the one he'd invented downstairs. Maybe the caller had been Carrie and not Margo.

He took the last flight of stairs two at a time and swung down the corridor to their room. He pushed open the door with a wide grin on his face and opened his mouth to speak. He knew that what he could see in front of him was really happening, but it was crazy—crazier than that old dummy downstairs.

Daniel Carradine was on one knee by the open window, the stock of the crossbow tight into his shoulder, his cheek snug on the polished walnut, one wide unwinking eye focused along the bolt. As the door slammed back against the wall of the room, his head jerked wildly and he glared over his shoulder. He found Bobby and fixed on him steadily and without emotion.

"Keep away," he hissed. "Keep away!"

Bobby recoiled. When he found his voice, he said, "What're you doing, Dan? What is it?"

But Daniel had turned away. He was on his knees again, the

bow snug to his shoulder, one eye squinting into the circle of the telescopic sight.

"Six," he intoned. The motorcade outriders slowed as they reached the double police cordons that formed a wall clear across Broadway. The accompanying cars moved up on them. There were no cheers.

"Two." The black open tops of the Secret Servicemen.

"One." The long black Cadillac in the middle.

Daniel squeezed the trigger. The bolt fizzed from the prod, flashed across the unheeding air, and struck the roof of the Cadillac just above the rear seat.

Inside, reclining in unwilling comfort, Aleksander Rostov, the First Secretary, and the Premier of the Soviet Socialist Republic, had been counting away the minutes to his arrival at the Chinese Mission against a fat, silver fob watch. On the intercom fitted to his car, he had heard the notification—in all three languages—of first, the Chinese Prime Minister's arrival and, two minutes later, the President's. Six words had entered his head at that moment and they were still there, echoing and re-echoing.

"Thank God, it all ended well."

He never heard the blast. He felt a movement beside him as the incomparable reflexes of his chief bodyguard jumped in warning, then came the shudder; he started to raise a protective hand to his face. In the split second between thought and the impulse to act, the world dematerialized in a cloud of blinding white light and the rear compartment of the car blew open like a paper bag.

Aleksander Rostov was swallowed up by flame even as that same ineluctable certainty electrified his brain: "Thank God, it all ended well."

The light came up to the window first, bright orange and gold and white. Then the explosion, booming like thunder between the sounding boards of the buildings on both sides of West Sixty-sixth Street and rolling its echoes into Lincoln Center and Broadway and Columbus Avenue. Then the heat. Then the shattering of glass as windows were sucked outward into the streets.

Then, quickly, one on the other, the howl of high-speed shrapnel and the discordant clang of dismembered metal on concrete and the screams of the maimed.

Daniel Carradine let the bow slip from his fingers and pushed himself to his feet. He turned to stare at Bobby, who had hurled himself against the far wall, arms wide.

Daniel's eyes filled with tears.

He didn't know why.

67.

Coincidence, thought Mr. Randolph abstractedly; it would soon be Thankgiving Day. They would still be there in their thousands, stiff and silent and dutiful, their curiosity sublimated by the act of homage and respect. For three days now, they had looped Red Square with their sinuous crocodile—the peasants who believed and the miserable *petite bourgeoisie* who came only so that they could one day boast to their grandchildren that they had seen the martyr and honored his lying-in-state.

Aleksander Rostov, the first since the Revolution to die by the sword—and at the hands of some American capitalist dog. That was what they had read in *Pravda* and *Isvestia,* and none of them would ever know the truth. They would be better citizens for that.

He let his eye dwell on the ebbing tides of promenaders by the Kremlin Wall. It would be months, years perhaps, before the last supplicant walked in awe past Rostov's open sarcophagus. That was as it should be—for Rostov, for them. They had such short memories: one minute they bared their heads before the dead savior of Russia, the martyr of détente, the next they were pooling around the eight hideous onion domes of St. Basil's or the Great Kremlin Palace or the Armory, blind as tourists to the real meaning of their pilgrimage. Five minutes later they'd be off to Gorky Street with their hands full of books and sausages and synthetic clothes.

"I think we're ready."

Chairman Orlov's growl sliced into Randolph's musings and he turned from the window quickly. Over the years Mr. Randolph had made a point of taking his inherited role as Master of Ceremonies at club functions very seriously indeed but never more so than today. There was a commotion over by the far door as the group arrived. Mr. Randolph moved behind the lectern and raised his hands high for silence. The babble in the bar fell to a conversational level as cocktail sausages were hurriedly speared and martinis and highballs replenished as provision against the inevitable speech.

A silver-haired West Indian in a kid jacket crushed an empty pack of Belair menthol cigarettes into an ashtray and patted his pockets for more.

"Try one of these, sugar." His lithe young companion twitched one false eyelash over her mahogany cheek.

The man shook his head. "Not me, sister. I fly higher on old white rum and Schlitz. No call for that grassy crap."

"Pleeeese," drawled Mr. Randolph, arms wide. "Ladies and gentlemen, please." To his left, the guest of honor pressed his way through the crowd, shoving good-naturedly at those who failed to grant him unconditional passage. Mr. Randolph came to him, hand outstretched, and the great broad-bellied figure, unfamiliar in sacklike civilian charcoal gray, pumped his hand.

"Grigory Loginov, how many years has it been?"

Mr. Randolph bowed. "Too long, Comrade First Secretary."

Orlov embraced the guest of honor warmly, and as he did so the chatter in the clubroom died and the faces assumed an air of studied detachment. It was not required of them to be any-

263

thing other than what they had trained to be, even for the new leader of all the Russians.

Mr. Randolph placed himself to one side of the lectern. Orlov nodded the go-ahead. "Ladies and gentlemen, your attention," said Randolph. "Chairman Orlov requests your attention and your silence for our . . . distinguished visitor."

There was no applause. Marshal Bunin clamped huge hands at the corners of the lectern and stared his audience into submission, eyes black under bushy black brows. He was wildly out of place among the Fifth Avenue business suits and elegant casual wear, but he needed no props.

"I am happy, and proud, to be among you today on what must be my first unofficial, official function." A ripple of tepid laughter. They were still not amused, just attentive. One bushy eyebrow rose to confirm the correctness of their judgment.

"First, I must congratulate your new Chairman, Comrade Orlov. This is a signal day in the history of the organization he is privileged to direct." All eyes turned on the squat, powerful Georgian. He inclined his head curtly to hide his pleasure.

"With his name, I couple that of our mentor Grigory Loginov." He touched his lips in mock horror. "I mean, of course, our dear club secretary, Mr. Randolph." There was a muffled cheer from the back of the room.

"But primarily we are here to witness a return. A triumphal, triumphant, return. I am here to welcome a comrade I have never met, yet one I feel I know better than my own family. One could even say that without our comrade some of us would not be where we are today." He stared blandly around at Orlov. "But I think I will not elaborate further."

Real laughter.

"Very well, or is the term here 'okay'? I ask you now to raise your glasses. First, to your new chairman." He threw back his head and took the vodka in one draft. Everyone in the room followed suit, except for Orlov, the object of their toast, who studied his feet. Then, below the lectern, a few at the front pressed forward and swarmed around the tall, spare woman, shouting their congratulations. She blushed deeply, lowered her eyes and mimed a thank you.

Vasili Bunin, First Secretary and Chairman of the Council of Ministers of the USSR, beamed down at the woman and gestured his delight to the audience. He beckoned with one hand behind his back and Mr. Randolph replaced his empty glass with a full one. Bunin raised it high above his head.

"Comrades, once more. To the greatest of all our sleeping dogs. To . . ." He paused dramatically with the glass at his lips. "To Anya Kolyesova, hero of the Soviet Union." He winked wickedly.

"Or should we call her Margo?"

68.

They talked all night.

By morning the saloon of the *Babalou* was wreathed with cigarette smoke and the chart table was littered with coffee mugs and overflowing ashtrays. It would have been sensible to eat something but the night was unplanned: spontaneous necessity. A little after five, a scarlet cuticle of light broke the sea edge and water, sky, boats, and buildings blushed red in the watery dawn. *Babalou* felt the stirrings of another day and rocked hopefully at her moorings, but the two men ignored the call.

Daniel had been in seventh heaven when Carrie asked him to stay the night with Bobby, and Hanlon and Carradine took it as a sign. They left the house a little before ten and walked to the pontoons and boarded *Babalou*. For a while, Hanlon had moved about the dark decks as if he really intended to take her to sea, but it was all show. He knew that to busy the body would be to leave the mind in limbo, maybe postponing forever what had to be said.

At first, like acquaintances meeting after years of parting, they had tested with hesitant sentences the old bridges that once linked them. When they were sure one would still stand the weight, they crossed with quiet satisfaction until they reached the next. It was a slow process, and revealing. Each of them fought shy of silences, rushing to fill them as if silence itself spoke of things better left unsaid. They had talked of old times at the Landing; days that now began to glow with each recounting until neither was sure whether they were remembering what was or what should have been. It didn't matter. It was the past and the past was safe and—if you didn't worry it too much—unchangeable.

They picked the past clean until it was a fleshless carcass. Then Hanlon raised Margo's name and the carcass shuddered.

Carradine had leaned his head into the oxblood leather of the pilot's seat and stared into the night until the darkness seeped through his eyes into his soul; and like a man recovering from a *petit mal*, he tried to exorcise the experience verbally.

The logjam broken, the rest came out in a steady stream. Margo, Daniel. Hatred, love. Friendship, enemies. Daniel. Love. Daniel.

In the first light, they both lapsed into silence and found it bearable, even comforting—the kind of silence that only true friends can share, that carries undertones too embarrassing to discuss and implications of brotherhood as outrageous as the dreams of childhood.

Hanlon stretched in his seat at the chart table, reached up to the cabin ceiling, and pressed his palms flat, arching his back as he did so with a grunt of relief. "You tired?" he asked.

"No. I should be, I guess, but I'm not. I've drunk so much coffee I don't think I'll ever sleep again." Carradine flicked the arm of the anchoring key under his seat to the release position and swung the pilot chair full circle.

The air in the saloon, visible now as a mass of gray smoke in the half light, was too much to bear. Hanlon made a pass at the cloud, skimming a billowing trail through it with a sweep of his hands, "Hey, come on, Frank," he urged. "Let's get some air."

They stood for a full hour on *Babalou's* afterdeck, sucking in the cool of the morning, heads snapped back on aching shoulders, eyes closed, chests heaving. From time to time, Hanlon grabbed the rail and pitched into a dozen deep knee bends.

Performance.

"Any more trouble with the shoulder?" Carradine asked.

"Uh-huh." Hanlon grunted, pushing himself upright. "I got me a good doctor. The best."

"Don't tell me," Carradine closed his eyes against the rising sun. "Well, that's great, Sam. But what d'you prescribe for a doctor in need?"

Hanlon dropped to the deck on all fours and began a series of fast push-ups. "What does he have that hurts, this doctor?" Hanlon panted.

"A ruptured past. A future you can't X-ray. Associated complications. You name it, he's got it." He watched Hanlon force himself into the thirty-first muscular push upward. He bounced to his feet, breathless and red-faced. "Well," said Carradine with a slow, reluctant grin, "do you have a prescription or don't you?"

Hanlon crossed the welldeck and swung himself onto the ladder. He beckoned to Carradine and stepped down to the pontoon. He pointed beyond the marina to the beach beyond Mackie's Point. "First thing, I say we grab some of that empty space before it goes away. Come on, Frank. Let's walk."

They had reached the beach and rounded the breakwater for the long exposed walk out to the headland, when the thin young voice pierced the shush of the surf and the harping of the breeze behind them. "Hey, you guys! Wait! Hey!"

Neither of them turned, but with their faces bunched to contain their pleasure, they strode on until the pursuers were in earshot. Then Hanlon twitched his mouth at Carradine and said loudly, "Don't say a thing, Frank. Ignore them or they'll be begging for some kinda handout—crazy beachbums."

"Hey!" A single word, shot through with mortification.

"Ignore them," bellowed Hanlon. "Maybe they'll go away."

Then, as the feet pattered close and fast, he fell into a grid crouch, one hand to the wet sand, pivoted on his heel, and lunged with a roar at the two figures. He caught them by their knees and they collapsed, limbs flailing. The three of them came up giggling.

"I told you he's a nut," gasped Bobby Hanlon. Daniel lay on his back, panting with the effort of trying to elude Hanlon's outstretched arm. Hanlon pushed himself up and regarded both of them with mock astonishment.

"I don't believe it! Frank, I don't believe it! I don't know about yours but mine looks like a kid called Bobby Hanlon who's never got himself out of bed before eight in the morning in his whole life. This guy's an imposter!"

Carradine plucked Bobby and Daniel to their feet. For a moment he studied his son. In the background, still on his backside in the sand, Hanlon's face tightened.

Easy, Frank. Eeeeasy. Don't rush it.

Carradine finally stuck out his hand, fanned the fingers, and moved them back and forth in front of Daniel's face. He stopped, frowned, and bent to stare the boy full in the face. "You're right, Sam," he said at last. "I'm sure this one's sleepwalking."

His face broke into a grin and he roughed Daniel's hair. The boy rolled his eyes up to the sky until he, too, could no longer contain his happiness. The laughter poured out of him in cascading waves.

"Know something, Bob," he gasped. "They're both nuts!"

Carradine made a grab at them both and they hurtled away

268

up the beach, screaming with amusement. Hanlon let his breath go. You made it, Frank. You made it. He got to his feet and, as Carradine turned to him, he winked. The tears came up in Carradine's eyes and stayed there until the breeze whipped them away. They followed the boys.

"It's going to take time," Carradine sighed.

"Not so long. You need each other too much for it to take too long."

"I hope you're right."

"I am."

Carradine sniffed and they strolled on, watching the boys who had started a game of tag in the grass-fringed dunes along the beach.

Carradine said suddenly, "We can't stay here, of course. Not now. I thought about it, but my patients made up my mind for me. There hasn't been a soul in my office for three days. Funny how naïve we can be about our misdemeanors. It took Washington months to decide I could stay in America, then I thought: Great! All forgiven. Start again. The law says Yes. The people say No. The supreme irony."

"Washington wouldn't want you wandering the world after this."

"Sure. At least they care about keeping me out of trouble. My patients don't care one way or the other. Anyway," he kicked at a pebble and set it rolling into the surf, "I'm getting out. I was thinking of California. Doesn't everyone?"

Hanlon slapped him on the shoulder, pretending the joke. "All that sun, surf, and—what's the other thing beginning with 's' they cultivate in California?"

"What about you, Sam?"

Hanlon swung his arms backward and forward, stretching the muscles, making them hurt. "Good question. We can't stay here either, and it's got nothing to do with the people."

"I don't see that. You've done nothing wrong. You're useful . . ."

269

"I'm about as useful here as apple trees in Eden. If it hadn't been for you—for Margo and the rest—I wouldn't have come here at all. That was my job, Frank. You were my job. It's finished."

"But there's the Center. Your friends here. You've got a whole life—Carrie, Bobby, everything. That's got to be worth something."

Hanlon bent, picked up a pebble, and skimmed it in a hop, skip, and jump across the advancing wavelets. "I've told you what I am, Frank. That's why I'm here and that's why I won't be staying. I'm a spy who works for spies. I don't parachute into Albania and I don't smuggle suitcases full of microdots across international borders, but it's one hell of a good reason for getting me out of here."

"You could quit."

"They don't accept resignations in this business."

"But you could ease off, surely. You're no chicken, Sam. When do they say, 'Okay, that's enough, Hanlon. Check your cards'?"

Hanlon grunted without amusement. "I'll tell you. You can maybe quit and they'll sit back and watch you build yourself a little business and wish you well. Then someday, you're packing your bags in Sacramento or Spokane for a trade fair in Frankfurt or Prague and all you're worrying about is overheads and expenses and whether your executives are going to rip you off in your absence, when—knock, knock, knock. 'Hullo, Sam. How's business? Hear you're flying to Europe. Now, what d'you say you deliver a little package for old time's sake. No sweat. No strings attached.'

"And the little package turns out not to be so little and there's a half-dozen lives depending on you. Who d'you think tells himself in that situation, 'Screw this, Mac—I sell tap washers'? I'll tell you in confidence, Frank. Nobody. Because they don't take No for an answer."

He threw another pebble into the surf and it skittered five times over the water before disappearing.

"Right now, I'm on suspension. Pending an inquiry. It's pure routine and all it means is they're deciding whether they can afford to run Sam Hanlon again and under what restrictions and at what level of security clearance. For the time being, a few months maybe, they'll let me go where I want. Maybe everybody gets to go to California."

He waved a hand at Bobby who stood at the summit of a dune, his arms semaphoring wildly.

Carradine said gloomily, "I'd like to keep in touch, Sam, whatever happens. It's important. Dan needs Bobby."

"No problem," Hanlon yawned hugely and stretched his arms wide. "It won't do any harm for you and me, Carrie and Bob and Dan to stick together. Langley'll go for that. Boy, surveillance free. No overheads. Carrie'll go for that, too. She cares a lot for both of you."

"What then?" Carradine watched his son roll helter-skelter from a dune.

"Sorry, Frank," Hanlon said. "There are no guarantees. You start clean, that's all. The rest is up to you."

"I hope to God he'll be all right." Carradine stared at the oozing sand. "After the . . . shooting . . . he was—he never said a damn thing, Sam. Not once. He asked where Margo was one day, but only that one time. When I told him she'd gone away he just accepted it. No more questions. Nothing. That's what really worries me stupid. I've been waiting for him to break. I keep asking myself: Was it planned this way? Was he programmed for it all along? Every move?"

Hanlon kicked a pebble up the beach with vicious intent. "Relax, Frank. It wasn't the way you think, I've told you that. This is the last time we go over this, okay? Just for the record."

"For the record, Sam." Carradine rolled up his sleeves as if preparing for physical effort.

"Right. Margo was a sleeper and so were Helen Shawn, Grace Fish, and Joan Cater. Deep penetration agents sown by the Russians in the late fifties for use as and when the need arose. Their orders were to become one hundred percent American and fast. First step: consolidate your position, establish an identity, create a bridgehead. How? Marry and settle down. But it's not that easy for agents working in an alien society, Frank. Everything has to be arranged because they have to be protected at all costs. So, husbands are arranged. Four of 'em, illegal immigrants who found their way to America and smack bang into the arms of women who loved them, nourished them, and built new identities for them with a flair that was little short of magical. But there's no such thing as magic, Frank. Just planning, preparation, and good old-fashioned farsightedness. You and Jack and Marv and Doug all came out from behind the Iron Curtain, all burning to get to America. The Russians spotted you before you left, ringed you, and nudged you gently in the right direction. And along the way they gave each of you something to be ashamed of, something to worry about, something to hide. And they had you hooked."

"But why? Wouldn't it have been safer for Margo and the rest to marry ordinary Americans?"

"No, it wouldn't." Hanlon looked at him pityingly from the corner of his eye. "You were insurance against the day when U.S. counterintelligence realized that there was a cell operating in Teague's Landing. What are we—agents and spies? I'll tell you, Frank: first and most importantly, we're *men*. And as men we expect to compete with men, oppose men, work for or against men. Women come into the equation but always as adjuncts to a male-dominated machine. That's what they were counting on in this case, and that's why they designated you and Doug and the others for the ultimate pratfall."

"I don't get you."

"Within months of the cell moving in, Langley had four surnames. They picked up a Russian communications link between Helsinki and New York. Very convenient. So we looked at the four names—just surnames, mind you—and we looked at you and Jack and Doug and Marv and bingo—four illegals from Soviet bloc countries, et cetera, et cetera. We were so grateful we didn't bother to look any further."

"Leaving Margo . . ."

". . . and the rest to play the perfect citizen bit, while I wore my butt ragged chasing their men with more technology than you could shake a stick at. You can't beat it for sheer nerve."

"But surely someone like Grace. . . ."

"Don't waste your sympathy, Frank. All right, Grace wasn't Margo. Margo *was* Kingfish and the others did precisely as she told them. That was the system. Grace and the others thought their husbands were just cover. Margo's job was to make sure that the husbands wore labels around their necks saying, 'I'm a spy. Follow me.' "

Carradine caught him by the arm and pulled him up short. "What was supposed to happen, Sam, if I—we—the husbands —made what you thought was a wrong move?"

Hanlon dragged his arm away and motioned him on. "That wasn't in my bag, Frank. Believe it. That was done way above my head. Merrit Leitch was briefed by Langley. They decided time was short and a simple execution or two solved all the problems." He sighed, hating himself and them. "It didn't exactly help that Moscow suggested the simplest way to root out the cell was to destroy it."

Carradine seemed far away. He said, "In Russia, I'd expect that to happen. When they talk about civil rights there they mean the value of an industrial wage and the availability of goods. Somebody gets shot by a faceless person in the streets and good citizens turn their faces to the wall. Sound principles. Your neighbor gets shipped to Siberia, you shrug your shoulders and remind yourself to keep your voice down when talking politics. But in America . . ." He shook his head. "I didn't think that happened in America."

Hanlon hissed through his teeth. "I don't feel comfortable on a high moral plane, Frank. Come down to earth and maybe we can communicate. I'm hired to fight a war. In the shadows, maybe. No battlefields, but a war just the same. In wars, people get executed without trials. Nowadays, it's not so easy to pick a citizen off the street and put him in cold storage for a while till the danger passes."

"So you kill him instead."

"Okay. You were pillars of the community, all four of you. How long d'you think you'd have been in jail for questioning before some smart-ass lawyer showed up with a writ? What do we say, 'These people have been spying on America for twenty years, but we can't prove it yet? They're dangerous, but we can't prove that either'?"

"I suppose not."

"You're damn right."

"So Jack and Doug and Marv had to die so you could be sure? Dear God, Sam, I thought that kind of stuff only happened in paperbacks."

"It should," grunted Hanlon. "That's where it belongs."

The boys, fifty yards along the beach, had found a friend. They were trailing a branch of driftwood and a tiny puppy barked after it, its paws leaving wolfhound-sized tracks in the wet sand. Carradine waved to the boys, but they were intent on their game.

"How could Margo . . . do it? And why, after years as a Russian agent, could she kill her own leader? It doesn't make sense."

Hanlon kicked the sand with his sneakers, gouging great holes that filled instantly with water. "Margo did what she was trained to do. She was a product of the Americanization Unit in Moscow. So were the others, but Margo was marked down as a leader, one of the elite. Oh, she was run by the KGB, all right, but her tutor, her mentor, was a guy called Grigory Loginov. At the Moscow unit he's known as Mr. Randolph, and he's the kind of hardliner who thought Stalin was soft. He has a friend, Dmitri Orlov, who's taken over as head of the KGB. The way Strauss sees it, Orlov wanted to sabotage the détente deal and topple his own leader in one easy exercise. Mr. Randolph provided the key: Margo and her cell. Kill a Russian leader on American soil at the moment he was bidding for peace and you have the perfect climate for a coup back home."

"But how did Margo persuade the others to . . . ?"

"She didn't. They were pawns. She designed the moves."

"Damn it, Sam. Margo was my *wife*. She had my *son*. How could some guy in Moscow hold her, keep her brainwashed, when she was leading a life that was normal and . . . and. . . ."

Hanlon dropped a hand on his shoulder. "Training and communication. Commitment. Why do you think I did what *I* did while I was living the same kind of life? Games, Frank. Games."

He shaded his eyes with one arm and watched Bobby and Dan and the pup. He was beginning to feel tired now and in a small alcove of his mind a thought nagged willfully. It was important, but it wouldn't speak its name.

"I can't believe it, Sam," Carradine said slowly. "I can't."

Hanlon shrugged. "Then look at yourself, Frank, and at Jack and Doug and Marv. All of you were what Margo made you. She and her group. They didn't just marry you. They re-created you. They gave you identities, papers, new lives. They taught you to look, feel, think American. They even killed your accents. Ask any speech therapist, Frank. That's one hell of an accomplishment on its own."

"And what was she doing with Dan?" Carradine asked.

"Who knows?" Hanlon fixed on a man in the long distance. "Maybe if Margo hadn't been awakened for this job, Dan might just have become the deepest sleeper of all time. A second generation sleeping dog. Personally, I doubt it." He pointed ahead to the dunes where the puppy was powering its way up the incline in hot pursuit of the two boys. "You're lucky. He's an individual. Remember, he's as much a part of you as of Margo. And he's one of the new breed—*our* society, not theirs. He and Bob are new people, Frank. You don't subvert them that easily."

They walked in silence for a while, then Carradine coughed nervously. "Last question. You didn't know I wasn't a spy, Sam. Everything you knew suggested I was. Okay, why did you get

275

me out of the country? You were putting your neck on the line."

Silence.

The veins on the back of Hanlon's hands were standing out like purple cords. His system was trying to tell him something.

"Yeah? Sorry, Frank. Just a minute. Take a look over there. Danny and Bobby. Anything strike you as odd?"

Carradine shaded his eyes. "No. They look fine to me. You think there's something wrong with Dan?"

"No. Nothing." He sucked in his lips. "Okay. I helped you *because*, Frank. Because. Christ, because I'm too old to let someone take my mind away from me. Because I'm selfish, stupid, and opinionated. I wanted you alive, Frank, because with you dead they were *right*. It made Leitch right. It made killing for convenience right. It made Leitch God. It . . . oh, forget it. Leave it be, will you?"

He stopped because the words dried up. The small voice finally got its message across to the forefront of his brain and boomed it loud and clear. He threw an arm across Carradine's chest, blocking his path.

"Stay here, Frank. Stay exactly where you are and don't move till I come back."

Softly, as if trying to mold his voice to the line of the beach, he hissed, "Bobby! Dan!" They didn't hear him. With the pup at their heels, they were weaving across a dune.

Puppy.

He began to run toward them, his feet slipping in the loose sand. He could see the markings of the little dog now—black and orange.

Doberman Pinscher.

"Bobbyyyyyyy!"

He yelled until his lungs had no more breath, a single shout that purpled his face and left him shaking. The two boys stopped, turned, and looked at him as if witnessing some weird adult ritual. They came to him warily.

"Something wrong, dad? We do something wrong?"

"Back to the beach, son," Hanlon said brusquely. "Go stand by Frank and stay there. Go now." The boys trotted off down the dune with only a sidelong glance.

It would have been comfortable to think he was just going crazy from lack of sleep, but that was too easy. He worked between the dunes until he found the rock path. He stopped and looked down. The little bay was an old and favorite haunt; he'd fished there often and his first instinct was one of proprietorial anger that his rights had been infringed upon. The motionless figure sat hunched on an outcrop of rock, a Fiberglas rod nodding gently in the tug of the sea.

The puppy, deprived of its new friends, sought out the latest prospect and danced between Hanlon's feet as he made his way down to the flat rocks, worn and polished like slabs of jet. The figure was in full fishing gear: old military-style jacket made of nothing but pockets, waterproof trousers tucked into waders, and a mottled forage cap rammed hard on its head. Hanlon stepped silently onto the outcrop, the roar of the sea in the bay covering his movements. When he was less than ten feet from the bent back, he stopped.

The puppy barked and tugged at the bottoms of his jeans, worrying the cloth between teeth that were needlepoints. The drop to the sea and the rocks below was twenty feet. The current down there was strong, unpredictable. A fully clothed man would go down like a lead weight.

Four paces and . . . No. He shook his head and at that moment the figure raised an arm and snapped his fingers. The puppy paused, considered the sound, looked up—and carried on chewing. Hanlon bent and picked up the pup one-handed. He straightened. The fisherman turned his head slightly, as if anxious not to be distracted entirely from his fishing.

"Don't worry yourself about him, Mr. Hanlon," said Merrit Leitch, the old smile softening his face. "He's quite safe."

"It takes time to teach a new dog old tricks."

277

Frank Ross is a pseudonym